THE
SHEPHERD'S
CALCULUS

Catherine –
Thank you for
sharing your stories
+ supporting authors
Enjoy!
C.S. Farrelly

THE
SHEPHERD'S CALCULUS

C. S. FARRELLY

CAVAN
BRIDGE
PRESS

Published by Cavan Bridge Press, New York, NY

Edited and designed by Girl Friday Productions
www.girlfridayproductions.com

Editorial: Emilie Sandoz-Voyer, Laura Whittemore
Interior design: Paul Barrett
Cover design: Scott Barrie, Cyanotype Book Architects

Cover images © beboy/Shutterstock; © Orhan Cam/Shutterstock

ISBN: 978-0-9987493-0-3
e-ISBN: 978-0-9987493-1-0

First Edition

Printed in the United States of America

For MJR & EVF

CHAPTER 1

When Peter Merrick's cell phone rang around ten on a Monday morning, his first instinct was to ignore it. Anyone who knew him well enough to call that number would know he had a deadline for the last of a three-part series he was working on for the *Economist*. It was his first foray into magazine writing in some time, and he'd made it clear to his wife, his editors, and even the family dog that he wasn't to be disturbed until after the last piece was done and delivered.

Several months had passed since his return from an extended and harrowing assignment tracking UN peacekeeping operations on the Kashmiri border with Pakistan, where violent protests had erupted following the death of a local Hizbul Mujahideen military commander. The assignment had left him with what his wife, Emma, solemnly declared to be post-traumatic stress disorder. It was, in his opinion, a dubious diagnosis she'd made based on nothing more than an Internet search, and he felt those covering the front lines in Iraq and Afghanistan deserved greater sympathy. He'd been a bystander to tragedy, he told anyone who asked, not a victim.

One morning as he'd stood drinking strong Turkish coffee on the terrace of his apartment in Jammu, he watched as a car bomb detonated in front of the school across the road. No children were killed. It was a Saturday, and teachers had gathered there to meet with members of a French NGO dedicated to training staff at schools in developing nations.

The arm landed on his terrace with a loud thud before Peter realized what it was. Pinned to the shoulder of what remained of its shirt was a name tag identifying Sheeraza Akhtar, presumably one of the teachers. At the time, he marveled at his complete lack of reaction to the torn limb, at the way his response was to read the letters on the tag, grab a pen, and start writing down details of the event—a description of jewelry on the woman's hand, the streak of half-cauterized flesh running from where it tore from the arm socket to the bottom of her palm, the way smoke curled from the remains of the school's front entrance, and the pitiful two-ambulance response that limped its way to the scene nearly twenty minutes after the explosion.

Even now as he recalled the moment, he wouldn't describe what he felt as horror or disgust, just a complete separation from everything around him, an encompassing numbness. His wife kept telling him he needed to talk to someone about what he was feeling. But that was just the point, he thought, even if he couldn't say it to her. He couldn't quite articulate *what* he was feeling, beyond paralysis. Making the most rudimentary decisions had been excruciating since his return. It required shaking off the dull fog he'd come to prefer, the one that rescued him from having to connect to anything. The pangs of anxiety constricting his chest as he glanced from the screen of the laptop to his jangling cell phone were the most palpable emotional response he'd had in recent memory. The interruption required a decision of some kind. He wasn't certain he could comply.

But in keeping with the career he had chosen, curiosity got the better of him. He looked at the incoming number. The area code matched that of his hometown in central Connecticut, less than an hour from where he and Emma now lived in Tarrytown, but his parents had long since retired to South Carolina. He made his decision to answer just as the call went to voice mail, which infuriated him even more than the interruption. For Peter, missing something by mere minutes or seconds was the sign of a journalist who didn't do his job, who failed to act in time. Worse, he'd allowed a good number of calls to go to voice mail while under his deadline, and the thought of having to sift through them all made him weary. The phone buzzed to announce a new message. He looked again from his screen to the phone, paralyzed by the uncertainty and all-consuming indecision he'd begun exhibiting upon his return from Kashmir. After several minutes of failed progress on his article, the right words refusing to come to him, he committed to the message.

He grabbed the phone and dialed, browsing online news sites as inconsequential voices droned on. His editor. His sister. His roommate from college asking if he'd heard the news and to call him back. Finally, a message from Patricia Roedlin in the Office of Public Affairs at his alma mater, Ignatius University in Greenwich, Connecticut. Father Ingram, the president of the university, had passed away unexpectedly, and the university would be delighted if one of their most successful graduates would be willing to write a piece celebrating his life for the *Hartford Courant*.

The news failed to register. Again, a somewhat common experience since his return. He tapped his fingers on the desk and spotted the newspaper on the floor where Emma had slipped it under the door. In the course of their ten-year marriage, Peter had almost never closed his office door. "If I can write an article with mortar shells falling around me, I think I can handle the sound of a food processor," he had joked. But lately that had changed, and Emma had responded without comment, politely leaving him alone when the door was shut and sliding pieces of the outside world in to him with silent cooperation.

He picked up the newspaper, scanned the front page, and moved on to the local news. There it was, in a small blurb on page three. "Pedestrian Killed in Aftermath of Ice Storm." The aging president of a local university was the victim of an accident after leaving a diner in Bronxville. His body was found near the car he'd parked on a side street. Wounds to the back of his head were consistent with a fall on the ice, and hypothermia was believed to be the cause of death.

To Peter's eye the name of the victim, James Ingram, stuck out in bold print. An optical illusion, he knew, but it felt real. He reached for the second drawer on the right side of his desk and opened it. A pile of envelopes rested within. He rooted around and grasped one. The stamp was American but the destination was Peter's address in Jammu. The script was at once shaky and assured, flourishes on the ending consonants with trembling hesitation in the middle. Folded linen paper fell from the opened envelope with little prompting. He scanned the contents of the letter, front and back, until his eyes landed on the closing lines.

Well, Peter my boy, it's time for me to close this missive. You may well be on your way to Kabul or Beirut by the time this reaches you, but I have no small belief that the comfort it is meant to bring will find its way to you regardless of borders.

You do God's work, Peter. Remember, the point of faith isn't to explain away all the evil in this world. It's meant to help you live here in spite of it.

Benedictum Nomen Iesu,
Ingram, SJ

Peter dialed Patricia Roedlin's number. She was so happy to hear from him it made him uncomfortable.

"I'd be honored to write a piece," he spoke into the phone.

"He talked about you to anyone who would listen, you know," she said. "I think he would be pleased. Really proud." He heard her breath catch in her throat, the stifled sobs that had likely stricken her since she'd heard the news.

"It's okay," he found himself saying to this complete stranger, an effort to head off her tears. "I can't imagine what I'd be doing now if it weren't for him." He hoped it would give her time to recover. "He was an extraordinary man and an outstanding teacher."

Patricia's breathing slowed as she regained control.

"I hope to do him justice," Peter finished.

It was only when he hung up the phone that he noticed them, the drops of liquid that had accumulated on the desk where he'd been leaning forward as he talked. He lifted a hand to his face and felt the moisture line from his eye to his chin. After several long months at home, the tears had finally come.

CHAPTER 2

While life on the Ignatius University campus was a flurry of mayhem and mourning, the world outside continued along its path, with priorities ranging from Hollywood starlets to political power struggles. Father Ingram's death had occurred nine months before the presidential election. His passing warranted only a brief mention in most of the tristate-area papers, while the efforts of the incumbent president to secure a second term dominated airwaves and newspapers worldwide.

Milton Casey, the reelection campaign's chief strategist, sat in his office in Washington, DC, poring over the latest poll numbers for President Arthur Wyncott, a Tea Party candidate who'd ridden a wave of postrecession anger to the White House, and his running mate, Philip Eldridge. The report, showing flagging results for Wyncott in Pennsylvania, Ohio, Connecticut, and Arizona, confounded him. He was well aware of the liberal bent in other states like New York, California, and Massachusetts. But according to his research, large numbers of fiscally and religiously conservative voters should have neutralized, if not surpassed, the liberal vote in the states he was currently reviewing. Connecticut voters, with many of their jobs dependent on Wall Street or big insurance, could be swayed to reelect Wyncott by his promise of generous corporate tax rates. Voters in Pennsylvania and Ohio were religious, largely Christian even if not Evangelical, so Wyncott's focus on social values and religious liberties should be helping to secure their votes, too. The campaign had been targeting social conservatives, making President Wyncott's belief that marriage was only between a man and a woman clear and guaranteeing that no federal funds under his tenure would go to support abortion at a time when family values were vital to a strong future for the nation.

This messaging and his incumbent status had so far handed him an early lead over the Democratic nominee, Jennings Osgood, a genial and benign opponent considered to be a Hail Mary choice. Political infighting in the DNC had created a leadership void, with various factions squaring off about their preferred choices. The party's few up-and-coming stars, namely a governor from Rhode Island and a senator from Oregon, were reluctant to squander their chances in a year when the party's upheaval was the bigger story. With just a few months to go before the convention, both had politely declined to put themselves forward, citing commitments to their home constituencies as their priority for the foreseeable future. Left scrambling, the Democrats settled on Osgood, whose primary contribution to the American political process had been his DNA: he was related through his mother's side to Cordell Hull, the secretary of state under FDR. Despite this tenuous connection to contemporary governing ability, the Roosevelt angle was a focal point in most of his campaign appearances and rhetoric. "America needs someone with vision to steer us through these turbulent times, just as FDR did," his candidate website proclaimed. And Osgood, with his anachronistic waistcoats and sweater-vests, was apparently the best the Democrats could muster to do so.

The American people, according to Casey's research, weren't buying it. Older voters had selective memories when it came to the public good achieved by the New Deal, and were hesitant to change direction midstream with a new president, while younger voters openly mocked Osgood for being anti-quated and out of touch. One late-night talk show host developed a running hand-puppet gag in which Osgood appeared as a Beatrix Potteresque rabbit, prancing across the screen and replying to audience questions with exuberant cries of "By Jove!" The Wyncott campaign seized on this skepticism and pointed to Jennings's years of study at Hotchkiss, Princeton, and Yale as evidence he couldn't comprehend the challenges real Americans faced. It worked. With several months left to go before he could even be officially named the Democratic candidate, Jennings was no longer considered a viable threat in most circles of influence.

But now, reviewing the latest poll results, Casey was nervous. While he and his team had been focused on establishing dominance over Jennings, a new threat had unexpectedly emerged. Just days before, they watched as the networks flocked to cover independent candidate Thomas Archer addressing a crowd in New Mexico. When Archer first burst on the scene, pundits and politicians alike had treated him as little more than an amusing distraction. Now, with less than a year to go before election day, Archer's popularity had begun to surge. At a rally in Albuquerque, hundreds had gathered holding signs of support, vying alongside over thirty television and print reporters for Archer's attention. The previous week, a Wyncott-Eldridge rally in the same location attracted only a small crowd and a handful of local media reporters. Archer opened his speech by thanking God and blessing the attendees, and when he followed his introductory remarks with a second speech entirely in fluent Spanish, the crowd went wild. Hours later, various television programs were still talking about it as though Archer had somehow invented both religion and the concept of foreign languages.

In interviews, Archer enthusiasts commented on his faith when describing his charisma. Part of Wyncott's image branding was around his own strong Lutheran upbringing and how it guided his decisions; Archer's gains on his religious territory were an unwelcome encroachment.

"We need to rethink how we approach these challenges," Casey said as his staff trickled in for the morning meeting. "Where are we losing votes?" he asked his dedicated team. "We've got strong messages. Ones we know resonate with these voters. What are we missing?"

That morning's edition of the *Washington Post* featured a photo of Archer on the steps of Saint Patrick's Cathedral in New York, taken as he left Sunday morning Mass. Casey waved the paper with irritation.

"What the hell is this?" he snapped, shoving the paper down the table. Casey was a tall, broad man born and raised in Tennessee. His accent seemed to increase in direct proportion to his blood pressure and agitated mood. "We've already pointed out how often he changes his mind on policy, let alone his religion. Why do they care where he goes on Sundays?"

An uncomfortable silence greeted him. "Nothing?" he bellowed. "Twenty brains in this room and not a one of you has something to say?"

"Sir?" A hesitant voice came to the rescue. "I think maybe . . . ," the voice trailed off. Casey glared down the table at the speaker, a milquetoast young woman, Ally Larkin, a graduate of Marquette University in Wisconsin. He hadn't been inclined to hire her. She didn't have the right credentials as far as he was concerned. But as the son of a Shell Oil executive, and a Duke University graduate, President Wyncott needed to demonstrate his everyman sensibilities and shift attention from his own affluent background. Having someone like Ally on board was consistent with his message about American democracy serving everyone, not just upper-crust graduates of Ivy League colleges. And, as strategists for the party mentioned, it was important to be able to say the team had some Catholics, a few Jews, and definitely a Mormon (or preferably two) on staff. So when a professional colleague asked him to consider hiring one of his former interns, Casey agreed. His friend assured him Ally was very obedient, very informed, and very Catholic. She would offer an interesting and possibly useful perspective. Thus far, however, she hadn't provided much beyond a nervous disposition.

"Yes? You think what?" Casey couldn't disguise the irritation in his voice. He hated it when people didn't finish what they started, whether it was a sentence or a campaign.

"The curiosity about Archer at church," she ventured. "I think it's tied up with the story behind why he goes to Saint Patrick's instead of Saint Thomas." She took in his confused reaction. "Saint Thomas—the pinnacle of WASP establishment, also on Fifth Avenue," she clarified. Her bluntness elicited a few chuckles from around the table.

"Archer is from a privileged background," she continued. "He's the son of a governor of Virginia, attended boarding school in Massachusetts, interned with the secretaries of state and commerce when most of his classmates were on spring break."

"I'm not hearing anything I don't already know, Ms. Larkin," he said, his patience swiftly running out.

"His ancestors helped found the Jamestown Colony. His great-great-grandmother was, like, *the* original Daughter of the American Revolution. They've been Church of England since they landed here, and Republicans for almost as long. And now he's Catholic? And an independent?"

Milton wasn't following. The minutiae of America's religious history bored him. America was founded on biblical principles, that's what he knew. Wyncott's ability to quote scripture at the podium alongside the most popular evangelists in the nation was far more important than whether King James knew his family or not. And he said so.

Ally shifted in her seat and began passing out copies of a situation analysis on their opponent's religious stance. It included a flowchart of the Archer family's seventeenth-century ties to the Virginia Company of London and culminated with Archer's conversion to Catholicism while attending Georgetown University in the late seventies.

"Archer's message about religion isn't just what he is—it's how he came to the decision to convert. He's sharing a spiritual journey. A narrative about having a genuine religious epiphany and how that has shaped the way he'll lead this nation if elected. That's a powerful message, sir. One that makes his faith a living thing, not just an entry on a fact sheet."

Casey flipped to the next page in Ally's report. It was an extensive biography of Archer's life prior to entering the presidential race. Archer entered Georgetown with the intention of pursuing international relations with the State Department in 1976. It was the height of the liberation theology movement led largely by Jesuits in South and Central America, many of whom visited Georgetown as guest lecturers. Archer had been so impressed by their efforts that he joined the Peace Corps after graduation, spending several years in El Salvador, then embroiled in a devastating civil war. "Archbishop Romero's physical body was killed," Archer said in an interview with *Time*, recalling the violence he had witnessed, "but his spirit, the essence of his faith was not. He died defending the oppressed in the same way he believed for his whole life that Christ had done during his short time on earth. That moment was when I

felt the call of Catholicism." Casey could barely keep from rolling his eyes at the saccharine piety seeping off the page.

"Not only that, sir, but Archer's religious conversion is tied
to living in Central and South America helping impoverished
communities. Even for Latino voters who aren't Catholic—
Pentecostals, Seventh-day Adventists—that means something. He cites his time there as the number-one influence on
his faith and his domestic policy agenda, from immigration
reform to stimulating job growth for struggling communities
across America. It has the potential to hit us in two key voter
pools: Latinos and jobless Middle Americans."

Casey asked for the latest demographic research. A young
man handed him a breakdown of shifts in Pennsylvania and
Ohio. Voters as recently as 2008 were largely Caucasian and
middle-class or retired. Eight years later the figures indicated
sharp increases in the number of Latino voters in most of the
battleground states like Pennsylvania and Ohio—critical states
with blue-collar communities brought low by jobs lost to the
global economy, and by widespread heroin addiction, and
where voter frustration with the two-party establishment was
high. Both factors could prove problematic for Wyncott.

Twenty-seven million US citizens self-identified as Latino
and were registered to vote. That figure couldn't possibly
begin to paint a full picture of the distribution of people hailing from nations south of the US border; for every registered
voter, there were bound to be others who were legal but not
registered. Realistically, identity politics alone wasn't going to
be enough to win this race—not this time. Gerrymandering
across the South, coupled with restrictive voter-fraud mea-
sures across the Midwest, guaranteed gains for the GOP. But
twenty-seven million ballots was still nothing to sneeze at.
Wyncott couldn't afford to ignore them, nor could he disre-
gard the inroads Archer was making with blue-collar voters in
postindustrial towns.

"We used to think these votes were concentrated in coastal and Southern cities where we either had the vote locked or we didn't. But now they're in every state, sir. Nebraska, Michigan, Ohio. In every class stratum. Mobilized to vote for candidates who understand their roots and identity. And Archer's message isn't just resonating with them. He's connecting with religious voters across the spectrum and in communities who feel left behind. So we have a bigger problem than why the *Post* takes his photo at Mass." She closed the binder she'd been consulting. "It's how to avoid losing the states we need just because Archer felt the hand of Jesus in El Salvador."

She was right. He was embarrassed to admit it, but she was right. The campaign had a team working on outreach to the Latino community, but he hadn't emphasized religion with them. That was a mistake. And this research showed that Archer was also gaining ground with Catholic voters of all ethnic backgrounds. When the meeting was over, he was going to need to follow up with his contacts in the Archdiocese of Boston. If anyone was going to know how to handle an immigrant Catholic problem, it would be John Cardinal Mulcahy.

CHAPTER 3

Bishop Owen Feeney contemplated the nature of death and its many forms from the billowy comfort of his leather chair at the United States Conference of Catholic Bishops in Washington, DC. James Ingram's accident had shocked many in his office, Feeney included. At times like this, he relied on the refrains of his life's devotion to explain away the fear and disappointment. Death, whether expected or sudden, was never easy. But comfort, he reminded the bereaved, came from faith and accepting the idea that whatever happened in this world—famine, war, even freezing to death on a quiet Sunday evening—was part of God's plan.

His assistant, Sister Anne Marie, popped her head in the door for the fifth time in an hour to ask if he wanted anything to drink. Some coffee or tea, perhaps? But he continued to stare at a framed map on the opposite wall, barely summoning the effort to give her an answer. He knew he ought to be kind to Sister Anne Marie and let her go fetch him coffee. It would give her a sense of comfort and purpose, something to do instead of pacing in front of his office door clucking like a hen over how tragic the loss of his best friend must be. She was a relic of the Church—a particular kind of woman with middling intelligence and profound piety, who entered the convent intent on furthering the faith of others, but ended up serving clerics who ascended higher in the ranks of Catholicism than she ever could, all at younger ages and with more esteem.

At age seventy-nine, Sister Anne Marie had long outlived any ability to manage the day-to-day practicalities of an office as large and influential as Feeney's. But upon the death of her previous ward, a ninety-three-year-old cardinal whose early-onset Alzheimer's relegated him to the dusty halls of ecumenical research, she was so lost that Feeney took pity and allowed her to work for him. She ruled the halls with the sort of palpable anger reserved for women who waited for opportunities and respect that never came. Although the clergy all disregarded her blustering with mild bemusement, she routinely terrified the younger staff and, in particular, the interns in ample supply who came from Catholic U, Loyola Baltimore, Georgetown, and occasionally Villanova.

But now, anxiously watching Feeney's face for a response, Sister Anne Marie broke into a smile entirely too wide, given the somber circumstances, when he finally gave an affirmative nod. "I'll be right back, Your Excellency," she bleated at the back of his head, which had again turned to the map.

It was an original from the eighteenth century, charting those parts of the world—Europe, Africa, Asia, and even South America—to which Catholic missionaries had extended their reach. Very little of the globe had been left untouched. The map was a gift from James Ingram many years ago, when Feeney had decided to leave academia and instead focus his clerical career on rising through Rome's ranks in America.

The news hadn't seemed to surprise Ingram as much as Feeney thought it would, and if he'd been speaking honestly (Did he ever? Even then?) he would have had to admit it hurt him to feel so predictable, so contrived, as Ingram might have called it. But then, that had always seemed to be the nature of their friendship. They had grown up just a few buildings apart on Kingsbridge Avenue in the Bronx. Knowledge, scholarly and human, had come to Ingram in ways that Feeney labored for many long hours to attain. Ingram could read the same passages from Saint Augustine's *Confessions* during class at their Jesuit high school, where they both were scholarship students, and summarize the meaning so instantaneously, so concisely, that the instructors often marveled at his acuity.

His homework would be completed in a fraction of the time it took the other boys. So much so that Feeney had learned to dread the sound of a basketball bouncing against the wall outside his bedroom window on the building's first floor, and the singsong of Jimmy's voice summoning him as he called out, "C'mon, Owen. Finish up and let's shoot some hoops!" The syncopated thwack of the ball against the bricks pounded like a musical interlude of failure in Owen's mind, a nervous feeling that followed him always so that even now, on those rare occasions when he took public transportation instead of a chauffeur, his heart twisted with inadequacy at the similar beat of the Metro train wheels thumping over the tracks.

What Feeney lacked in raw ability he made up for in hours spent at the offices of first his local parish, then the nearby monsignor, then his bishop, and on up the line until his admission to Columbia for an undergraduate degree in political science. By junior year he had announced his plans to join the Church, and not long after graduation, he was headed to the Pontifical North American College in Vatican City.

Years later, when Feeney announced his intention to transfer from a post at Villanova to work on governmental affairs for the Archdiocese of Chicago, Ingram had cautioned him not to lose sight of why they chose to take orders. "This map," he said as Feeney unfurled the gift, "doesn't represent the physical dominance of our church, Owen. It represents the strength of its ideas. That's what lasts—through oppression, through earthquakes, through constant change. After we're gone and the art, the real estate, all of it has passed into other hands, it's the ideology that will endure."

He thought about his last conversation with James, just days before his accident. At the disappointment on the Jesuit priest's face as he addressed him. The only thing more infuriating than James's disappointment was his continual surprise at the discovery that people were flawed, imperfect beings. "Flawed is not what I would call it," Ingram had said at the time. "Flawed implies that some part of it is beyond your control, Owen. We're talking about negligence here—the willful and deliberate refusal to act even though you knew you should have." Then James had pushed a battered brown envelope across the table at him.

"You have a chance to do the right thing now," he said. "Don't make me wonder if you got lost in your zeal to become cardinal, or if you were this way from the start."

Even if he'd wanted to give his full attention to the contents of the envelope (he didn't), or to the loss he felt at his old friend's death (he did), Feeney had more pressing matters before him. The gray accordion folder on his desk was bursting at the seams with issues that wouldn't be ignored. Each day, more and more files arrived at the Conference's offices. Notices to subpoena records. Notices of intent to file class action suits against this diocese or that, to file against this defrocked clergymen or his monsignor. Nearly ten years after the widespread scandal had erupted, victims of sexual abuse at the hands of clerics across the nation continued to file nuisance claims against the Church, seeking monetary recompense for some sense of security or comfort that would never come, no matter the size of the settlement. That was what he found so exasperating about the exercise. They should be looking for the answers in God, in his opinion, not a bank account.

"Which God would you recommend they consult, Owen?" Ingram had asked when Feeney called him to vent one night, feeling overwhelmed by the sheer volume of claims and paperwork. "The one served by the priests who did this to them?"

Feeney could almost see Ingram shaking his head in that oh-so-disappointed way of his through the telephone cable. "Comfort for these children became unattainable the minute those priests touched them," Ingram had said after Feeney's failure to respond created an uncomfortable silence. "It's justice they need now."

Feeney opened the gray folder and began slogging through the most recent financial impact analysis prepared by their internal auditors. In a worst-case scenario, if judgment in all the current claims went for the plaintiffs, the Church was looking at a payout in excess of $700 million. This was on top of approximately $2 billion paid out over the past ten to fifteen years. He looked at a pile of papers on the opposite side of his desk—counterclaims, motions to dismiss, and filings citing precedence to treat the Church as a limited liability corporation, all prepared by the Conference's legal team. Judging from that pile, stacked twice as high and twice as deep as those he'd just finished, justice would be a long time coming.

CHAPTER 4

The window announcing successful transmission of the file popped up on the laptop screen at last. The *Economist* piece had been filed, and Peter now turned his attention to the difficult task of trying to summarize the life of a man whose influence was seemingly too vast to be contained by words on a page.

He was rocking back in his chair, bouncing a miniature soccer ball off the wall, when Emma came in.

"I saw the news about Ingram," she said gently. "Are you okay?"

"Okay's a relative term these days," he said without looking at her. He couldn't stand to. Couldn't stand that expression of hers, the way her eyes pinched together in pity whenever she smiled at him. "But I'm doing, and that's something at least," he said, throwing her a bone, his tone more dismissive than he'd intended.

Emma flinched. "A Patricia something from the college," she began hesitantly. "From Ignatius—she, uh, called earlier."

He wondered when Emma had stopped being able to complete entire sentences without stuttering. She rocked back and forth on the balls of her feet, a nervous habit from her days as a dancer in high school. "She left a couple of messages on the home phone."

"I got it." He turned and looked at her. "I've already called her back."

"Oh," Emma said. She seemed disappointed that she couldn't even be useful as a messenger. He wasn't trying to make her feel that way.

"She called my cell. It's the first time I've checked those messages in days," he offered in a conciliatory tone.

"I'm writing a piece about him now," he added. "A eulogy of sorts, I guess." He saw her face brighten. She got excited over the littlest things he did these days, like he was an infant clapping his hands for the first time. He was swift to quell her enthusiasm. "I'm stuck on the first paragraph, so don't even bother to ask how it's going."

"You don't always know what I'm planning to do or say, Peter," she said sharply. It was a nice change from the way she'd been tiptoeing around him for weeks on end.

He began bouncing the ball again. "I'm just trying to make some headway here and—"

"I know, I know. You don't want any interruptions." Emma grabbed the ball in midair as it ricocheted off the wall. "I don't see how you're going to get anywhere sitting here staring at a screen."

"It's what I do. It's how I write."

"It's how you write an article, yes," she said. "But this is different. Ever since I've known you, this man has been important to you. More important than anyone else, I think. How can you get that right from here? Maybe it would go more smoothly if you went somewhere else to write it. Ignatius, even."

Peter felt a flush of anger and irritation rising in his cheeks. "Tell you what, Emma. I won't tell you how to be a crayon shrink or whatever it is you do, and how about you let me be the writer?"

The words had their intended effect. Her body closed in on itself like the shrinking violet she'd been for months, but she wouldn't fold without a parting shot or two. "Art therapy, Peter. I do art therapy."

She put the soccer ball down on his desk, just out of reach so he had to shift position to reach it. She'd been winning that way for years, knocking him off-balance when he least expected it.

"And that's the difference between you and Ingram," she said, moving toward the door. "He didn't just sit around writing about the things other people do. He actually got up and did them."

He didn't notice until he heard the sharp clang of pots and pans being unloaded from the dishwasher: this time, she'd left the door wide open.

CHAPTER 5

Miles away in snowy Boston, a package from Milton Casey sat on Cardinal Mulcahy's desk. It contained the results of an independent poll conducted among Catholic voters about what they looked for in a political candidate. The information was encouraging. Key voter issues and trends among Catholics were easier to track than for most groups. A limited number of issues seemed to drive them more than others, and although economic policy was important, so also were moral questions routinely addressed publicly by the Vatican and its leadership in the United States. The cross influence couldn't be denied, even if it was impossible to capture hard numbers on the full extent to which it drove voting decisions.

Mulcahy had predicted as much when Casey contacted him about the findings in Ally's report, and Mulcahy suggested the poll. It wasn't a long conversation; Mulcahy thought these things were better discussed in person. He'd assured Casey that the Church shared certain interests with Wyncott and that a meeting between the two groups could prove productive for everyone. Then Mulcahy arranged for Casey to meet with Bishop Owen Feeney in Washington, DC. "Owen's the right man for this," he told Casey. "Trust me—he's got the sharpest business mind I've ever seen." Casey was amused to hear him speaking about a bishop as though he were the head of a tech start-up.

Mulcahy wouldn't be able to join them. His schedule was (and would continue to be) jam-packed with meetings, depositions, testimony preparation, and public appearances expressing remorse, all related to a number of sexual-abuse charges that had been levied against priests in the cardinal's archdiocese. When the accusers first started coming forward Mulcahy hadn't bothered to address them publicly. Throughout his many years in parishes around the United States, he'd encountered accusations and rumors before, but seldom accompanied by any compelling evidence.

Now, from his seat in Boston, ghosts from his years as a monsignor in Baltimore and a bishop in Chicago were materializing into flesh-and-blood problems with legal representation. These sorts of accusations seemed always to erupt in waves, and usually came from men and women who had exhibited unstable conduct in their youth and were hardly faring much better in adulthood. It was difficult to determine which ones were telling the truth and which ones were just looking for a way to pay for whatever substance they were addicted to. At the time, Rome had supported his handling of the issues. He would quietly remove the cleric involved and let things smooth over.

But this time it was different. This time the victims were going to the press. And once the press started calling, the pressure to issue a formal apology, make monetary restitution, or even turn the accused over to civil authorities increased. Mulcahy had inherited his post in Boston only six years before, many years after most of the claimed incidents of abuse there had taken place. He didn't think it was entirely coincidental that his predecessor entered early retirement shortly before various news outlets got ahold of the complaints—hundreds in the Boston archdiocese alone, and thousands nationwide, the highest number made public in the history of the American Church. At last count, an independent research report had identified more than four thousand priests accused in nearly eleven thousand incidents since the 1950s. Where they were getting this information from was a mystery to Mulcahy. Rising through the ranks in the Church, he learned that he and the others were expected to refer sexual-abuse cases to their superiors for handling rather than to the civil authorities. The suggested guidance on such cases was rooted in a Vatican decree called *Crimen Sollicitationis*, which addressed solicitation of sexual favors before, in, or after confession. According to the decree, all parties involved—including the victims—were expected (if not directly ordered) to maintain silence about such incidents and any associated investigations under threat of excommunication. In the absence of formal instructions on how to treat abuse that took place outside confession, Mulcahy's superiors had tended to follow *Crimen Sollicitationis*. For his entire career, this guidance had been respected. But that had changed, and with it, Mulcahy noticed, so had other areas under the Church's control.

When evidence of widespread abuse began to gather attention, for every outraged parishioner, there'd been one who remained true and committed to the Church. These supporters shared with church leaders the information about cases they came across in the police precinct, in the schools, and in attorney's offices. ("Several accusers came in together," one woman had recently told Mulcahy, speaking of a visit to one of Boston's sharpest civil litigators, where she was a receptionist. "It doesn't take a rocket scientist to figure out what they're doing there.") Tip-offs of this kind helped neutralize unwanted surprises that would knock any other leadership off-kilter. But now, Mulcahy had noticed a cooling of support. Attendance numbers for weekly Mass, including the one he presided over, were down. And more than a few telemarketers reaching out for the bishop's annual appeal at Christmas had been given surly responses to requests for money. "So you can pay for the lawyers, you filthy bastards?" said one angry message left on the archdiocese's general number, and the caller demanded to be taken off the call list. It was a request the telemarketers immediately obliged.

No, it was obvious to Mulcahy that the leaders in Boston and DC had known this might be coming when they approached him with news of his transfer to the Northeast, back to his hometown and memories of growing up in South Boston with his parents and their soft Galway accents. With his large belly, red cheeks, and twinkling blue eyes, Mulcahy was the perfect figure to assume leadership in a situation like this and quell the fears of their followers. Nothing about him spoke of sexuality at all—normal or depraved—and his record was stellar. In his many years serving believers in every corner of America, he hadn't once been directly involved in an accusation from a parent or child. And the one and only time he encountered what might be a problematic priest, he took care of the situation.

Father Mike Pechowski was a dynamic teacher who connected with his middle school students, when Mulcahy met him in 1986. Mulcahy, a monsignor then, had thought this was admirable. He had grown up in a more stern tradition of Catholicism, one populated with perpetually enraged Irish and Polish nuns who taught you to fear Jesus more than revere him. Forgiveness wasn't something to be sought as a means of growing closer to God. It was something to tearfully beg for, or risk facing the flames of hell, which the nuns described in excruciating detail.

He found Mike's approach refreshing. He noticed the way Mike reached out to kids who came from broken homes, kids who needed the Church to help reinforce what was right and good. Mike was a devoted basketball coach, and Mulcahy thought his idea to take his students to the local Catholic high school games was a good one. They would look forward to ending their time at Saint Gabriel's primary school and moving on to Sacred Heart High, where they could enjoy the more extensive extracurricular activities it offered as a larger and coeducational school. One evening after a game, Mulcahy went to dinner with Father Bill Schroeder, the principal at Sacred Heart, to talk about his top students and where they might be steered for a college education in line with Catholic teaching ("Keep them the hell away from Saint John's," Mulcahy told him. "That place is about as Catholic as the state of Israel."). After dinner, Mulcahy realized he'd left his scarf in the gym. Schroeder offered to take him. He took Schroeder's building keys and left him in the warm car while he jogged across the deserted parking lot and went in the side door of the gymnasium.

The scent of industrial cleaning solution mixed with ammonia hit him as he entered. A lightbulb dying in a wall lamp thrummed loudly and warped the ceiling's reflection on the floor, so it appeared as though he were walking not on the hard, waxed squares of a hallway, but on a shallow, watery surface. A high-pitched wail broke the silence. It sounded a little like the whine of a steam pipe. But he turned the corner, away from the ceiling pipes, away from the lightbulb's hum, and heard it again, echoing down the empty hallway where light spilled from the gym door.

In the narrowing hallway, his footsteps no longer echoed down the long corridor. He could now hear voices coming from the gym, ghostly whispering, clearing of the throat, and, interspersed throughout, what seemed to be laughter or crying. He reached the double doors of the gymnasium, finding the right one slightly ajar. Shadows of movement interrupted the ray of light, then they stopped. He pulled open the door slowly and peered in. The gymnasium appeared to be empty, but he knew he had heard and seen something.

"Hello?" he called. The words bounced from the glossy floor to the ceiling and back. "Hello?" he tried again, this time louder. He walked toward the bleachers where he'd been sitting and climbed the stairs. Down the long narrow length of the row he spotted his scarf.

He was wrapping it around his neck when he saw it—a swift movement through the slats of the bleachers beneath him, accompanied by a whimper. Someone or something was there. He dropped to his knees and peered into the dimly lit area below, and there it was—the knobby leg of a crying child.

"Come on out, now," he said through the gap. "You know you're not supposed to be here."

The shallow sobbing stopped. "I said come out, son," he repeated. "It's all right. You just need to go home."

He walked down the stairs and rounded the corner to the small space between the wall and the bleachers. By now the boy, who looked to be about eleven years old, was standing up and looking at him with fear, tears streaking his cheeks. His left hand was clenched around something while his right fingered the top of his pants, moving quickly to pinch the snap button closed. It happened so quickly, it barely registered in Mulcahy's mind.

"Do you need a ride home?" He'd seen situations like this more often than he would have liked. Kids who ended up lingering at libraries, schools, even the rectory while they waited for parents, babysitters, or aunts and uncles who couldn't be bothered to come.

The boy looked nervously to his right. His gaze was fixed there. Mulcahy walked closer, but the boy broke into a run all the way down the bleachers to the other side. Mulcahy jogged after him, slowed by the need to dip and dodge beams that threatened his six-foot frame.

He caught up with the boy on the gym floor, grabbed him by the arm, and twisted him around. A half-eaten Snickers bar flew from the boy's hand and skittered across the wooden floor, part of the wrapper still clutched in his hand. Suddenly, the boy vomited onto his shoes, the contents of his stomach looking like he'd raided a candy store. Mulcahy recoiled.

"I'm not going to hurt you—" Mulcahy looked around the room for a paper towel dispenser, anything to clean up the mess. "I just want to make sure you get home safely, all right? Father Schroeder is outside in a nice warm car, and we'll have you home in no time." The boy blanched.

"I'm—no, thanks. Please," he whimpered. His protest was interrupted by the squeak of a door on its hinge. Mulcahy turned in time to see one of the doors swinging shut. He marched the boy over and pushed through the doors with more force than usual.

"Are you here with a friend? Huh? Planning a prank? Come on!" He shouted the words into the dim hall. "Come out now! It's over! Time for you to go home!" He wasn't accustomed to being disobeyed. When the second boy did not appear, irritation bubbled into his voice. "Get out here *now!*" he yelled.

Mike Pechowski rounded the corner at that moment, a sports bag slung over his shoulder and a basketball in hand. "Everything okay, Monsignor?" he said, but the words didn't have their usual pep.

"I think so, Father. Just a couple of hooligans who need to get home. I forgot my scarf and happened upon them." Mulcahy tried to walk the boy closer to Mike, but the boy dragged his feet, squirming and twisting. "Do you recognize this young man?"

Mike smiled broadly at the boy. "Of course I do." The boy vehemently resisted Mulcahy now, wrenching himself this way and that to escape.

"He's Tommy Gilroy," Mike said. "And he's usually not this much trouble, are you, Tommy?" He hunched down and looked at Tommy. "Stop causing problems. Come on, I'll take you home." He reached for Tommy's arm, but the boy withdrew, turned his head sharply, and began retching again, fierce dry heaves that racked his small body and made him cough.

Mulcahy felt alarmed. Tommy Gilroy was ill, that much was clear, but when he reached out to feel the boy's forehead, Tommy shrieked. "I think maybe it would be best if Bill and I, if we take him to the hosp—" He paused when he saw them through the mesh pocket on Mike's bag: a handful of Snickers bars.

"What are you doing here?" Mulcahy asked slowly. Mike's body jolted.

"Me?"

Mulcahy chose his words carefully. "I thought you left when we did." He looked around the deserted hallway. "There's no one here except—" He nodded at Tommy, who had stopped fighting and limply swayed in his grasp. His hand nervously played with the top snap of his pants. He looked at Mike and began whimpering again. "Is there something—" Mulcahy could barely bring himself to ask the question. "What's going on here?" he finally managed. The color drained from Mike's face.

"What—" Mike sputtered. "How do you mean?"

"Were you in the gym with Tommy? Just now when I came in?"

"Uh, look, Monsignor." Mike's voice cracked as he spoke. "I'm just here for—"

"Were you under the bleachers with this boy? I heard someone else in the gym and you're the only person here." The subtext of his questions thudded in the back of Mulcahy's brain. His mouth felt dry as he formed the words, but they came out with urgency.

"I'm getting the basketballs we need to borrow for drills tomorrow. That's all." At Mulcahy's lack of response, he tried again. "Hey, now. I'm not sure what you mean here, but I'm just helping out—"

"What I mean, Father Pechowski, is that I've got a deserted building and a sobbing child who seems to be scared to death of you. Is there something I need to know about why that is?"

Mulcahy knew immediately that he'd given too much away. Mike's head snapped forward and his eyes narrowed. "I don't think so, John." The use of his first name caught Mulcahy off guard. "And I'd be careful about what you imply."

Mulcahy was taken aback. He'd never had a subordinate speak to him this way. "What did you just say?"

"You heard me, John." Mike, who was shorter than Mulcahy but seemed to be growing before his very eyes, walked forward, stepping so close that Mulcahy could feel his breath on his neck. Tommy writhed, bucking wildly to get loose. "Seems to me," Mike said, "I'm the one who came around the corner here and found this kid trying to get away from you with his pants half unbuttoned." He nodded at Tommy. "So I'd think again about what you say."

Mulcahy's vision whited out. He felt himself move, heard noises, and vaguely perceived the pressure of a few blows. When his sight returned, he had Pechowski pinned to the wall, one hand crushing the younger priest's windpipe while the other punched him repeatedly in the gut, angry jabs that sank deep into the soft parts of Mike's abdomen and battered the hard bones of his rib cage. Sound flew from Mulcahy's mouth as he delivered the blows, but his head was swimming, he couldn't make anything out. Mike's eyes bulged as he gasped for air. When Mulcahy finally released him, he did so by shoving him across the hallway so he bounced off the far wall and tumbled to the ground. "Do you hear me, you son of a bitch?" he growled, his senses at last returning. "No more after-school help, no more basketball with the kids, no more Snickers bars, and I swear to God if I hear you've given anyone a ride home"—he hovered just above Mike's face, fist drawn back—"I will bury you. Understand me? I will fucking bury you."

The sound of footsteps pulled him away. He turned to see the silhouette of Tommy Gilroy growing smaller as he ran down the length of the hallway and out a swinging door to the frigid temperatures outside. "Now get up." Mulcahy spat the words at Mike. "And go clean the vomit in that gym."

When he walked out to the brightly lit parking lot, he found Tommy near Bill's car. Bill was wrapping Tommy in a blanket and putting him into the backseat.

"Everything okay?" Bill asked, his gaze falling on Mulcahy's hands, already swelling and turning a sickening purple.

"It's going to be," Mulcahy replied. Bill's intuition told him this was a conversation best continued later, if ever. He shut the door on Tommy and got back behind the wheel. Mulcahy's knuckles wouldn't cooperate when he tried to open the passenger-door handle. He was just about to give up when the door popped open. From inside, Tommy had reached over the seat and pulled the handle. Mulcahy tried to smile at the boy, but for both of them it came out as more of a grimace.

Two days later, on the recommendation of his superiors, Father Michael Pechowski was enrolled for a transfer out of Saint Gabriel's to pursue missionary work in the rural mountain villages of Brazil. For his prompt action and discreet handling of the situation, Mulcahy received commendations from his church superiors. Nearly fourteen months later, in a move those same leaders would many years later have to defend in a separate abuse investigation, Mulcahy was made a bishop.

This same discretion served him well when he was contacted by Milton Casey looking for advice. Given the amount of attention focused on the Boston archdiocese's sexual-abuse scandal and on Mulcahy in particular, he knew it would be best for Casey and Wyncott if he remained in the background. But he also knew what Owen knew and what was at stake for the Church. More importantly, he knew how badly Casey needed votes. There had to be a way for both sides to get what they needed, and Mulcahy had just the solution.

The proposal should come from Owen. Mulcahy had discussed it with him, and Owen agreed. And although archdiocese attorneys had developed it along with an impact-and-feasibility analysis, it was decided that Casey should be guided to arrive at the clever solution on his own. Political egos were sensitive, Mulcahy had learned in his many years with the Church, and navigating them could ensure success or failure with the same amount of ease.

In the end, if the plan worked, the Church would avoid over $700 million in losses, and Casey would avoid a defeat on election day. And seventy million Catholic votes were worth at least that much, weren't they?

CHAPTER 6

Abingdon Hall, which housed the president's office at Ignatius University, was a large eighteenth-century stone building that sat in the middle of campus. The top of its stained-glass cupola sprouted a large cross on which seagulls and pigeons usually perched (and sometimes defecated) in an act of defiance not even the most irreverent of Ignatius students would consider. In front of the building, a statue dedicated to Cecil Calvert, Lord Baltimore and founder of Maryland as a haven for Catholic colonists, stood piously gazing at the sky. Behind the building, a less stately statue of Saint Ignatius himself sprang from a misshapen knoll left over from an archaeological dig some fifteen years before. This Ignatius stood on what resembled a golden diving board, hilariously posed not unlike the *Birth of Venus* with swiveled hips and outstretched hands. The forefinger of the saint's right hand was twice the length of all his other fingers and pointed in a freakish way at the cupola's cross. Ignatius's nose was obscenely long, and it wasn't unusual to find banana peels, beer cups, or even a condom hanging on it after a weekend of drunken debauchery. Ingram had hated the statue. In his letters to Peter he referred

to it as an erectile dysfunction advertisement and lamented the
need to place it somewhere visible simply because it had been
sculpted by the feckless son of a prominent donor.

Peter hadn't walked the campus grounds in quite some
time. The sight of the statue and the accuracy with which Father
Ingram had described it amused him. He'd made arrangements
through Patricia Roedlin to visit Ingram's office. "I'm not sure
what you'll find there, Mr. Merrick," she said, perplexed by the
request. Less than a week had passed since his death, and feelings about the news remained raw.

It hadn't sounded nearly as meaningful when he tried to
explain it to Patricia, but after he said he thought it was important to include the on-campus element, she realized its merits
for promoting the college and endorsed his decision to visit the
office. She even offered to send a photographer along if Peter
thought it would be helpful. The truth was, his clearest memories were of how many books Ingram had in his office. When
Peter met him, Ingram had only recently been made a dean.
Until a larger office became available, he continued to use his
office in the basement of the Theology Department. He'd chosen the basement office because it had a lot of bookshelves.
While Peter's other professors generally ignored texts that
weren't written by them, Father Ingram's books all appeared
well used and well loved. Splatters of tomato sauce streaked
the page edges like a Pollock painting, and moisture rings dotted the front and back covers.

First introductions to the priest could be intimidating. He
paced in front of the class, expounding on theories of psycho-
religious cultural development and lobbing tough questions
at unsuspecting students. But in his office, he would come
shuffling out from behind a tower of books and papers, which
somehow set a friendlier tone for interaction.

Peter wanted to see that office again. To read the titles
on the spines and use that for inspiration as he struggled to

articulate what Ingram's life meant and the loss caused by his death.

He pulled open the heavy cast-iron doors of Abingdon Hall, where Ingram had relocated after becoming president of Ignatius University. The hallway to his office was flanked by portraits of past Jesuit priests who had served as president, a few French names at first, followed almost exclusively by Irish names. Father Ingram appeared to be the only variation among them. "Don't feel bad," he'd said to Peter once. "I sometimes felt like the only kid in the Bronx who *wasn't* Irish, too."

Patricia was kind enough to meet him at the office. Ingram's secretary, Jane Kemp, was there to meet him as well and introduced herself with more bravado than she clearly felt. She was still shocked by Ingram's death. He couldn't remember if she'd been around when he was an undergraduate. In those days, he hadn't spent much time with the university president, an elderly Irish man who mingled with the undergraduates from Jesuit high schools first and foremost, Catholic high schools next, and, if he had time left, kids like Peter, who had gone to public school. Peter never said so, but he sometimes wondered if Ingram would have taken an interest in him if he hadn't managed to outshine the other students in a theology class freshman year. Even so, he didn't look back at the uneven attention bitterly. To priests and students alike, it hadn't seemed unequal. It was just the way things were.

Jane led him into the cavernous office. He was surprised by how little seemed familiar. He looked for the items he knew best: a brass rubbing of a German knight he'd coveted for years, and the framed photo of an Anglican bishop blessing a fox hunt in Devon that, upon closer inspection, included a hound urinating on the bishop's opulent robes, its lithe leg lifted high for maximum coverage.

Ingram used the photo, he said, to "weed out the students rendered spineless by piety." During Peter's second or third class with Ingram, the vibrant priest had held the photo up for students to see. "What do you think of it?" he said excitedly. From his seat in the third row, Peter had spotted the hound and was trying to disguise the shock on his face.

"What do you think, Ms. Healy?" Ingram asked a bubble-gum-chewing blonde sitting near Peter. She wore a tight tank top with the pink lace of her bra straps slung down both shoulders. Green shamrocks dangled from her ears, and around her neck a sterling silver string of Celtic knots came to a point just above her epic cleavage.

"Of what, Fawther?" She snapped the words in a nasal Long Island accent.

"The photo, Ms. Healy. The photo!"

"Oh, I . . . Well . . . ," she struggled.

"What spiritual essence does it evoke in you?" Ingram prodded her.

"I, uh, like maybe God and nature?" she mumbled.

"Really?" Ingram's tone indicated his belief was anything but real.

Next up was a Fordham Prep graduate on the water-polo team.

"A metaphor for the Church's historical hunt for heretics," he said, oozing intelligence and confidence well beyond his eighteen years.

"Mmm." Ingram's head wobbled with noncommittal consideration. He paused in front of the first chair in Peter's row. "What about you, Mr. Merrick. What does it evoke in you?"

Peter had a cogent thought on the matter, but the obvious nature of it gave him pause. He thought there must be something wrong with him for not seeing something more profound.

"Confusion, sir?" Peter expected a rebuke.

"Why confusion?"

"Because the hound is, uh . . . relieving itself on the bishop?" Peter uttered the words with trepidation. He waited for the priest to call him juvenile.

Instead, Ingram whooped with laughter and clapped. "Indeed, Mr. Merrick. Perhaps the hound was confused. Those Anglicans—you know, especially the English ones—can be very wooden!"

Ingram explained that most students were too self-conscious to say what they actually saw. "Don't overthink it," he barked at them. "Don't overthink yourselves into a stupor of silence." He wandered slowly back to the desk at the front of the classroom.

"Sometimes a dog urinating on a bishop is just that—a dog urinating on a bishop! The most important element of worldly faith, ladies and gentleman," he continued, "is that though we represent God, we are but men and women made in his image. Human and, at times, vulnerable. Even to the bladder of a canine. I don't want you to say what you think I want to hear. To regurgitate what someone else with more letters after his name has already said. I want you think about what human frailty means for religion. Show some ambition!"

By commenting honestly, Peter had evidently impressed Ingram. He heard from subsequent classes that Father Ingram's hound photo was a ploy he used to break in every class of freshmen. That's why Peter was so surprised that he couldn't find it now as he looked around the office, while Jane Kemp and Patricia Roedlin anxiously watched his face for any sign of emotion. He didn't give them one, not at first. It wasn't until he noticed the boxes around the room, half open and half filled, mostly with file folders, papers, and the occasional book, that he cracked a little.

He gestured toward the boxes. "I didn't realize they'd appointed a new president already. Isn't that—" He tasted bitterness as he spoke. "Isn't it a little soon?"

Jane rubbed his shoulder in a maternal fashion. "Oh, I
know. Believe me. I've been having trouble trying to put things
away myself. It's not to make room for his replacement. At
least not yet."

Patricia stepped forward smiling brightly. "We've had a
request from His Excellency Owen Feeney at the US Conference
of Catholic Bishops to send Father Ingram's papers and correspondence to them. It's quite an honor. We're sending it today."

Peter was perplexed. "What do they want his papers for?"
But Patricia was no longer listening. She'd begun taking photos
with her iPhone.

Peter had never much cared for Owen Feeney and other
career-climbing clergy like him. He first met Feeney a few
years after graduation, at dinner with Ingram one evening in
Manhattan. He was a little man, slight of build and possessed
of the inadequacy complex that usually afflicts such men. His
rust-colored hair was thinning into transparent wisps, leaving the pale and freckled skin of his scalp peeking through the
tufts like bits of skull. Dark brown eyes peered out from behind
severe round spectacles that seemed better suited to a 1920s
silent movie. A small reddish caterpillar mustache sprang
from his upper lip. Like him, it seemed to struggle to grow. His
speech patterns were incongruously grandiose, and when he
spoke, he deliberately deepened his voice in a way that forced
him to puff out his chest like a bird.

"What an *absolute* pleasure it is—*really*—to meet one of
James's best students. Do you drink sherry? I *do* hope so." He'd
taken Peter's hand and shaken it too emphatically.

Could he possibly know that much about Peter? Ingram
only ever mentioned Feeney occasionally in their years of men-
toring and friendship, and it usually came courtesy of another
battle the Church faced in the press. "Owen must be having
an awful time with this," Ingram would say, the earnestness
in his voice almost paining Peter. This earnestness was one

of the qualities Peter most admired, envied, and puzzled over in Ingram. He knew firsthand how often people based their beliefs and convictions on what was most personally advantageous to them. He felt certain that from his privileged post inside the DC Beltway, Feeney felt little or none of the genuine concern or guilt that plagued Ingram. A year or two after that, he ran into Feeney at a National Press Club function in Washington, where Feeney said much the same thing as when they first met.

"Oh, Mr. Merrick, what a *pleasure* to see you. It's an *absolute delight* to run into one of James's best students, *really*. I *do* hope you still drink sherry?"

No, he didn't like Feeney one bit. He found him fake and unctuous, and he told Ingram as much.

Ingram only mildly protested. "You mustn't be so hard on him," he said.

Peter scoffed. "I'm not. He's a shady powermonger and a poster child for everything that's wrong with the Vatican."

Ingram, with his reservoir of patience and understanding that Peter had been born without, sighed deeply, his eyebrows furrowing more in concern than consternation. "Owen is a good man at heart. I truly believe that. Even if, at times, he allows ambition to cloud his judgment."

Peter disagreed. As far as he could tell, Feeney's most notable contributions to society had been to show up at political functions, dodge questions from the media about mistakes made by the Church in handling abuse accusations, and go on talk shows to criticize the use of stem cells. It didn't help that early in Peter's journalism career, Feeney had written a letter to the editor of the *Chicago Sun-Times* characterizing an article Peter wrote about union-busting to preserve profit margins at a nearby Catholic hospital as defamation and demanding an apology.

Peter resented what he thought was hypocrisy and knew
how to hold a grudge. "If he's so interested in the morality of
these issues and saving America's soul," he carped to Ingram
during one of their catch-up sessions, "why isn't he at the
Capitol fighting for legislation himself instead of hiding behind
Jesus and cocktail parties?"

Ingram's raised eyebrow told him he'd gone too far. "Don't
pretend to be so naïve," he chastised his protégé. "Politics,
Peter, has always been the second role of religion. Occasionally
it's even been the first. You're kidding yourself if you've ever
thought otherwise. You're right, though. Owen would've made
a formidable congressman."

"But Rome is an easier mark," Peter muttered with disdain.

"Maybe so," Ingram conceded. "It's a complicated relationship—politics and religion. One I don't pretend to understand.
But also one that can't always be defined by convenient sound
bites."

Nonetheless, now that Peter was standing in the office of
his former friend looking at the remains of his life being boxed
up, he felt angry. In that moment he didn't just dislike Owen
Feeney for his self-promotion and habit of placing political
machinations above doing good. In that moment, he also hated
him for being so quick to put the pieces of James Ingram away.
Worse, to put them on a shelf in his *own* office, as if by doing
so he could ever hope—through proximity, through osmo-
sis, through pure envy—to glean any of the grace that had so
clearly bypassed Feeney himself.

Peter watched as a pair of burly men parked a hand-
cart outside the door and began carrying sealed boxes into
the hallway. Patricia took a break from packing to answer a
phone call while Jane gave instructions to one of the mov-
ers. She kept saying the words slowly and loudly and point-
ing with gusto. The man, whose uniform said he was named
Eduardo, blinked at her with the benign patience of someone

accustomed to assumptions about his English fluency. At the end of Jane's (downright aerobic) display, he nodded and said, "Yes, ma'am. We got the address in DC and will make sure it's hand delivered."

Peter walked from box to box, peering with some jealousy at the physical objects that had outlived his friend: books, three-ring binders, a chipped mug with a pun about Descartes. A large bound volume, *The Collected Works of Joseph Conrad*, had been crammed into a nearby crate. Peter absentmindedly picked it up and flipped through the pages. Sentences were underlined throughout, the margins riddled with running commentary in Ingram's handwriting. "Causality and redemption!" he'd scrawled on a page of *Lord Jim*. "The convenient ignorance of power . . . ," he'd written midway through *Heart of Darkness.*

Peter smiled and closed the book, making to return it to its crate, when from the back sleeve of its battered jacket, two small envelopes slipped out and fell to the floor. As he picked them up, Peter recognized the pale cream linen stationery and wavy script from the many letters he'd received from Ingram. But he was struck by large red rejection messages pinning Ingram's words to the page: "Return to Sender" on one, and "Address Unknown" on the other. In his nearly twenty years bouncing around at least fourteen countries, Peter couldn't remember missing one of Ingram's letters. Even when he was in a small village in Malawi, Ingram's letters had reached him. His mentor had been as devoted to keeping his address book updated as he was to keeping epistolary traditions alive. Peter stared at the letters, suppressing the urge to read them. He stuffed them in the book and reached to put it back in the crate when he spotted—in the hole left when he picked up the book—more scattered letters.

Maybe it was his all his time in war zones, or the memory of getting caught reading comic books during Mass, but Peter somehow knew that he wanted to examine the letters and that he would need to do it discreetly. He retrieved the letters from the book, grabbed a few more from the crate, and tucked them all into his jacket pocket.

He stepped into the hallway and took advantage of the privacy to look more closely at the letters. Two were addressed to a Kevin Garrity in Olmsted, Wisconsin. The "Return to Sender" was handwritten in each case, apparently by the same person. It seemed odd to Peter that the message didn't indicate it was a wrong address or that the recipient no longer lived at that location. This was a personalized, individual refusal to accept the letters. The date and time stamps showed they had been sent two years apart. The third letter was addressed to Angela Terzulli in Parkchester, Illinois. Her envelope bore the "Address Unknown" stamp. The last, addressed to Erik Bader in Claremont, Pennsylvania, had been stamped "Return to Sender."

He tucked the envelopes away and returned to Ingram's office. Patricia was pulling books down from their shelves, and Jane was labeling boxes with a fat Sharpie. Its tangy chemical smell wafted through the air. Her letters were large and thin. *Illinois*, it read when she finished. She turned to the box next to it and drew a tall *W*.

"Excuse me, Jane," Peter said. "What's in those boxes?"

"Papers and files from his various parishes," she answered. "Homilies, research notes, you name it. He sure loved to write, didn't he?"

Peter was surprised. "His parishes?"

"Yes—the various cities where he spent time as a novitiate. Before he came to Ignatius."

Peter thought about the letters. "Would it be possible to get a list of those locations?"

Jane and Patricia looked at him quizzically.

He smiled tightly and said, "I'd like to be able to mention his work elsewhere. The piece is meant to be a retrospective on his entire life. From the moment he decided to join the Society of Jesus up until his—up until now."

Jane's face crumpled again at the reminder. "Of course, yes," she said. "I can get you that information now, if you'd like." She walked briskly to the antechamber where her desk sat, a look of focused determination and efficiency on her face. It was clearly a relief to have something else to do. He soon heard frenzied tapping on the computer keyboard.

"When do you think the piece will be finished?" Patricia tried to ask the question nonchalantly, but failed.

"It's almost done," he lied. "Eight hundred words isn't a lot of space. I'm afraid it won't even scratch the surface of who he was and what he accomplished. But I'll provide you with a copy by tomorrow," he said, careful not to commit to rewriting anything based on her review. Normally he didn't mind word limits. They had a way of restraining a writer, of forcing you to remove self-indulgent flourishes and get to the most important information. But this time he would have liked a little more room to play with. It didn't seem possible to limit James Ingram to less than a page.

Jane returned with a summary of Ingram's priestly career—where and when he joined the Jesuits, what he studied, and where he taught in regency. Olmsted, Wisconsin, and Parkchester, Illinois, weren't on the list, but that didn't necessarily mean anything. Garrity and Terzulli might have met Ingram as students at Ignatius the same way Peter had. Terre Haute was on the list, but Peter had no idea where Parkchester was in relation to the Indiana border. More out of curiosity than anything, he decided to look closely at both the letters and the list Jane gave him later.

He put the list in his satchel and began to pack up. It wasn't exactly what he'd planned to find when he arranged to visit

Ingram's office, but he did feel closer to being able to start than before.

"Thank you so much for letting me visit," he said, shaking Jane's hand. "It feels right to have been here."

By the time he walked across campus back to his car, he'd already queued up Google on his phone to search for Kevin Garrity in Wisconsin.

CHAPTER 7

The office housing President Arthur Wyncott's reelection campaign was a frantic scene most days. An ever-expanding population of volunteers, full-time consultants, and staffers had long outgrown the original space. By either fate or design, overflow offices were scattered in other parts of the city. Milton Casey was apt to be at one of three places at any given time, and strict protocol governed who knew where he was and when. "Don't worry about finding him," Ally's manager, Mark Weintraub, had told her when she started. "Someone can always get in touch with him, but that someone is not you. Not yet." On her first day of work, Mark gave her a list of dos and don'ts when it came to dealing with Milton Casey, compiled by staffers who'd been there far longer.

Its two pages ranged from the truly informative ("Do read every newspaper, magazine, or blog you can before you get to work") to the banal ("Do NOT take the last Diet Orange Crush in the refrigerator, no matter how thirsty you are"). Other rules repeated Wyncott's stance on various issues with a reminder to espouse them at all times: "Do promote strong moral messaging in innovative ways." Ally smirked, imagining the list as

Martin Luther's *Ninety-Five Theses* tacked to the front doors
of the Capitol, the words marching across the page in strong
Latin script. *Ne abdūcite ultimum Diet Orange Crush nītrum.*

Those first few days, she noticed the office was a bit like a
high school Advanced Placement class. There were the staffers who did most of the talking, tripping (sometimes tram-
pling) over each other to get as much attention as possible.
Then there were the quiet ones who kept their heads down
and plowed through, choosing to let their written memos and
research reports speak for them instead. In between was a
sampling of the sharp, the witty, and occasionally the dumb
but well connected. The office was swimming in piles of paper.
Casey did not want to receive e-mails related to sensitive campaign matters (number seven on the "don't" list), which had led
to an explosion of folders and files in a limited space. Anything
he was expected to read needed to be hard copy only. "If you've
got something so brilliant or sensitive to say," Casey bellowed at
the room after a tech-savvy staffer suggested his refusal to use
e-mail made him seem out of touch, "you can damn well say
it in person. I'm not suggesting we *never* use technology. But
I don't understand y'all." He waved an arm around the room.
"You sit fifteen feet from one another and you send e-mail. Get
up and have a conversation, for Chris'sakes. E-mail's a bigger
pain in the ass than it's worth."

Due to Wyncott's status as incumbent president, communication with various members of his team in the White House
was almost constant. In nearly a year and a half with the campaign, Ally hadn't been assigned to a specific division or task.
She wasn't so low on the rungs that she didn't get to work on
interesting projects. It was just clear that she was a floater—
meant to pitch in with whatever was needed.

When staffers left for the day, anywhere between 9:00 p.m.
and 3:00 a.m., all effort to keep their workstations clean had
typically fallen by the wayside, leaving an impressive trail of

paper carnage behind. A few days after her presentation on Thomas Archer, Ally was one of the only people left in the entire building at 2:30 a.m. and the sole one in her immediate office. She knew she wouldn't be for long. If her transition to life in DC had been rocky thus far—she hadn't yet found a core group of friends and felt out of place as a conservative Catholic—she admired the work ethic many other young Washingtonians exhibited. She possessed a nervous energy that spurred her to get up and work on random projects at random times and always had. In high school, she would sometimes rise at 3:00 a.m. to clean her room, certain she couldn't possibly focus on an upcoming trigonometry exam until she'd accomplished something like rearranging the bookshelves or long-forgotten stuffed animals piled in the corner.

Her analysis of Thomas Archer's religious narrative had come to her in much the same way—as a burst of energy flashing early in the morning as she stared at the ceiling from the comfort of her Ikea bed. She'd been living in the DC area for just under two years now and, unlike most of her colleagues in the office, she did not live in a fashionable part of town. Her basement apartment in Takoma Park, Maryland, was a thirty-minute walk to the Metro in a no-man's-land between the nicer part of Takoma and a grubbier corner of Silver Spring's easternmost border. Many if not all of her immediate neighbors were new arrivals to the United States. Bodegas at the end of Maple Avenue sold strange foods—pigs' feet in brine and vegetables she didn't recognize. On weekends, her neighbors played soccer in the park near her apartment, their families turning out to cheer them on.

For Ally, who felt far from her own family back in Michigan, this was one of the things she liked most about living there: the ability to soak up the family atmosphere even as an interloper. But she hadn't yet learned how to interpret the puzzled reaction she got when she told people where she lived. "That's an *ethnic* part of town, isn't it?" was something she heard often. It was a phrase she found confusing in Washington, a city with people from every corner of the world. What they meant, of course, was that many of the families around her were from Mexico and Guatemala.

Her fluency in Spanish came as a shock to many as well, but learning the language in high school and college had been a natural and practical choice. As the granddaughter of a soybean farmer, she knew how much her family's business and those of her neighbors relied on migrant labor. Learning Spanish wasn't required or expected of her, but the idea of seeing people every day all summer long and not speaking with them seemed inhospitable and unnecessarily rude.

This ambition to speak with people she didn't know was a change for her. As a small child, she had been shy. Every Sunday at Mass with her family she shrank in fear and anxiety during the exchange of greetings prior to the Eucharist. The entire tenor of the service changed when the ritual began. Total strangers stuck their total strangers' hands in her face, murmuring in a weird, offbeat cacophony. "Peace be with you," they said, the words melding in a hushed mumble that grew to a roar when fifty people uttered it at once. It was, by far, her *least* favorite part of attending Sunday services. It wasn't until junior high that, at her mother's urging, she chose to see Mass as an opportunity to learn how to be more outgoing, swallowed her fears, and overcame the anxiety. But even now, an inescapable discomfort erupted in her whenever she heard people murmuring in close proximity to each other. She much preferred political rallies, where people shouted.

Talking to the seasonal workers who appeared each spring was a similar opportunity to face something that intimidated her, to connect with strangers speaking and displaying emotion she could sense, but whose words she could not comprehend. She went to the language lab after school to listen to Spanish language CDs. When she tried to speak to the workers, faltering at first, she got a thrill from the way they smiled and nodded at her attempts. Their tempo, too fast for her to follow at first, soon became familiar. She was able to practice her language skills outside the classroom, and by the time she left for college at Marquette University in Wisconsin, she tested into an advanced Spanish literature class.

Both the extent of her fluency and the history behind it baffled many around her and occasionally impressed them. But that was the nature of Ally Larkin's experience in education and life in general. She defied tidy categories without trying to and possessed an analytical thought process, which most people, Milton Casey included, seemed to overlook. Ideas formed constantly in her head the way one had formed on this night, keeping her in the office after hours. Since lunchtime she'd been tracking down research on voting patterns in midwestern states with fast-growing immigrant populations. The information was all out there, just not in the same place. And she didn't always know what to do with it once she found it. With a sigh, she turned on one of the many televisions in the bullpen and flicked through the channels until she landed on Univision. On-screen, a man in a suit rattled on in Spanish. She repeated his words out loud to follow along and keep her listening skills sharp.

A rustling from Casey's office stopped her midsentence. He poked his head around the door and blinked, the light from her upturned desk lamp causing him to squint. "I didn't know anyone was still here," she started, poking frantically at the remote control to turn down the volume. While a few of the more prized staff generally spent time in his office, she wasn't considered one of them and had never seen the plush brown couch he'd been napping on. In fact, up until the meeting where she distributed the analysis of Archer's familiarity with

South and Central America, she wasn't sure Milton Casey even knew she existed.

"Don't you have a home to go to?" Casey's voice interrupted her thoughts.

"Oh yes. I just wanted to—I'm trying to cross-check information from a Pew Trust analysis of migration patterns in Wyoming and Utah."

"Which one?"

"The new one—from the Pew's Hispanic Trends Project."

He nodded. "I've heard that's an excellent resource."

"You haven't seen their research?" She meant it as a genuine question but was aware how snide it sounded almost as soon as she said it.

"As a matter of fact, Ms. Larkin, I have not. That's what I have you for." He said the words kindly, but not without an edge. "Where do you live? Woodley Park? Tenleytown?"

Ally prepared to answer. This was usually the part where she'd have to smile nicely in response to the description of her neighborhood as "ethnic."

"No, sir. In Takoma Park."

Casey laughed. "Takoma Park? What the hell are you doing all the way out there? Are you a lesbian?" He bellowed the question, a reference to Takoma Park's reputation for being a liberal community where diverse families were more the norm than the anomaly.

"Not a problem if you are," he went on. "Hell, I'd trot you out in front of the cameras if you were."

"Uh, no, sir. I don't actually live in that part of town. I'm more on the outskirts."

"Why aren't you closer to downtown?"

Ally wasn't all that surprised by the question and its unspoken assumption: that someone well connected enough to work for Casey could naturally afford to live in a trendy neighborhood. She'd grown accustomed to the inescapable connection between wealth and opportunity in Washington, DC. Never before had she seen young people so educated, working for such low wages, yet managing to live in opulent apartments. That many of them were subsidized by their parents or their trust funds or a combination of the two shouldn't have surprised her, but it did. Still, in moments like this, she puzzled at how people in politics—whose livelihoods depended on understanding the realities of their constituents—could be oblivious to them. Mark had given her an answer when she asked him about it a few weeks after she started. "Because they can be," he said simply. "Once they're here, they're here. Actually understanding the realities versus just appearing to understand them is a zero-sum game." There was a good chance Mark had learned that explanation from working in Casey's office.

She shrugged. "It's affordable," she told Casey. "And I like the community. People talk to each other there."

"It's full of hippies, isn't it?"

"Well, is it full of lesbians or hippies, sir?"

The question shocked her. She'd been thinking it, of course, the words bubbling to the top of her internal cauldron of simmering class resentment. But that her mouth formed the words and her vocal cords pushed out the sounds necessary to say them aloud—to her boss of all people, a man who had barely spoken six words to her before now—astounded her. She felt her cheeks flush. Casey regarded her, narrowing his eyes as though he were going to deliver a rebuke, and then burst into laughter, a mighty guffaw that took her off guard.

"Well, I guess they could be lesbian hippies, now couldn't they?"

"Yes. Yes, they could."

"Don't suppose you could talk a few of them into voting for Wyncott, could you? That would be an absolute gold mine," he said.

"I'm not sure I—uh, I don't really know." She could just imagine it. Sitting at dinner with her neighbors Carol and Sadie, eating a meal prepared with vegetables from their garden and meat from the local co-op, talking about education reform. At just what point, she wondered, would it be appropriate to casually mention they might consider a vote for Arthur Wyncott? To throw their backing to a man who didn't consider their twenty years together raising a son to be a valid relationship or acceptable parenting, while he himself was on his second marriage with a daughter addicted to Oxycontin?

Casey had spun the discovery of the addiction deftly. "Don't think of this as a weakness," Casey told the staffers when CNN ran an interview with the dealer who supplied Wyncott's daughter. "This doesn't make Arthur Wyncott an inferior candidate. This makes him just like you and me." Within hours, Ally watched as pundits on Wyncott's side applauded his courage in tackling the important issue of addiction in America and noted his intimate familiarity with the troubles faced by the American people. It was one of many lessons she would learn during her time with Casey's office.

Ally herself had no objection to Carol and Sadie or the life they had built together. But as a lifelong Catholic, she did believe that a marriage in her church had to be in accordance with its teachings—whether that meant she couldn't marry a man who wasn't Catholic, or couldn't marry a woman. If Carol and Sadie wanted to marry in another faith that held a different opinion on the subject then that, in Ally's mind, was a decision for that faith, not her. This position put her apart from many around her. Caught between those who believed she was wrong to deny marriage in any instance and those who said she was condoning a grave sin by not condemning Carol and Sadie, Ally chafed at the lack of flexibility. She learned not to express her opinions about it at all, a defense mechanism that

guaranteed her peace in the passionately political climate of
DC, but also made her feel all the more isolated.

Casey went on. "Well, it would certainly be a coup if we
could get a lesbian couple up there to say they supported
Wyncott. It wouldn't hurt our numbers at all."

Ally smirked. "I'll keep an eye out for one, sir."

"It's Milt. You're not checking me into a hotel, for Chris'
sakes."

Ally laughed in spite of herself. "Okay then, Milt, I don't
think I'll have much luck finding many lesbians who want to
vote for Wyncott, but I'll try."

"Take them to brunch and talk it over with them. They love
brunch, don't they?"

She cocked her head and gave him a confused smile, unsure
whether he was truly that obtuse or just being funny. A quick
wink gave her the answer.

"But in all seriousness"—his expression grew focused—
"you've got some good ideas. And you're fluent in Spanish?"
He nodded at the television behind her, where the mustached
anchor was now reviewing soccer scores.

Ally nodded. "Yes. It was on my resume. At the bottom."

Casey waved his hand dismissively. "I don't pay much
attention to resumes, darlin'. Half of what people put on 'em
is horseshit. They spend six hours volunteering at a community garden and by the time it gets to my desk, they've saved
the Brazilian rain forest." He darted back into his office and
returned with a packet of materials in hand.

"I'd like to see you get involved with this." He handed her
a folder labeled "Faith-based Initiatives." "John Mulcahy said
you've done a lot of work with religious organizations."

"Cardinal Mulcahy?" She didn't mean it as a correction.
She was just unaccustomed to hearing him called by his casual
name.

Casey rolled his eyes in exaggerated embarrassment. "Yeah, yeah. I forgot. *Cardinal.*"

She tried to recover by moving on. "In Boston. The summer I worked for him. He put me on a team working with Catholic schools."

"How do you feel about Philadelphia?"

"As the US capital of type-two diabetes?" She'd just finished a research project for Wyncott's childhood-obesity prevention team.

He laughed. "Ah, now, I think Memphis has Philly beat there. But keep that opinion—both of 'em—to yourself. We're already on thin ice with Philly voters as it is. I mean what do you think of it as somewhere we need to test the waters with voters?"

She gave him a raised eyebrow. "What kind of voters? We're already on the ground there."

"Voters with a particular interest in Archer because of the very things you've already identified—faith and immigration." He nodded at the TVs. "I assume you watched his rally in Fairhill a few weeks ago?"

Ally nodded. It was a brilliant PR maneuver from Archer's camp that hit its mark perfectly and infuriated Casey, sending him on a rampage through the office. Early on in the campaign, Archer had decided to tackle the question of his religion head on and make it a focal point. Instead of wasting time trying to downplay it, Archer put it front and center, explaining it as the source of his commitment to building strong communities and serving the American people with justice and compassion. Tucked away in northeast Philadelphia, Fairhill was Philadelphia's dominant Hispanic neighborhood, colloquially known as El Centro de Oro, with 70 percent of the community hailing from Puerto Rico, the Dominican Republic, and Colombia.

Fairhill was an ideal location to launch Archer's message. Several months beforehand, Philadelphia voters had elected a Democrat named Milo Garcia as mayor. The grandson of immigrants from Oaxaca, Mexico, Garcia was the first Hispanic mayor of a major northeastern city and signaled a change in the traditional power structure, not just for the Boston-to-DC corridor, but for critical swing states like Pennsylvania.

Archer and his advisers strategically held a rally at a community center in Fairhill to talk about immigration and improving the quality of life for those in impoverished parts of the country, with Mayor Garcia providing the introductory remarks. Welcoming the attendees not just to the rally but to America, Archer reached out to the city's immigrants and Catholics all at once. "Being Catholic compels me to work to eradicate poverty," he said to a cheering crowd. "Being American compels me to welcome those who have come here to work hard for a better life and to restore opportunities for that life. Not just for them, but for all Americans. I hope you'll join me in preserving Philadelphia's heritage and celebrating it. Together, we can build strong, diverse communities across this great nation, starting right here in El Centro de Oro." The crowd roared even louder in approval. The event had received enormous coverage.

"Yes," Ally told Casey. "I remember."

Casey was blunt. "John sai—I mean, the cardinal said you might be the right person to speak with community leaders there. Find out if they're still leaning toward Archer now that the fanfare has settled."

She sat up sharply, unable to disguise her excitement at the opportunity.

"I'll need you to go Monday." He moved on before her enthusiasm became too embarrassing. "And you'll have to go with Steve Tilden." He caught the flicker of irritation on her face when he said the name. Steve was one of her least favorite coworkers. He didn't know it, but Ally had overheard him making fun of her on more than one occasion for being too uptight. Steve seemed particularly preoccupied with the status of her sexual experiences ("Must be like having sex with an igloo," he remarked once. "Even if it happens, it's not likely to leave a dent.") and openly questioned her ability to contribute to the office. To an extent, he was right. Her parents back in sparsely populated Piedmont, Michigan, were not politically connected. They could not, like Tilden's parents, pressure others to hire their son who, as best as Ally could figure, had little beyond an aura of entitlement to offer. The irony of Tilden's disparaging whispers was that he was oblivious to how often everyone referred to him as "Daddy's Checkbook."

"He's been here longer. He'll be a good resource," Casey coaxed her. "I just need someone to take the temperature there. See if you can get some good sound bites for us to throw in. But just so we're clear—whoever comes back with the most information gets the prize. So consider the challenge issued." He put on his jacket and headed for the door.

"Sir?" she called out. He stopped, but didn't turn around.

"Milt?" she tried again. This time he spun to face her with a smirk.

"What's the prize?" she asked.

"Why, knowing you're better than the person I pitted you against, of course." He pulled open the door and stepped through it. "And a free trip to Philadelphia," he said over his shoulder.

She was still laughing when she heard his voice echo from down the hallway.

"Goodnight, Ms. Larkin."

CHAPTER 8

The scent of soup or stew greeted Peter when he got home. His glasses fogged up from the change in temperature. It was so cold out that the short walk from the end of the driveway to the front door was enough to cause him pain. At eighteen degrees (according to the thermometer hanging from the mailbox) it was still several degrees warmer than on the night James Ingram died. Peter stopped in his tracks at the thought. He was processing the news the way he did most things he found unpleasant—in little pieces that tripped him up at the strangest times, but by doing so, only made him stumble and not fall. He wondered what Emma's circle of fellow therapists would say about that.

Grady, a border collie–golden retriever mix with one blue eye and one brown, had come clomping down the hallway even before Peter got the door fully open. Through the haze of his fogged-up glasses, he could make out the form of the dog, his wagging tail and the way he boxed with his front paws in an invitation to play. The eagerness with which Grady greeted him pinched a little. It reminded him of how Emma used to be when he got home from being on assignment. When he returned from Jammu, she'd been so relieved to see him. She knew it was awful, she said, but all she could think about was that he was okay, even though she knew she should be thinking about those who died in the explosion. He accepted that this was the nature of most people—they could conceive of something terrible happening to others but remain utterly focused on if they had been personally affected. But with the acrid scent of roasted flesh and melting plastic still fresh in his mind, he'd snapped at her instead of telling her how glad he was to be home. Now, as he buried his head in Grady's warm, wriggling side he willed himself to be nicer to Emma. He hadn't always been so sharp and argumentative with her. Part of him knew he was pushing her too far, and once the limit was reached she would be gone.

It had happened once when they were dating in college. She was preparing to leave for study abroad in Paris. Rather than tell her he was convinced she would meet some fabulously wealthy, sophisticated, and intelligent European man, he had acted like a jerk. Sniped at her the way he'd been doing lately, laughed at her every contribution or suggestion, as though belittlement would somehow persuade her she was unworthy of any attractive man she met in France.

She had argued at first. He was being ridiculous, she told him. Then she appealed to his ego, explaining she wasn't in love with being in a relationship like most girls in college were. She was in love with *him*. None of it, not the screaming matches or the genuine expressions of affection, made him feel any less powerless to control what happened after she got on the plane. "You're not supposed to control it or me," she'd reminded him firmly on the one and only occasion he came close to telling her what was really bothering him. "You're supposed to trust me." Even then, at age twenty, she was so much more emotionally articulate than he'd ever been, and she still was. Trying to explain that he didn't trust his ability to compete with men he imagined to be more attractive and worldly had come out all wrong. "Then stay here, so I don't have to worry about it," he told her. "Stay and it won't have to be over." That was when she gave up. After weeks of almost daily bickering, she wouldn't take the bait anymore. He kept trying to pick fights with her, to prove she still cared enough for him to be provoked, but she just wouldn't respond. She looked at him one afternoon and said, "That's enough, Peter. Really." Like he was a small child stamping his feet in a shopping mall. A few days later, about a month before she was due to leave, she just disappeared. He called her house. She wasn't home, her mother said. He called her office, a summer job at a financial firm on Wall Street he knew she hated. She wasn't available, a secretary said.

By the fifth night of silence, he had driven to her parents' house in Tenafly, New Jersey, and parked outside to see if she came home. After a few hours her father came out and knocked on the window. "Peter—nice to see you, but it's a bit odd, isn't it? Parking outside the house like this?" Emma's father, Hugh Merriman, was a friendly man with bright blue eyes that crinkled when he smiled, which was most of the time. He was a high school English teacher and seemed always to address Peter as he would his more favored students. "Why don't you come in for a minute?"

Moments later Peter was seated awkwardly at the Merrimans' circular kitchen table with a mug of hot chocolate.

"She's not here," Mr. Merriman said with a bluntness that took Peter aback. "I'm not going to tell you where she is, but I can tell you that she's not here so you don't waste any more time parking out front and scaring the neighbors. Not that I mind it all that much—Mrs. Kearney two doors down is a terror in her own right." He took a sip of hot chocolate. "I just love the miniature marshmallows, don't you? They're like a cluster of little surprises," he said with a warm smile.

"Why is she—why can't I—"

"Oh, I think you know the answer to that, Peter," Mr. Merriman said without a trace of anger or admonition. "Would you want to be around you right now?"

Peter felt the color spring to his cheeks. He was certain he emitted more heat than the old iron teakettle bubbling on the stove.

"I'm sorry," he said. And he meant it. "I don't really know what to say, Mr. Merriman."

"Well, for a start, you don't need to apologize to me. Seems to me Emma's the one you've been hurting lately. Am I right?"

Peter nodded.

"She's not even mad right now, Peter. I think she's done. I know my daughter. She'll give something a hundred tries if she thinks she can get it right. But once she decides there's no use . . . well, she doesn't waste any more time on it. See what I'm saying?"

"I didn't know," Peter said. He could feel tears springing to his eyes but refused to cry in front of his girlfriend's father. "I didn't know she was done."

"I know. But you had to know it was upsetting her. Now look," Emma's father went on, "I think you're a pretty good guy. So get it together if this is what you want. She'll give you another chance if you do." He stood up and patted Peter on the shoulder. "And stop parking out in front of the house or I'll call the cops, okay?"

Peter nodded in a way that made him feel like he was disembodied, watching the entire scene from the ether. He took the mug over to the kitchen sink and reached to turn on the water. It was a product of his time as an altar boy. Cleanliness was a sign of respect, and there was very little that couldn't be fixed by cleaning. Twelve years later when the World Trade Center was hit by two jetliners, Peter would spend every minute he wasn't filing a freelance story vacuuming the apartment he shared with Emma. He would wash the windows from the fire escape and do the same laundry he'd done the day before as if creating a sterile environment within the confines of his home could keep the chaos and fear outside at bay.

"Leave it," Mr. Merriman said of the mug. "I'll get it. I do some of my best thinking when I do dishes." He had smiled at Peter, a warm smile that said everything would be okay if he was willing to let it be.

Now, standing in the front hall nuzzling Grady, Peter realized that Emma wouldn't tell him when she'd had enough this time, either. He would come home some afternoon and find the house empty. She'd probably even leave everything behind for him—except maybe for Grady. She loved that dog. And in fairness, she spent more time with him than he did. In his mind, Peter could already see the Emmaless house. The hallways dark when he came home, the scented candles he mocked her for unlit or gone.

"Honey, is that you?" Emma called from the kitchen. He rounded the corner and found her standing at the gas burner stirring the pot of stew. Heat rose from the wall-mounted oven behind her where he could see rolls browning under the coils.

"They're Pillsbury," she said apologetically. "I can't take credit for them." She beamed a smile at him—her father's crinkle-eyed smile. Peter reached out and pulled her into a hug. He felt the hesitation in her response, so he held on even harder, gave an additional squeeze, waiting for her to return it. She didn't. After a few moments she pulled away. "Well," she said somewhat uncomfortably. "I don't want dinner to burn." She turned back to what she was doing, and Peter watched her for a moment more before retreating to his office. Without thinking, he knocked the door shut with his heel as he entered but caught it before it slammed against the door frame. Outside, the sound of Grady's nails on the kitchen floor rattled down the hallway alongside the syncopated clink of a spoon in the pot.

As he sat down at his desk, he felt a crackle of paper in his pocket. He pulled out Jane Kemp's list of locations where James Ingram had spent time as a novitiate and then as an ordained Jesuit priest before he arrived at Ignatius as a professor. The column next to the locations listed general dates—May 1982 to March 1983—beginning with his entrance into the Society of Jesus in 1970.

Next to the locations, Peter wrote the names of the letter recipients and their towns and states. So far, nothing about Kevin Garrity seemed connected to Ingram's movement. The closest Ingram had ever been geographically to Wisconsin was the brief stint teaching in Indiana.

He looked at the other two letters—Angela Terzulli in Parkchester, Illinois, and Erik Bader in Claremont, Pennsylvania. Terzulli's address was about 140 miles from Providence Cristo Rey High School in Indianapolis where Ingram taught, according to Jane's list, between 1982 and 1985. And Erik Bader was the most direct hit of all. If he was still living in Claremont, he was in the same town where Ingram had volunteered as a retreat coordinator for Good Shepherd Catholic Church while he completed the first of his two PhDs (English and, a few years later, theology) at the University of Pennsylvania.

On the drive back from Ignatius, Peter's search for Kevin Garrity on his iPhone brought up 9,820 hits. He'd decided to wait until he could be a little more specific in his search parameters. He now tried a search for Kevin Garrity and Wisconsin. It still brought over 2,000 hits, although not necessarily in ways that related well to each other. He didn't need to know, for example, that there was an entire town named Garrity in northwestern Wisconsin, or that the Garrity Gators basketball team usually went to regionals each year.

He felt a weary sense of overload as he clicked through the pages, an endless stream of information that had no meaning to him but had meaning to someone somewhere. He tried Erik

Bader, typing in his name alongside Claremont. No immediate luck finding a connection. A slew of articles came up related to Erik's status as a powerhouse player on the Claremont high school baseball team. Articles in the local paper as recent as a month ago referred wistfully to the golden days of Bader's reign as a shining athlete by comparison to the dry spell now affecting the region. Based on the date he graduated from Claremont, it was unclear what sort of interaction Bader would have had with Ingram. At most he'd have been five or six by the time Ingram finished at Penn and moved on. He tried a search on Erik Bader and Good Shepherd. The hit list suddenly went from 282 to 19.

That reduction alone would have been attention grabbing, but Peter didn't have time to contemplate statistics. The first heading that came up under Erik Bader's name alongside Good Shepherd wasn't a list of athletic accolades. It was an article on an abuse survivors' network website in which Bader was quoted. Under the terms of a settlement reached with the Archdiocese of Philadelphia several years beforehand, Bader explained, he was unable to discuss the specifics of his abuse or his case. However, he stated to the author, he could generally confirm that the incidents had taken place in the Archdiocese of Philadelphia. The article commended Bader for his willingness to speak, but appealed to other victims to refuse to sign confidentiality agreements and instead speak openly and publicly. Agreeing to silence, the article argued, prevented other victims from coming forward.

He opened another search window and entered Kevin Garrity's name—this time with "sexual abuse" alongside it. This, too, narrowed the search. Garrity was on a list of individuals who received out-of-court settlements from the Archdiocese of Milwaukee. As with Bader, however, under the terms of the settlement, the details of his case were confidential. He opened a third search and entered Angela Terzulli's name with the same phrase. He wasn't expecting much—from what he'd read about the abuse scandal that had been swirling for several years in America, the victims had tended to be mostly young boys who were now grown men. If he'd been willing to admit it, in his mind Angela Terzulli seemed more like a seventy-six-year-old town librarian than an abuse victim.

He wasn't wrong, but he wasn't right either. The search didn't bring up a list of victims with her name on it. The first article to pop up listed Angela Terzulli as surviving her late son, Anthony Terzulli, whose body had been pulled from the rushing depths of the Meskousing River. According to witnesses, the twenty-nine-year-old man had voluntarily plunged from the crossbeams of a truss bridge nearly fifty feet above the water. Funeral arrangements, the article concluded, were being handled by Martinelli Bros. Funeral Home.

The next few articles were related to the suicide—factual, mostly. Small blurbs in the police news sections of two of the local Parkchester newspapers, followed several days later by an obituary in one and an advertisement in the other praying to Saint Jude for Anthony's soul and expressing sorrow for the entire Terzulli family.

The sixth article tied it all together. Anthony Terzulli was listed as a plaintiff in a suit brought by more than eighteen men in Illinois who claimed they had been sexually abused by a Father William Hartnett while attending the Academy of the Holy Cross parish school or participating in parish activities. The suit named the Diocese of Greeley as the defendant and cited failure on the part of its leaders to remove Hartnett and at least one other abusive priest who had rotated through the parish despite numerous written complaints from parents. After an article about Father Hartnett's abuse at Holy Cross was reposted to an abuse survivors' site, parents from two of his previous parishes in Rochester and Baltimore had come forward to say they notified his superiors of similar abuse and cc'd the archbishop's office on subsequent complaints after failing to receive satisfying resolution. In an interview with Parkchester's local paper, the parents of a victim from the Baltimore parish claimed it would have been impossible for the individuals who transferred Father Hartnett *not* to know he was a risk before relocating him to his post in Illinois.

The plaintiffs' attorney had filed court papers to compel the church to share internal documents regarding who knew what about Father Hartnett's predilections and when, but an attorney representing the Diocese of Greeley had filed a series of motions to deny the request. It wasn't the first time Peter had heard about this sort of thing happening. Since the scandal erupted, a number of dioceses facing scrutiny had declined to cooperate fully with attorneys, citing internal investigations already underway and privacy entitlements for the clergy involved to refuse to turn over documentation about their actions to the victims' legal representation.

Peter remembered talking to Ingram about it the last time he saw him, not long before he left for Jammu. It was the only occasion on which he could recall Ingram expressing genuine inability to understand the choices of the church he'd devoted his life to. It wasn't easy to watch. Ingram's face hadn't contorted in rage or even protest the way it typically did when he talked about something he felt passionate about. Instead, he'd sunk deeper into the chair in his office and scowled at his fingers, arching them against each other to create a misshapen circular cage. It was the first time Peter asked him directly about his thoughts on the subject. Not specifically about the nature of pedophilia. Ingram was clear it was a crime of the worst variety and that anyone who committed it, priest or not, should be punished. Perhaps more importantly, anyone who committed such crimes should be absolutely and utterly prevented from having the opportunity to do it again, no matter what that took.

They'd had that particular conversation before. But out of respect for his friend more than anything, Peter had refrained from asking Ingram his thoughts on the Church's larger role. The Church was being blamed in a number of ways. Peter, who'd been raised Catholic but didn't consider himself that religious, thought he'd been pretty fair about deciphering criticisms with merit and those without. He didn't believe, for example, that by refusing to let priests marry, the Church had effectively hung a neon sign in front of its doors saying "Child Rapists Welcome Here!" And he was even willing to entertain the idea that with charges as serious at these, it was necessary to afford accused priests a certain amount of due process—a silent investigation of sorts to determine what the truth was before destroying someone's career or reputation.

But when he read articles about a diocese refusing to turn over church records related to accused priests, even when they were subpoenaed, he was floored. Such conduct was detestable when CEOs of companies that mortgaged their staff's pensions did it. When a religious organization employed the obstructionist tactics of a Fortune 500 company, it somehow seemed that much more distasteful.

A Montana Supreme Court ruling was what set him off that hot July afternoon when he and Ingram met. The court had ruled that a Catholic diocese didn't have to turn over its records on a priest who was charged with deviant sexual intercourse with a minor. The prosecutor obtained a subpoena to review the priest's personnel files and establish if a pattern of similar conduct had been reported to his superiors. The diocese refused to surrender them, offering instead a private inspection of select records in the judge's chambers and only in the presence of the chancellor of the diocese. The priest, the diocese argued, was entitled to reasonable privacy. The Montana Supreme Court had agreed.

Peter wasn't interested in whether the Church was correct from a legal standpoint. It didn't matter that the prosecutor was still able to get the information, either. What mattered was that the Church demanded special treatment and expected its own ideas of justice to trump the civil laws governing the rest of American society. To him, it was a moral imperative to cooperate with that system because it was the right thing to do, not just because it was the law. Hiring lawyers to split hairs and prevaricate like executives at Enron or Brown & Williamson wasn't acceptable under any circumstances. "Why would you argue about something so clearly black and white?" he asked Ingram during their discussion. "I don't understand it. I just don't."

Ingram stared at his fingers, a vexed expression on his face. "If there's one thing I'm beginning to learn throughout this entire mess, Peter," he said, "it's that none of what you know about the Church—about the people in the same pew as you or the priests you've known since your baptism—is the complete truth." Ingram looked at him sadly but firmly.

"I'm sure there are genuine moments," he continued. "But when these men stand in front of that parish every Sunday and talk about the power of forgiveness—that we are all blessed with the grace to ask for it and to receive it—they're not being completely honest."

"That's for sure," Peter grunted. "There are just some things that can't be forgiven."

Ingram shook his head. "No, not that exactly," he said. "Everything can be forgiven. And I do mean everything— my acceptance that Christ was the son of God hinges on it." Ingram had unconsciously begun to rub the topmost button of his shirt, where his Roman collar normally peeked out from under its side binding, though Peter couldn't remember the last time Ingram had worn the garment. "But there are some people who will never have the humility to ask. And without that, nothing—not forgiveness or healing—can be offered."

Ingram had been more troubled by the discussion than Peter had ever seen him. At the time, Peter assumed he was struggling to reconcile his feelings about the abuse with belonging to the religious community that had committed it. But now, as he looked up the names associated with the letters, he wondered. He stared at the envelopes, pondering whether to open them and read the contents. The owners had either returned them or didn't know of their existence. And Ingram was gone. Peter wasn't exactly worried about his friend finding out and chastising him, but he was superstitious enough to envision Ingram staring at him from whatever form Heaven or the afterlife took, and shaking his head in disappointment.

As often happened, Peter's curiosity got the better of him. He opened the first letter, to Terzulli, and unfolded it. Based on the introduction, it appeared to be one of a series. It made reference to how long it had been since last he wrote and his hope that the words and sentiments he expressed in that letter had achieved their desired effect.

Peter scanned the page, looking for anything that might offer a specific explanation. None popped out. The phrasing was, it seemed, intentionally vague and made almost constant reference to the earlier letters. When he got to the end, Peter froze. Ingram once again expressed regret—his remorse for what had happened and his hope that Terzulli might someday be able to forgive him and the others to find peace for herself and her son's memory.

The page shook in Peter's trembling fingers. He read the words again. *Words cannot express how sorry I am for what happened or my personal regret for what my failings have created in this life for you.*

Ingram's failings? A flaw in him that left another person's life irrevocably changed for the worse? Peter tore open the next letter, to Erik Bader. Once again, Ingram offered a personal apology for what happened and expressed hope that someday Erik could find a way to offer forgiveness. This letter too appeared to be one in a series. In ornate script that stretched across the page, Ingram said he'd been giving much thought to what happened and why. That he was trying to find the answers in himself to offer an apology with more merit, because apologies without explanation were the most dissatisfying and disingenuous kind.

Peter blinked repeatedly, refocusing on the words each time as though doing so could change their meaning. It didn't. Each time he looked at the pages in his possession, he found his longtime friend and mentor apologizing to young men who had been sexually abused, or to their families, and asking for their forgiveness. From down the hall Emma called out to come to dinner. Grady entered the room and urgently nuzzled Peter's knee. But all Peter could feel was his churning stomach and the weight of his last conversation with Ingram about the sexual-abuse scandal.

Peter had read aloud from a newspaper profiling a priest in upstate New York who was being investigated for abusing children on a retreat. He'd been there less than a year after transferring from a parish in Pennsylvania. The community was in absolute shock, the article stated. The townspeople were in disbelief about the charges. "He helped set up the battered women's shelter downtown," said one resident. "Went door to door to find the money until the women of this community had a safe place to go." Another one, a widowed father of four, described how the priest lent him his personal car so he could go to work after his truck broke down, and it took him two months to save up enough money to pay for the repairs. "This just isn't possible," the grateful father told the reporter. "Someone that good just doesn't do this kind of thing."

74 C. S. FARRELLY

But that was the main point of this entire situation, Peter knew. Folding up the paper, he looked up at Ingram. "He's right. How does that happen? How can someone be so devoted to helping others and do this at the same time?"

Ingram looked straight at Peter for the first time since the discussion began. "That's a question we've been trying to answer since Cain and Abel," he said. His eyebrows curved inward in an expression that bordered on pity as he rose slowly from his desk chair. "Ah, Peter," he said, leaning over to pat him on the shoulder. He picked up Peter's copy of the newspaper. "May I?" Peter nodded. Ingram glanced once more at the article before expertly folding it in preparation for his Metro-North ride home and stuffing it into his jacket pocket.

"The truly terrifying thing about evil isn't that it exists, Peter," Ingram had said. "It's that it manages to coexist with good in the places we least expect it. And always has."

Peter thought about the other letter he'd found but could not take, and what Ingram had been hiding, the trail of recipients he left behind who'd been owed apologies for some reason. Staring at the letters in his hand and unable to deny their meaning, for the first time Peter believed him.

CHAPTER 9

Ally arrived at the office the morning after her Philadelphia trip to find an embossed invitation sitting in the incoming mail basket on the right-hand corner of her messy desk. The United States Conference of Catholic Bishops was holding a series of lectures and discussions on the modern face of Catholicism and would be delighted if she could join a reception at the Oval Room to launch the series. She beamed at the invitation, imagining how excited her parents would be when she called to tell them she'd get to go. A quick glance at the schedule of events precluded any hope she had of attending the lectures. All fell during hours she would inevitably be at the office doing any number of tasks. In fact, even the launch reception itself might be difficult to attend, but she decided it was worth mentioning to her manager, Mark, to see what he said.

"Absolutely not," Mark replied. "I'm going to need you here."

"For what?" Ally said with slightly more irritation than she meant to.

"Stuff—you never know what's going to come up."

"Mark, it's one evening. It could be a good place to talk to people, and I know for a fact I'm not so vital to this place that everything will fall apart if I'm gone for three hours."

Milton Casey walked by just then and, spotting the invitation in her hand, interjected mildly, "Oh, you're headed to that? So am I. It will be good to have you there."

Mark looked at her in defeat. "Fine," he muttered before turning to sift through his own mail, clearly searching for an invitation of his own.

"How did it go in Philadelphia?" Casey asked, walking her back to her desk.

"I'm finishing the summary now," she said. "The director of the center we visited seemed mostly concerned with recent church and school closures in the area."

"Mmm," Casey said with uncertain interest. "Times are tough, I guess. If they don't have the money to keep going, it's hard."

"Wyncott's going to continue the Faith-Based Initiatives office, right? Can't we say we're exploring ways to support religious education as a tie-in for his overall ed policy?"

"Ah, well, we can't go promising money to Catholic schools," Casey said, shaking his head.

"We don't have to say we'll give them money. But can we say the Office of Faith-Based Initiatives will look at developing partnerships to support them?"

Casey nodded in measured agreement. "Yes, Ally. We can. Just keep it vague and noncommittal."

He turned into his office, leaving her at her desk to research the number of school and church closures. It was going to figure prominently into her write-up for Casey.

When she met with Ernesto Horta at the Saint Rita's community center in Philadelphia, she had been unprepared for the amount of information he lobbed at her. In her mind, the purpose of the meeting was to establish what the members of that community were looking for and why the message Wyncott's team was sending didn't seem to be landing.

This was not, of course, the first time Wyncott's camp had reached out to grassroots organizers in the Latino community. There was an entire task force dedicated to sculpting Wyncott's finely nuanced stance on immigration, amnesty, and border control. Since Archer's rally in Fairhill, they'd stepped up the efforts significantly. Campaign flyers were being inserted in *La Voz Hispana* and *El Diario*, while a new television ad had begun running on Telemundo and Univision. In the advertisement, a serious voice spoke in Spanish about Arthur Wyncott and what he had accomplished. At the end, Wyncott looked into the camera and said, "Por un mejor y brillante futuro!" forming the words with an uncomfortable expression of constipation on his face. The words fell awkwardly from his mouth. Ally cringed every time she saw it. It was evidence that Wyncott had made a huge mistake by packing his staff with Spanish-speaking white kids like herself instead of finding politically active Latinos to weigh in. Mark explained it was a point of contention between Wyncott and Casey. "I don't need to trot these people out on the podium with me," Wyncott had apparently said at a meeting long before Ally joined, shocking everyone. Casey hustled him away from the rest of the staff before he could do any more damage, but Mark said they could hear Wyncott shouting, "I won four years ago without them. I'm not going to be held hostage by them this time either!"

The night before Ally and Steve left, Casey reminded them to find out not just what Latino voters were saying, but what Latino Catholic voters were saying.

"I know they're not the only Catholic voters—and I do want you to work with the faith-based team for broader Catholic outreach—but I want to try to zero in on what makes these voters tick. I mean, Archer's a pro-choice candidate who supports stem-cell research and won't criminalize euthanasia. Does that register with them at all, or are they entirely focused on immigration? Does it outweigh his experience in El Salvador? The more information we have to regroup, the better."

Wyncott, he explained, was showing stronger polling numbers when asked about his status as a man of faith and moral principles, and they needed to explore if this was a good way to increase his standing with Latino voters. They weren't trying to increase the religious vote, necessarily. They wanted to find the religious conservatives already in the community and target them, every week if possible, in case they were on the fence about voting for Wyncott because of immigration.

Ally was grateful for the opportunity. Her relationship with Casey seemed to turn a corner after their blunt discussion that late night at the office. From the start of her employment with him, she'd felt at a disadvantage. She thought Casey probably saw her as chattel, much the same way he viewed her colleagues like Steve, who was hired after a well-timed campaign donation from his parents. Everyone she worked with either knew someone or knew someone who knew someone who got them the job, herself included. She'd applied for at least twenty-two jobs in the Washington, DC, area her last semester at Marquette. Resumes and cover letters went to nonprofits, federal government postings, and think tanks. And she got interviews for only four, none of which resulted in a job offer. She was just about to give up on DC when Mulcahy contacted her to say he'd be in Milwaukee to speak at the annual National Catholic Development Conference.

He invited her to dinner with him and an old friend from the Bishops Conference. Bishop Feeney was a nice man—genuinely interested in her experiences at Marquette and her thoughts on how the current generation saw Catholicism fitting into their daily lives. Did she go to Mass every weekend, he wondered? She did. Did she tithe? Yes, she certainly did. How did she feel about abortion? It was a grave sin and damaging to society.

But unlike Feeney, she didn't think homosexuality was inherently wrong, even if they agreed that gay marriage didn't have a place in the Catholic Church. She'd felt this way even before she met Sadie and Carol. When she was growing up, she and her mother routinely stopped by to check on their neighbor Silas, an older man who, now that she was older and more worldly, Ally realized was probably gay. It was nothing obvious that she could point to. Just some mannerisms that set him apart from the other men she knew and a strained relationship with pronouns when he discussed people who came to visit him. No one lived with Silas and he never married. In the months before he died at age sixty-eight from lung cancer, Ally felt sorrow that he didn't have anyone to take care of him. To keep him company on those nights when his breathing labored, the gasps rattling in his chest like a countdown to the end. Even if he was gay and couldn't be married in the eyes of God at her church, surely he shouldn't have to spend his last days without companionship because of it? She'd phrased it more tactfully when she spoke to Feeney, but her example was clear. Feeney appeared disappointed in her response, moving on to topics with Mulcahy that were well beyond her scope of knowledge, like intricate theological principles and papal encyclicals. While Mulcahy stopped every so often to offer some short explanations here and there, Feeney continued unabated. The rapid-fire pace of his speech seemed almost like a challenge. Eventually, she'd tuned out a little, just in time for him to turn to her and ask, "And what's your opinion on this, Ms. Larkin? Are you able to discuss Church teaching in an intellectual way, or do you just respond to *feelings*?"

She'd been mortified. She struggled to offer an answer, but didn't actually know what he'd been talking about. Feeney looked at her expectantly, watching her fumble with a certain amount of amusement. After a disastrous minute of incoherent rambling, she gave up. "I guess I don't really know, Your Excellency. It's not something I've considered fully." Feeney's demeanor immediately changed. He smiled warmly at her. "And that's okay, Ms. Larkin. That's why the Church is here. To help guide you to the right answer in these situations. Question it, challenge it even, but accept that it's grounded in knowledgeable interpretation of our Lord's words and messages." Ally hunched meekly over her plate. "Yes, Your Excellency," she murmured.

Several weeks after the dinner, Mulcahy contacted her to say he had a lead on a position with Wyncott's campaign and that he and Feeney were both willing to act as references for her. While grateful, she was also surprised, given how she'd failed to measure up. "I've never worked in politics," she confessed to Mulcahy. He assured her it was only very entry level and she could make as much or as little out of it as she chose. "But the job's yours if you want it, Ally. Just let me know." Part of her felt being handed a job for which she hadn't competed was in opposition to the values of hard work and opportunity drilled into her American psyche for the bulk of her childhood. But the thought of beginning her postcollege life back in Piedmont without a job terrified her. Thanking Mulcahy, she accepted the position.

She struggled at first to fit in, as much in the office as in DC. Her coworkers weren't cold exactly, but they had all been working on the campaign for some time before she showed up, an interloper thrown into their well-oiled machine by a prelate hundreds of miles away in Boston, a city they already knew wouldn't go for Wyncott. It was understandable, and the notion of trying to force them to accept her instead of just tolerating her was more aggressive than Ally had any desire to be.

But now that she'd asserted herself at a meeting with Casey with some success, she felt more at ease. More importantly, she felt she could connect to what Casey was looking to find out about the voters they seemed to be losing. By bestowing the honor of this trip to Philadelphia on her, even if she'd had to share it with Steve Tilden, Casey acknowledged her worth. The job in his office was no longer a handout she struggled to justify. It was now something she had earned, and she planned on continuing to deliver.

That's why she was so rattled by how unprepared she was for the conversation with Ernesto Horta. She'd spent a good amount of time researching the economic and ethnic makeup of the neighborhood by Saint Rita's. She was certain she'd be able to cover anything he asked about and make some strong arguments in favor of Wyncott. He seemed like a nice enough man, and she felt they probably would have liked each other more if they'd met under different circumstances.

She studied her materials the entire way there, stopping to look up only once, just in time to spot the vandalism lining the walls of rundown buildings as the train pulled into Thirtieth Street station. Steve was still flipping through his notes even as everyone had begun to rise and collect their belongings.

"I just don't know that we're not wasting our time here," he had said at the start of their journey from DC. "I mean, Philly is probably going to go for Archer no matter what we do."

"The point isn't to get Philly to vote for him," Ally replied. "It's to make inroads with the community here and figure out how to make Wyncott more attractive to similar groups in other cities."

Apparently they weren't the only ones thinking about this. When Ally and Steve arrived at the community center, Ernesto commented immediately on how popular his office had become since Thomas Archer delivered his speech in the neighborhood. "I only seem to hear from you guys when it's election time." He said the words with a smile, but it knocked Ally and Steve off their game a little. It didn't help that during

the subsequent discussion, Steve kept calling the neighborhood's voters "demographic patterns" and "migrant populations" in basic conversation.

Ernesto had eventually interrupted him and, with a warm
smile, said "Yes, yes, Mr. Tilden. Of course, I know that your
candidate's current interest in me and the groups I work with
is based on the strength of our voting numbers." He'd leaned
back in his chair. "But please. Do try to remember that we are
people first. Though we may occasionally lean toward certain
issues as a community, we are not all the same person, and if
we do vote collectively on occasion, we do so in the hope that
someday we may be recognized as people, not a sociological
trend."

Ally saw an opportunity to wrangle back control of the
discussion and jumped in. "Understandably, Mr. Horta. That's
why we're here. We want to know what the members of your
community want and need from a candidate. Arthur Wyncott,
as you know, is a man of great faith, and we think that helps
him be a better president, to make governing decisions that
serve humanity and preserve a strong moral core. What do the
people in your community need from a candidate possessed
of faith?"

"Your colleagues have heard all this from me before,
Ms. Larkin. I'm not a good judge for your campaign strategy
because I don't have a black-and-white answer."

She cringed inwardly realizing her first mistake. Of course,
Steve screwed up by calling them a demographic, but she was
hardly faring better by labeling them one-issue voters.

"Oh no, we're not looking for black-and-white answers.
We know that different people have different needs. From
what you see in general about your community, what's important to them?"

He seemed to relax a bit. He leaned forward and doodled
on a piece of paper. "Well, obviously, they're looking for better

opportunities. Education, employment, health care. It's easy to chalk this all up to immigration, but that ship has sailed, Ms. Larkin. Immigration is here to stay—whether Wyncott and Archer like it or not. The question is what to do now. They are and want to be part of their communities." He gestured around him. "This is part of it. They're a devout group of people. The people in this community don't make a lot of money, Ms. Larkin, and maybe can't offer much to help finance a campaign. But they always find time to get to Mass, whether it's Saturday night or Sunday morning. And regardless of what they don't have, they always manage to give money to the collection plate. I think that's what makes it all the more insulting."

Ally heard the last word like a slap. "I'm so sorry, Mr. Horta—I don't mean to be insulting at all."

"Not you. All of this. You asked me what matters about the faith of a candidate to the people I serve. Okay. For them? What the Church teaches. The Church tells them to come every Sunday, so they do. It tells them to give money, and they do. And what has the Church done for them lately?"

Ally interjected, "But Archer is a pro-choice candidate. Wyncott is aligned with what the Church teaches on this subject."

Horta nodded. "I'm sure that matters to an extent. People feel strongly about it ideologically, but look at this neighborhood, Ms. Larkin. Crime rates are high, graduation rates are low. Poverty is the norm. They don't devote a lot of time or effort to the pro-life/pro-choice debate. It's not a luxury they can afford."

He took in Ally's shocked expression. "That said, they still listen to the Church and make a place for it in their lives. See my point?"

Ally nodded. "That's always been one of faith's strongest elements," she said earnestly. "Creating and reinforcing a sense of communal morality."

"And one of its most easily manipulated," he responded. "I don't know if any of what I'm saying helps you all that much. What I can tell you is that while I like Wyncott well enough, and I appreciate what he's doing with his interfaith initiatives, what Archer plans to do for communities like mine matters more. And I'm not shy about saying it to the people who come to me."

"And what's that, exactly?" Ally could see Steve flipping frantically through his packet of preparation materials, searching for information on what Horta could be talking about.

Horta gestured around the room. "This—the community center—it's attached to the school across the street. Saint Rita's primary school. And the archdiocese identified it to be closed down by the end of the fiscal year."

Ally was confused. As they had walked past the building, she had seen what appeared to be a thriving school with a flurry of activity through the windows of every classroom. "Is enrollment down?"

Horta laughed, and she felt herself blush. "Oh no, Ms. Larkin. There are plenty of students in that school. Plenty of people in this community who scrape together the money to send their kids there because a Catholic education is important to them and they feel they need to in order to fulfill their obligations to the Church."

He leaned back in his chair. "The problem is that the Church feels no such obligation to them. You passed the new apartment building on your way here, I take it? And the Starbucks that just opened on the corner?" Ally and Steve nodded.

"They can operate the school and serve the people of this community for a profit of barely seventy thousand dollars a year. Or they can sell it—the church, the school, the community center—to a real estate developer for four million dollars. And another apartment building that the people here couldn't possibly afford to live in will open. And another one. And another. Until they have to move and the only time they come back to where they raised their children is to clean the apartments their displacement built. And you don't suppose the Church would share any of that profit, do you?"

Ally's mouth was dry. She'd read articles about the Church being forced to close parishes and schools all over the country. Some closures were reportedly prompted by large settlements for abuse cases. Others were the result of falling enrollment.

But looking around the neighborhood, she saw a viable community. A place where churches and schools still held the neighborhood together. And where closing them would tear at the seams of a community already struggling for mobility.

"Archer has a plan. He's going to direct funds toward helping communities like ours get first-buy options. And demand that if the Church insists on closing and selling, it'll be taxed at a higher rate, with the revenue going to assist communities affected by the closure. What's Wyncott willing to do?"

It was a reasonable question and one she couldn't answer. Put on the spot, she did her best. "He's got a panel looking at that very question right now," she blurted out. "That's why your input is so valuable," she added for good measure. Writing quickly in the margins of her binder, she made a note to find out what Wyncott's religious affairs team had in mind to balance Archer's proposal. It was clear from the conversation with Horta that Casey would have to put that front and center in any promotional materials to urban Catholic congregations feeling pinched.

She left the meeting feeling like they'd failed. Steve told her to stop worrying so much. "These people? They're small potatoes. Casey wouldn't have sent you and me if he was that worried about getting their votes." They were sitting in a sandwich shop at Thirtieth Street station waiting to board the train back to DC. Ally chewed her meal sullenly while Steve mocked her for being so dejected.

"Then what was the point of coming here?" she asked him. "To make fools of ourselves?"

Steve rocked back in his chair. "No—not to make fools of ourselves. But to make them feel like they got to tell us off. To feel like they got one up on us so that when Casey announces whatever it is he has up his sleeve, they can feel like they had a part in it."

But during the meeting, Ernesto had asked them a lot of questions she'd been unable to answer. That bothered her the most. "Frankly, I don't know why they're closing Saint Rita's, Mr. Horta," she told him, the words coming out more exasperated than she'd intended. "I don't work for the archdiocese. I don't know what's behind their business planning."

"That's just it, isn't it, Ms. Larkin?" He'd smiled triumphantly. "When did it become a business?" The question made her uncomfortable. Her worries went beyond the confines of their meeting and seeped into the larger doubts she'd begun having about her church.

On the train back to DC, she mulled things over. What if, she posed to Tilden, they took an approach that seemed less punitive and more collaborative?

"Not sure how that'll fly given anger about parish closures and the bigger abuse situation," Tilden said in one of his few examples of astute analysis. "I mean, I think Archer's approach is as popular as it is because he's basically telling his own church that they're going to have to pay for their mistakes. That the parishioners, those who experienced the abuse and those who had nothing to do with it, aren't going to have to pay the price for the Vatican's screwups."

He was right—the punitive undertone to Archer's plan was appealing, even to Ally, who despite her devotion to Catholicism felt out of sorts after her meeting with Horta. But while she wasn't entirely certain what Wyncott's or Casey's relationship with the Church in America was, one thing was fairly obvious:

they weren't interested in alienating either Catholic voters or the leadership that served them every Sunday. Whatever solution Ally developed would have to address the concerns outlined by Horta but avoid offending the Church.

"I know *that*," she said as they exited Union Station and hailed a cab back to the office. "That's why we need something that seems friendlier. Something that says we're going to help the parishes in need instead of punishing the Church. His first concern is making sure people in his community get what they need. I think he and voters like him would be fine with something that keeps the Saint Rita's center open without necessarily giving the Church a spanking."

She thought Tilden looked unusually impressed as he held open the door to the office. Usually he regarded her with the condescension of an older sibling forced to let the baby tag along. Their growing office rivalry caught her by surprise. Tilden didn't perceive her as a threat at first. She figured he enjoyed feeling superior to her and knowing that, in almost every way that mattered to elite America, he was. But ever since she shared her analysis of why Archer was winning votes, Casey had paid more attention to her, and Tilden's demeanor around her had changed. Deep down, she suspected, what offended Tilden most wasn't that she had ideas or that they were good. It was that he should have remained superior to her in spite of it, that his supremacy should have gone unchallenged simply because of who he was and where he'd come from, not because he wasn't coming up with ideas as good or as often. Ally's America may have been one in which opportunity was open to everyone, but Tilden's, financed by a hedge-fund father and defined by Phillips Exeter and summers sailing, was one in which opportunity wasn't just handed to you. It also protected your roost through well-placed limits on the Ally Larkins of the world.

This was likely why he went out of his way to ridicule her. And possibly why one night after they returned to the office from a reception, he had propositioned her in a thoroughly unappealing fashion. It was a social misstep born, she imagined, of curiosity and inebriation more than carnal desire. She had left the reception alone (she thought) and returned to her desk to pick up her ratty backpack. Going back to Takoma Park between work and evening events wasn't usually possible, and the JanSport pack, with her since freshman year of college, carried her facial cleanser, a toothbrush, and makeup. It was where she had left it, tucked neatly beneath her desk.

The majority of her colleagues were still at the reception, and the office had a strange atmosphere of desolation, the sound of her every movement magnified so she felt like an elephant crashing through a sleeping village. She turned at a noise in the hallway. Steve rounded the corner and steadied himself on the wall.

"You don't *have* to spend every minute at *work*, you know." He was slurring his words, but only slightly. His boisterous volume was more indicative of his state.

Ally smiled patiently. "Not working. I'm just about to head home."

"You don't honestly expect me to believe this quiet saint act of yours," he scoffed, heaving himself into an office chair and landing in a disheveled heap. "Casey doesn't take on anyone who isn't cutthroat. There's nothing wrong with wanting what you want and going for it, Larkin," he said. "You want an invite to his boating party as much as I do. You just won't admit it."

Ally stared blankly at him.

"The boating party?" he said. "Casey's annual soiree that determines whether he's going to build your career for you or not?" It was a question but sounded more like an insistence of fact. She shook her head no. She was aware of Milton Casey's past—born to an influential Tennessee tobacco family with a tradition in politics that stretched back to a great-grandfather's run for governor in 1880. And Mulcahy had certainly been clear that she should be prepared to network and take advantage of any helpful contacts she could make through the position. But the mysterious boating party eluded her.

Steve shook his head in disapproval more than disbelief. "Fucking classic," he said, standing up and brushing off his clothes in agitation. He walked to his desk and pulled a folder out of the filing cabinet. "Twenty other kids out there dying to get a job in this place and you don't even bother to look him up." He tossed the folder, full of articles about Casey, onto her jumbled desk. It couldn't have held more than twenty pages, but it landed with a thud of condemnation.

"Why are you here, Ally? What are you looking for? You don't care about politics. Not the way the rest of us do." He dismissed her absently and checked the pocket of his suit jacket for cigarettes. "You're not going to find a rich husband to take care of you here," he said, lifting one to his lips. "You're not up to the competition. So you may as well go home to Minnesota."

"Michigan," she corrected. "I'm from Michigan." An uncharacteristic anger in her. "And sleeping your way to security is something I'd ask your mother about, not Milton Casey." She watched the cigarette drop from Steve's mouth, his normally pursed lips slack with shock. "You must be so proud." She punctuated the insult by grabbing the folder and flipping off her desk lamp, leaving him silent in the darkened office.

Halfway down the hall, Ally reached into her pockets for her gloves but found them empty. She remembered placing them on top of a filing cabinet. She pushed back through the office door into the darkness, adeptly feeling her way around until she made contact with the familiar knitted folds. Far less familiar was the feel of two arms wrapping around her waist as she stood with her back to the door, frozen with the sensation.

Those same arms turned her around so she now faced their owner, Steve, who moved his face toward hers with surprising fluidity, his eyes closed as his lips pressed sloppily against hers. Ally's mind was in a fog as Steve groped her. His hands slipped under her shirt, and her body involuntarily responded to his fingers tracing around her breasts and down to her hips. She'd begun kissing him back, she knew, but could not recall ever desiring him, even now. When he pushed her up against the wall, pressing into her, sliding his knee between her legs while pinning her arms at her side, Ally Larkin knew this was a deciding moment. Steve was accustomed to getting what he wanted. He had spoken often and disparagingly of his exes. Girls whose fathers owned corporations and private islands and who bored him not long into their short-lived relationships. Ally suddenly realized she'd be just another conquest for Steve and saw the true nature of the situation. Any brute physical desire she may have felt for him dissipated, fading like the heat from her embarrassment.

She gave him an aggressive shove. "Not a chance, Tilden." He slumped against the filing cabinet, his head lolling back in a precursor to the headache that would greet him in the morning. She ducked out the door and skip-hopped down the hallway, looking over her shoulder once to see him shuffling into the hallway with labored steps.

The incident had happened months before, and while he still spoke to her with a mocking superiority, beneath his attitude ran an undercurrent of shame and, Ally sensed at times, fear.

It was also most likely why, when they went to the office to type up notes after returning from Philadelphia, Steve had lingered after she'd left, and opened the file outlining her strategy for answering Archer's proposed tax on religious institutions. The next morning, she noticed that the printouts didn't seem to be as tidily organized as she thought she'd left them, and the folder was now on the side of her desk where she usually kept inane items like train ticket receipts.

She pulled out her copy of the strategy and reviewed it. Late last night as she was trying to sleep, another idea had occurred to her. Her original proposal called for churches engaged in business transactions to develop a local development corporation model—nonprofit/business hybrids that often engaged in projects with for-profit potential but enjoyed tax benefits because of their mandate to work for specific communities or neighborhoods. Anytime the parish intended to make a significant profit through its activities, the development corporation would facilitate the transactions. The profit would be taxed, though not at as high a rate as Archer was calling for, and it sent the message that Wyncott still respected the special role of religious entities in American society, while forcing those organizations to reinvest a portion of the profit into their immediate communities to receive the highest tax break possible.

But as she mulled the day's events over, she felt restless about all of it—her conversation with Horta, the closures, her proposal. She still believed that the campaign's response had to address the "Church as profiteer" perception. And that to keep his supporters in organized religion happy, Wyncott would have to do so without fundamentally affecting how much money they actually made. But thinking back to Horta, she tried to figure out what had so discomfited her about his comments. It was the way he implied there was an ethnic or even maybe class bias to the closures. Maybe he was right. It was hard for her to imagine the Church closing a school in one of Philadelphia's more affluent neighborhoods. She understood that what angered Horta, as much as if not more than the actual closures, was the way the communities appeared to have no voice in the decisions or any ability to respond—the Church wielded unilateral power over what happened to them.

Archer's staffers were shrewd, Ally knew. They had already proven themselves ahead of her team by reaching out with their tax proposal. Any response from Wyncott that didn't include a community voice in decisions would have limited impact. She'd sat up in bed around 3:00 a.m. and begun scribbling notes. After filling several pages she moved to her desk and laptop.

Her modified proposal called for a split governing structure. The actual churches and affiliated parishes would maintain their status and tax breaks, while financial transactions with third parties would be managed by a nonprofit with an operating board of directors. The nonprofit would pay the monthly bills for the churches—phone bill, rent, electricity—which would qualify as charitable giving. Having an operating board would create accountability, showing that the Church wasn't possessed of sole power to do anything it wanted with no thought for the consequences. In all likelihood the board would consist of figureheads or allies personally chosen by church leaders. But having at least one community member serve on it would create the perception of outreach and allow dissenting opinion to go on record—even if it was guaranteed to be outvoted when it was time for hard decisions to be made.

Ally had mixed feelings about the proposal. She knew it was like so many other aspects of politics and governance she had discovered in her short time with the campaign—a paper tiger meant to convey a call to action that would never actually materialize. But having an independent operating board at least afforded certain avenues for members of the public to challenge church decisions, something that didn't currently exist.

Parishioners would have the chance to do something about it if they wanted to. Whether that was ever likely to happen wasn't really the point. Neutralizing the idea that religion was a machine and that Wyncott was in bed with it was. Giving

Wyncott a platform to place the onus for change on the American people and make him their vehicle for it was. She had begun typing at 3:30 in the morning, napping only briefly before coming into the office, so receiving the Conference reception invitation gave her the extra burst of energy she needed to finish her changes before the morning meeting.

Her computer clock moved closer to the 8:30 mark of the meeting. As she typed, her eyes darted to the corner of the screen, registering the advancing time and calculating how close she was to finishing. She hit "Print" at 8:24 and was at the photocopier by 8:25. The collated, stapled copies were still warm with the tacky scent of fresh print when she rolled into the conference room two minutes later. She passed Casey's office on her way and spotted him on the phone. He had a folder on his desk and was talking animatedly. The entire staff was assembled by the time he walked into the room several minutes later, unusually tardy.

"Let me just begin by saying I know the past few weeks have been a lot of work," he began. "We were behind on the religion front and we didn't even know it. But you've all come up with some really great information and ideas."

He turned to Steve and smiled. "Did you bring enough copies for everyone?" Steve rose and began passing out a document. Despite sitting kitty-corner to Ally at the table, he didn't look at her once. She soon figured out why.

Steve's handout was almost verbatim what Ally had prepared and left on her desk after they returned from the meeting. Recognizing it immediately, she looked up and tried to catch Steve's eye. His gaze remained cast down anytime he turned in her direction. When he finally raised his head to speak, he spoke over her, focusing on the back of the room or on objects, never on the people sitting at the table, Ally included.

For much of Steve's presentation, Ally sat in stunned silence. She wasn't so naïve that the concept of something like this happening hadn't ever crossed her mind. But that he had done it so brazenly shocked her. More importantly, so did Casey's failure to question how someone whose ideas had been consistently mediocre had suddenly come up with a brilliant plan now. Steve's duplicity left her livid, but Casey's inability to spot the sham surprised and disappointed her.

After several minutes in a daze, she recovered, thanks to Steve's thoroughly undynamic presentation style. She scanned the page to see how he'd phrased the tax break element she'd replaced this morning. She couldn't distribute what she'd brought with her. It was almost exactly like Steve's and, given Casey's public acknowledgment, she couldn't pass hers out without expecting colleagues to assume she had pilfered the idea and not the other way around. Even if Casey figured it out or agreed with her, she had no desire to embarrass them both in a public meeting.

At the end of Steve's presentation, Casey nodded approvingly. "There are a few specifics still to work out, but assume that this is the counterproposal we'll eventually be going with and start thinking about the best ways to market it." Steve took a seat, and while Casey beamed with pride, Ally inhaled slowly and raised her hand. Steve finally looked at her, a cross between fear and smug triumph on his face.

"It's a very good proposal," she started. It physically pained her to have to publicly acknowledge her idea as someone else's. "But I wonder if we're not missing an opportunity to demonstrate Wyncott's concern for church communities by giving them a more direct voice."

Steve's eyelids fluttered. "In what way?"

Ally went on to highlight the components of her modified proposal, the idea that establishing this board would provide members of the community with a say in how financial matters of the church that impacted their communities were handled. She concluded with her analysis that it would ultimately be up to the original churches whether they used it as a genuine agent of change or stacked the deck against the community. But at least Wyncott would be seen as facilitating a direct line of communication and accountability in a way that even Archer's plan did not.

Casey nodded in agreement. "Works for me." He turned to a legislative research assistant. "Have a look at how we'd need to structure it in reality, but in the meantime"—he nodded at the press team—"start writing a press release to highlight Wyncott's commitment to helping preserve faith-based communities."

He dismissed them. Steve took off, anxious to avoid Ally. She packed up her folders, her lips pursed in anger. Casey stopped her as she headed for the hallway.

"I know, by the way," he said evenly. "I'm not an idiot." He squeezed her arm and ushered her out the door with a smile. But it wasn't enough. Not by a long shot.

CHAPTER 10

Owen Feeney stared at the saddlebag he had brought home from the office. Peeking out from under the leather flap was the edge of James Ingram's folder. He leaned forward to reach for it, thought better of it, and settled back onto the couch with his glass of wine. On the television, a nondescript pundit with a pudgy belly and shock of silver hair was ranting about something. In recent months, he'd begun tuning them out in much the same way he tuned out Sister Anne Marie. But he also knew he should try to remain well informed. Turning up the volume, he sat up straight and tried to focus on the words, but the presence of the folder kept pulling his attention back to the bag. At the commercial break, his distraction was almost unbearable. An advertisement for irritable bowel syndrome medication didn't help. A couple, not much older than Owen himself, frolicked in a montage of septuagenarian bliss. Riding their bikes along the sea, walking hand in hand with ice-cream cones, seated on a blanket with a basket and bountiful spread before them. Suddenly from the lush tree above them, a red-suited gremlin labeled "IBS" descended on their picnic, cackling, kicking the plates of food in a drunken jig, and wreaking havoc as both husband and wife looked ill, clutched their stomachs and took off running for the restrooms.

The giggle started in the bottom of his chest and rippled slowly to the surface, erupting into full-blown laughter that came in waves again and again until tears streamed down his face. He doubled over, gasping for breath, and reached for his phone, his thumb punching in the last number as he raised it to his ear. It rang once, twice, and then picked up. "You won't believe this ad!" he panted into the receiver.

The icy voice of an operator informing him the number was no longer in service stopped him in his tracks. The phone felt suddenly heavy in his hand. Of course the number was disconnected. James had been dead for well over a month now. He knew that. In his heart and mind he knew it, but his body didn't always remember. He slammed the receiver into the cradle and yanked the brown folder James had given him out of his bag. The first letter in it brought color to his cheeks. He knew it well. He'd dictated it to his secretary when he was serving in the Archdiocese of Chicago for a brief period before moving to Rome. His words, terse, matter-of-fact, and completely stripped of his usual oratory indulgences, assured a Mary Keenan of Parkchester, Illinois, that her concerns had been registered and that Father William Hartnett was being removed from the school and would no longer have contact with children in any capacity. The letter closed with his assurances that her concerns were valued and a wish for God's peace to be with her.

Behind that letter, printed on formal stationery, was another letter from him dated just days after the response to Mary. It was meant, it said, to serve as an introduction of Father William Hartnett to a Monsignor Sexton overseeing the parish of Good Shepherd in Claremont, Pennsylvania, where Hartnett was due to begin his assignment as the youth retreat coordinator. Father Hartnett, Feeney emphasized in the letter, was a well-respected member of the clergy who had distinguished himself in service many times over and would be a fine replacement for the outgoing retreat coordinator. The parishioners of Claremont, Feeney stated in conclusion, would benefit from his time serving them. At the bottom left of the page a CC list jutted out. The third name down read *J. Ingram, SJ.*

Even now, Owen had no idea how James had put the pieces together. The phone in his office had rung one afternoon just about nine months ago. Sister Anne Marie stuck her raptor-like head around the corner and informed him that Father Ingram was on the phone.

"I'm a bit busy at the moment, Sister. Please take a message."

A few moments later, he again heard her deferential shuffling outside the door.

"Yes, Sister?" he called out.

"Sorry to bother you, Your Excellency," she croaked. "He says it's quite urgent and he does sound distressed."

He shooed her away with an acquiescent nod and picked up the phone. It wasn't like James to be so insistent.

"Jimmy? Are you okay?"

"No, Owen. I'm not." His voice was hard. Gone was the usual warmth that seemed as much a part of him as a vital organ. "How long did you know?"

"Know what? Jimmy—what's wrong?"

"About Hartnett. How long did you know?"

Owen's chest constricted. He opened his mouth to speak but held back, reminding himself that he needed to figure out just which incident James was talking about first.

"I'm afraid you're going to have to be a little more specific," he said smoothly.

"What I want to know, *Owen*"—the way Ingram said the name was sharp and bristled with disgust—"is if you knew Hartnett was molesting kids before or after you recommended him to replace me in Claremont. Before or after you asked me to introduce him around."

Owen hadn't been expecting that. James clearly knew more than he thought. He took a breath and collected himself.

"Look, Jimmy. Of course I didn't know. And as soon as I found out, I made a few calls to move him out of there as soon as possible. You know that."

"When did you find out?"

"We moved him out of Claremont just as soon as we could. So maybe a month before he left. April of that year, I guess. Look, you'd been gone for ages by that point so none of this casts a shadow on you."

"Well, that's a relief," James said with a trace of sarcasm. "But that's not really the point."

He sounded less angry now. Owen relaxed a little. "Believe me, we didn't see it coming."

"Do you ever?"

"Exactly!" Owen slammed his hand down on his desk. It was part of what drove him crazy about public reaction to this sort of thing. It was as though people thought he was supposed to have some sort of superhero X-ray vision to tell him who was a pedophile. The first time charges had been brought against a priest serving under him, he couldn't have been more shocked. He'd spent hours around the young man, planning events and filling out paperwork. Never once did he sense anything was off with him. In fact, he had disregarded the charges as a modern-day witch hunt led by overbearing and hysterical mothers. Only when the archdiocese's legal representative came to see him did he reconsider. The attorney came into the office with a furrowed brow. He tossed a document on his desk—affidavits from three different children intimately describing a birthmark on the priest's right inner thigh, mere inches from the scrotum. Feeney was still trying to wrap his head around the graphic descriptions—one boy said the birthmark changed color in the summer, grew darker after hours in the sun spent swimming naked in the retreat house lake—when the lawyer slapped another one down. A photo of the priest's leg with the telltale birthmark. Owen recoiled at the image.

"Trust me on this, Owen," the lawyer told him with an air of defeat. "We're going to have to settle this one out of court." And they had. To the tune of $40,000 for each boy and a guarantee they wouldn't make any public statements about the abuse.

"That's exactly it!" he shouted again at James through the phone. "We never know until we *know*. It's awful. I don't like it any more than you do. But it's like being allergic to bees. You don't know if you are until you're stung, and you better hope you're close enough to a hospital to get through it and be all the wiser after."

There was silence on the other end.

"Jimmy?"

Continued silence.

"Jimmy, you still there?"

"I'm here," Ingram spoke finally. "Did you—did you really just compare molestation to a bee sting?"

"Don't be obtuse, Jimmy. That's not what I was saying and you know it."

"Inappropriate, Owen. Still wildly inappropriate."

"You see what I'm getting at, right?"

"Your metaphors, Owen, are—and have always been—abominable."

The day before, even a few hours before, this comment would have prompted a laugh or some good-natured verbal sparring like they'd done since their days growing up in Kingsbridge. But this time there was an edge to Ingram's voice. Owen couldn't quite read him.

Ingram piped up again. "So you didn't find out about Hartnett until March of that year, and then you got rid of him?"

"Of course—we couldn't have him working with children."

"Where did you send him, Owen?"

"You mean where did he go?"

"Yes—did you send him to treatment?"

Owen refrained from answering. He knew he had to handle this one carefully.

"I recommended he be placed in treatment," he began slowly. "But once he was removed from Claremont, it was really up to his new superior to decide."

More silence greeted him.

Finally Ingram spoke. "So that's a no, then. You didn't send him to treatment."

"Not directly, no." Every inch of Owen was tense, every muscle flexed in a subconscious attempt to control the direction of the conversation.

"And you didn't feel the need to follow up on it? To give his new superiors a call to make sure they'd sent him?"

Owen stifled an exasperated sigh. He should have seen that one coming.

"Look, Jimmy—do you know how many priests I'm responsible for at any given time? Dozens. Too much to manage. And I know if there's one, there are probably more. But what am I supposed to do? Drop everything to pursue one guy to the ends of the earth?"

"You don't have to pursue him to the end of the earth, Owen. You just have to pursue him somewhere away from children. And maybe even try to help cure him."

Owen pushed back from his desk in irritation. The wheels of his chair slid across the plastic base under his desk, stopping abruptly where the carpet began and nearly pitching him onto the floor.

"Damn it, Jimmy!" The shout ricocheted off the ceiling, amplifying to the point that Owen shrank from it. "So I go after him and leave everything else to fall apart?" He took a breath and started again, speaking more softly, more gently to his old friend.

"You can't just drop everything, Jimmy. You have to think of the whole picture, the whole community. That's what it means to be a good shepherd in every way. You're out on a mountain and you come upon a wolf that has killed one of the herd. You want to chase it off—you do. You want to kill it. But you have all the others to think about. And now you know there are wolves out there. Because where there's one, there's bound to be another, of every kind, shape, and color. So what do you do? Do you leave the rest of the flock alone? Sacrifice them for one that's already gone? Or do you accept that you can't save it now and focus on protecting everything else? It's a calculation, Jimmy. Figuring out how much we can possibly control. We do the math every day. You can't do and be all things all the time. You have to choose. Even you, Jimmy."

He heard Ingram take a breath. For a moment he felt it—the triumph of having for once beaten his cerebral friend at his own game. But it didn't last long.

"Jesus, Owen," Ingram said after a long pause. His voice sounded quiet and far away. "You sacrifice yourself, then—if that's what it takes. You look after the others *and* you pursue the one with a taste for blood. Every day, all at once, until it breaks you if you have to, but you do it all. Every last thing that it's physically possible to do. Because that's your job, Owen. That's your responsibility. Your *duty*. Without it, you don't deserve to wear a collar or call yourself a man of God."

Owen covered his mouth. He couldn't even summon breath, let alone words to respond. After an interminable silence, he licked his parched lips.

"Jimmy." His voice cracked as he said the name.

"I know, Owen. I *know* you knew about Hartnett. I've got a copy of your letter to Mary Keenan right here in front of me.

You know when it's dated for? Do you remember? January fucking third, Owen."

The profanity sounded foreign issuing from Ingram's lips. It was so crass and harsh that Owen winced.

"You even close it with best wishes for a healthy, happy New Year. You knew he was raping kids, and you still sent him to replace me. Used *me* to show him around. I handed him the keys to the kingdom, set up a camping trip at the retreat center as the last thing I did before moving on. I served those kids to him on a platter, Owen, and you tricked me into doing it."

"It wasn't like that, Jimmy. I'm telling you, it wasn't."

"And I'm telling you I know, Owen. I know about this. And like you said, where there's one, there's others. Others you covered up for. Others you protected when you should have been protecting those kids. I'm going to find them, Owen—every last one of them—and make it right. And when I'm done? You're going to make it right, too."

The room started to spin. Owen reached for the desk to steady himself and take a deep breath. But by the time he recovered, it was too late.

James was already gone. Nothing but the angry whine of a disconnected phone line greeted him when he held the handset back up to his ear.

Even now, as he stared at the information James had compiled in that brown envelope, he couldn't figure out where it all started. How James had stumbled upon Hartnett. He was hardly the first or most egregious of victimizers out there. The case in Claremont had been handled quietly. Each of the families involved accepted out-of-court settlements and agreed not to speak publicly on the subject. The abuse problems in Boston, California, even Ireland had garnered far more attention than anything that went on in the communities where William Hartnett was relocated. That James should have looked into something so minuscule by comparison remained a mystery.

But what mattered most now was that the folder was here with him. And the rest of James's materials were sitting safely in boxes at Owen's office, delivered obediently by Ignatius University, waiting for him to sift through them. The letters, the affidavits, the paper trails that James amassed would stay just as they were meant to remain. Far from the prying eyes of a public searching for someone to blame for what happened. His memory of James's words, of the accusation that he didn't deserve to wear a collar, still stung. Owen prided himself on doing exactly what was required of him, of performing his duty to protect the Church. It was what he was born to do. Even if it hadn't come early or easily the way it had to James, Owen Feeney had known instinctually in childhood that he was destined to be in the service of God. Without the Church there was no serving Him the way he was meant to. Without the Church, there was nothing. He pondered how James could have spent so many years as a priest without recognizing how inextricably the two were linked. He could not, Owen firmly believed, be a priest in the truest sense of the word without serving the closest thing to God on earth in every possible way. When his church called, he would always answer.

With a shake of his head, he put the folder on the end table and rifled through his bag again. This time, he pulled out a binder that bore no resemblance to Ingram's pile of ratty papers. It was sleek with tabs and foldout charts. And like many of the other documents in Owen's life, it called on him to serve his church. He opened it and began reading. A grid labeled "Projected Impact Analysis" splashed across one page, and a bar chart followed on the next, the fingers of the data reaching skyward with labels like "Immigration," "Abortion," and "Homosexuality." According to the summary and corresponding chart, a majority of Catholic voters paid attention to a candidate's stance on these issues. While it was difficult to trust hard numbers on how many of them allowed this stance to sway them in the voting booth, they had answered yes to it on a survey conducted by an independent polling company retained by Milton Casey at Arthur Wyncott's campaign offices. Perhaps most important was the response to the last question on the survey. When asked how influential their religion was in making political decisions, well over 65 percent rated it as high on the list.

"Now again," Casey had cautioned when he delivered the binder, "it's not clear what aspect of Catholic religion—abortion, social justice, international relief work, even gay marriage—is having that influence. And that's a real pain in the ass. But the point is, they're listening. Whether they're in the pew every Sunday or not, they're paying attention to what religion tells them."

Feeney shook his head. "No, Mr. Casey. They're paying attention to what *we* tell them."

It was exactly what the campaign was looking for, what they'd needed to confirm before moving forward. Now Owen could make his counteroffer. He laid it out. Exactly what the Church needed, how they wanted it done. Casey first offered to sponsor sympathetic judicial appointees. "Then we can funnel the cases to them." Feeney wasn't impressed. Too much left to chance. He repeated what they were looking for, this time being more specific. At the end of the description, he said, "I've seen some of Wyncott's proposed legislation, Mr. Casey. If it's possible for him to do it for Fortune 500 companies, he can do it for us."

Casey mulled it over. "And in exchange, you'll back our candidate?"

Owen nodded, but not without reservation. "Just so we're clear—I can't promise you that every person who walks in is going to cast a vote for Wyncott."

"And I wouldn't want you to. That would be election tampering," he said, "and illegal." Feeney gave him an incredulous look.

"But that said," Feeney went on, "we can and will extol the virtues of your candidate anytime we can, and in exchange . . . Well, you know what we need."

Casey nodded. The proposal was right in front of him, complete with a mock-up memo written on United States Conference of Catholic Bishops letterhead.

"We'll have to pick our timing wisely," he said. "Anything we try to rush through now, before the election, is going to be scrutinized even more than usual. It could be a risky move."

Owen chuckled. "I try my best to avoid watching too much television, but even I know how long Wyncott's health-care bill was. Over a thousand pages, I believe?"

"Closer to two," Milton admitted.

"And who actually reads every last word?"

"No one—less than . . ." It dawned on him what Feeney was suggesting. In spite of himself, he broke into an enormous grin. "That's something we can manage." He resisted the urge to slap Owen on the back. Something about the man's diminutive stature and the stiff way he sat in his chair, almost like he was taxidermied, made him worry the priest would break into a thousand pieces at the slightest touch. "You should've gone into politics." The way Feeney smirked made Casey realize he already had.

Now in his living room, Feeney nodded at the memory and flipped the page. On the television screen, the pudgy pundit was talking about Thomas Archer and his latest tussle with church authorities over something said in a speech. Religious leaders across the board, not just in Catholicism, had exclaimed disapproval over his proposed taxation of church business transactions as though they were performed by corporations.

Archer wasn't taking any of it. Through his spokesperson, he replied that his proposal would put money directly into the communities that helped create the profit in the first place. "I'm not sure I understand why religious authorities would have a problem with this. It's in line with what the majority of them preach. Unless, of course, the money is supposed to be going to something else. I'd love to sit down with any of them and have them explain what they think the money should go to instead. In fact, I'd love for them explain to me where it's all going right now."

Archer knew how play to his audience and the paranoid pulse of American voters. Feeney had to give him that. But if Archer got elected and limited the real estate profits they originally anticipated, it was going to take forever to pay out all the claims and other liens against the Church. Preventing a win for Archer was going to save money no matter what. Getting Wyncott to push through legislation that capped the church's civil damages offered even more. In an ideal world—and here Feeney thought of James Ingram and the parallel universe of altruism he seemed to occupy for most of his life—they would be able to ferret out the worst of the offenders on their own and implement a better system for dismissing them at the very first sign. Suits filed against the Church for abuse would eventually dwindle as more and more problematic priests were removed in an organized but discreet effort to clean house. But until then, money would keep going out the door. And his job, his *duty* as James had so snidely put it, was to keep that from happening. Until he was called on to do differently by his superiors, it would remain his focus.

He looked at the clock, calculating how late he'd have to stay up in order to reach Rome first thing in the morning there. What he saw on television wasn't enough to keep him entertained that long. And the folders and papers around him held only bad memories, recrimination, and regret. He leaned back on the couch and shut his eyes. A few hours of napping would give him just enough rest to be alert for his conversation with the prefect of the Congregation for the Doctrine of the Faith. The timing should be coordinated like a set of dominos. The Pope would publicly reiterate his position. The United States Conference of Catholic Bishops would issue its memo. And Archer would be publicly humiliated.

CHAPTER 11

Weeks after Steve's stunt, Ally was still seething. She arrived at the office one morning to a flurry of activity. It was now mid-April, and the hordes of tourists drawn to DC every spring by the cherry blossoms made it harder than usual to get to work. For most of her employment with Casey's office, she'd arrived at work earlier than the others. But for the first week after the sabotage, she'd gotten to the office at her usual time to find Steve and one other person already there. The uncharacteristic rage she felt after his stunt increased tenfold with this close proximity, and her revenge fantasies ranged from juvenile (spitting on the salad he left in the refrigerator) to criminally insane (cramming him headfirst into the industrial-size shredder). Delaying her arrival twenty minutes hardly caused the collapse of the office, but it did enable her to better control her anger. That's why she was surprised when she opened the office door to find her manager, Mark, already there. "Where the hell have you been?" he snapped.

"It's not even eight thirty yet, Mark. I've been home. Eating breakfast." Gone was the deferential employee she'd been when she started.

"I hope you were watching the news."

"Don't own a TV, Mark." She walked to her desk and began unpacking her bag. "You don't pay me enough to buy one."

"You're going to want to see this." He turned up the volume on the largest of the TVs mounted on the wall. On CNN, an anchor leaned toward the camera and thanked his colleague for joining them from the scene.

"Well, Dan, this is huge news, but it's also the first time we've ever seen a formal directive of this kind." An attractive young woman with bookish glasses spoke into a microphone on location in a plaza ("Olivia Fontana Reporting Live from Rome," the screen read). "Public reaction is difficult to predict. Churches that obey it could be in violation of the Johnson Amendment, a tax code provision barring nonprofits and churches from endorsing or opposing political candidates. And as you know, in the past the American political tradition has not taken kindly to foreign attempts to influence our government or electoral process."

The anchor leaned forward. "But does this really qualify as a foreign attempt, Olivia?"

"That will be the question, Dan. Catholicism is the only major Christian faith in America to still have its seat of power in a foreign country. No one's arguing that voters in America who happen to be Catholic aren't still American, but a move like this is bound to ignite some controversy about if or how much the Vatican should be allowed to interfere."

Ally looked to Mark in confusion. "What are they talking about?" Mark shushed her and nodded back at the screen.

"So what does this mean for Thomas Archer and Arthur Wyncott?"

Behind Olivia, a flock of pigeons rose like a dark cloud, swooping over her and muffling her voice. She covered her head with one hand and hunched down a bit, shouting into the microphone.

"It's hard to tell at this point, Dan. President Wyncott, of course, is not Catholic, so he's not directly impacted. For Thomas Archer, the effect could be immediate. The memo issued by the prefect for the Congregation for the Doctrine of the Faith states very clearly that"—she lifted a sheet of paper and read from it—"a Catholic would be unworthy to present himself for Holy Communion if he were to deliberately vote for a candidate with a permissive stand on abortion and/or euthanasia. Catholics who don't share this stance but vote for that candidate for other reasons are guilty of remote material cooperation."

She lowered the paper and looked back into the camera.

"Under the terms of this memo, he's not only saying that Thomas Archer is unworthy to receive Communion because of his pro-choice stance, he's saying that Catholics who plan on voting for Archer, regardless of how they feel about abortion, are committing a sin and should also be denied Communion."

"Has that happened yet?"

"Well, copies of the memo were released to the public just today, but it's dated last Wednesday, so American bishops have had several days to digest it. It's not clear at this point if any of the bishops have instructed parish priests to follow the edict or not. So far, there have been no reports of denying anyone Communion, but that's not to say it won't happen. The Eucharist is a cornerstone of Catholic faith. This memo is a direct order about a vital component of being a practicing Catholic."

"And tell us, Olivia, what does this mean for the presidential election?"

"It could impact voting patterns. Realistically, the process is too private for anyone to know who you cast a vote for. But it's possible this memo will make Catholics and possibly other religious voters think twice about casting a ballot for Archer. We're not really going to know until November."

"Thanks very much." Dan turned back to the camera. "That's CNN correspondent Olivia Fontana reporting live from the Vatican, which has issued a memo instructing bishops and priests to block pro-choice candidates and those who vote for them from receiving Communion during Mass. To read the memo in its entirety, visit our website, and join us later tonight when we discuss this latest development with political strategists and clergymen."

The volume bar appeared at the bottom of the screen and decreased slowly until Dan's words could no longer be heard. Based on the images of dairy cows and the closed captioning, he'd moved on to a segment about regulating growth hormones in livestock. Ally didn't particularly care. She was still trying to wrap her head around the announcement.

Instinctually, she knew this was a very good thing for Arthur Wyncott. At least with regard to their low numbers with Catholic voters. And even Ernesto Horta had admitted that members of his community responded to what the Church dictated. They would have to take a new poll and see how or if the news had any demonstrable impact on voter opinion.

Mark turned to her. "Well?"

Ally sighed. "It's a big move. Any idea why the Vatican decided to get involved now? We've been lagging on religion in the polls for months. Casey had us in Philly weeks ago and placed coverage at Catholic churches in six other cities as well."

Mark shrugged. "My guess? Archer stepped up the rhetoric on the right to choose in his interview with *60 Minutes* last weekend."

He was right. When Thomas Archer had emerged as a possible contender for an independent run, she was a senior in college. She couldn't remember his stance on choice being a focal point in any of the coverage then. She knew he was pro-choice, but he either had the cooperation of the reporters who interviewed him, or he refused to answer questions about the subject because it wasn't what had come to be associated with him. His relief work in Central America got much more coverage. In fact, despite how monumental and public this assault on his position was, she wasn't convinced it would be able to eclipse the image of Archer as the candidate who understood how many middle-class and low-income Americans were struggling.

Milton Casey strolled through the door at that exact moment, an enormous grin on his face and looking less stressed than Ally had ever seen him.

"This, ladies and gentlemen, is a beautiful day, isn't it? It's what we like to call a gift. A gift from Heaven." He clapped Ally on the back as he glided, as if floating on a cloud of unexpected victory, through the bullpen and into his office. The phones that had rung only occasionally the past few days began ringing all at once. A shrill wave that prompted everyone to dive for their desks to grab them. Around her, a chorus of greetings ("Arthur Wyncott for President!" and "Good morning, how can I help you?") and responses ("Please contact our director of communications" and "No comment!") stopped and started, sounding uncannily like a third-grade music class round of "Three Blind Mice."

On one of the TVs, political commentators gathered for a roundtable shouted each other down about the ramifications of the memo. They ran clips of Archer discussing his stance on abortion and slapped a breakaway graphic of a statement from his campaign director across the screen: "It is Thomas Archer's contention that America's future should be determined by American citizens and American citizens only. While he remains devoted to his faith, he stands by his pledge to represent and serve all Americans of all faiths, no faith, and everything in between if elected."

Back at the roundtable, the head of a pro-life organization applauded the memo and said she'd endorse the Pope as a write-in candidate if doing so could save even one more of the unborn. Across from her, a red-faced columnist yipped that Rome needed to stay out of American politics and do what it did best: deny responsibility for rampant pedophilia. The entire office watched the coverage. The atmosphere vacillated between relief for the extra boon to Wyncott ("We're already up six percent in the latest poll!" Mark shouted after hanging up his phone) and discomfort at the way civility had deteriorated on every channel, with commentators and pundits shrieking at each other. Eventually, Mark hit the mute button. "I can't take it anymore," he said and sat back down. Casey was still in his office with the door shut. They hadn't seen him since his entrance, but every time Ally walked by, he was on the phone or scribbling in the margins of an enormous document.

Ally was reading a copy of the actual memo online when Mark tapped on her desk to get her attention. He nodded to the TVs and cranked up the volume again. Fox News was interviewing Bishop Owen Feeney about the recent announcement. The host of the show, Storm Whitby, was a preppy, clean-cut man in his forties as well known in Ally's office for his ludicrous name as for his consistent promotion of Arthur Wyncott. The camera cut to the right of Storm's desk, where Feeney was seated. The skirt of his stately bishop's simar robe fanned elegantly in stark contrast to the plush pillows of the large chair that seemed to swallow him. Ally recalled how shocked she'd been by his diminutive stature when they met the first time, and couldn't resist a glance at his feet.

The majesty of his robes didn't just create an aura of piety; it successfully drew attention away from the way his feet dangled off the chair, almost but not quite reaching the floor. He stood when Storm approached, rocking himself forward off the chair with a robust push. After handshakes were exchanged and each expressed how delighted they were to be there, they got down to business. It was strange to see Feeney on TV. The night she met him in Milwaukee, he was dressed in plain clerical blacks, and when she saw him at the reception two months ago, she had been too intimidated to say hello. He was always surrounded by a gaggle of admirers, holding court with a speaking voice too practiced to be genuine and a raucous, booming laugh.

Now that she watched him with Storm, he was, as usual, an impressive speaker, answering each question with confidence and ease. This memo, Feeney explained, was not an effort to subvert the democratic process. Rather, it was a reminder to Catholics of their "obligation of conscience" not to cooperate with practices that, even if permitted by civil legislation, were contrary to God's law.

Storm gamely tried to play devil's advocate, reading from Thomas Archer's statement on representing all of America, not just Catholic America. Feeney looked into the camera. Morality, he said, was a condition of humanity and transcended ethnicities and faiths.

"Murder," he concluded, "is wrong for America and wrong for every citizen of this world."

Storm let him have his moment to allow the words to sink in. Ally couldn't contain a smile. He was impressive. And as she usually kept her opinions about controversial topics to herself, she got a small thrill from hearing someone articulate her feelings about abortion without embarrassment or compunction.

Feeney concluded by endorsing Arthur Wyncott as that rare breed of politician who legislated and voted in a manner consistent with morality and God. It was, he said, a supreme kind of irony that a man who votes according to respect for God as man's maker, and not according to man's whims, should be the exception and not the rule. Storm, ever objective, nodded his head as though he were seated in the audience of a self-help seminar and not conducting live journalism. He thanked him, and Feeney stood to bow piously before exiting the soundstage. Ally looked around the room and knew instantly that they'd all seen it—the mesmerizing presence of a clergyman, dressed in ceremonial attire, speaking to the very core of their souls about what it meant to have been made in God's image. Most of her colleagues were not Catholic, and if they were religious at all, very few of them were as devout or conservative as Ally. Still, as she peered at their faces, she knew they couldn't help but be impressed. Feeney was more than a mouthpiece for Catholic dogma. He was a force and a presence.

At the same time, her own enjoyment of the moment was tempered by an uncertain opinion about this turn she was witnessing. Wanting Wyncott to win and being pro-life was one thing—turning the ceremony of Mass into a political playground was quite another. She wasn't necessarily offended or disturbed. But she couldn't help noticing that she'd never seen Feeney appear on television to address the church's role in sexual-abuse cover-ups. Figuring out just how she felt about this, however, would have to wait.

Casey emerged from his office and told them all to cancel any plans for the next few weeks. Arthur Wyncott was ready to resubmit his bill on tort reform after months of tweaking it to garner more support. It would be his last bill before the election and, if they got it right, would be passed just two months before the voting booths opened, leaving voters to enter the booth with an image of Wyncott as a doer, not a talker. This meant the White House would be focused on building support for the bill with various members of Congress. He was going to need all hands on deck to help balance the campaign's needs with those of Wyncott's White House staff who were working overtime on the bill.

"Remember, folks," he said. "Tort reform could be a key piece of Wyncott's legacy. We need to put everything we can into making this a success."

Ally audibly scoffed. Wyncott wasn't so much looking for a legacy as he was delivering a kickback to his largest donors. Pharma and Big Tobacco had spent a lot of money on his first campaign, and it wasn't a coincidence that he was now proposing limits on the kinds of litigation that cost them time, money, and business. Casey must have heard her. Too late, she realized he was looking directly at her when he said, "That's the party line, people. So stick to it." Her cheeks flushed. The smirk receded from her face.

After Casey left for his lunch meeting, Mark pulled her aside for a lecture. "That kind of thing can sink a career, Ally," he said. "I like you—I think you're bright and you've got a lot of good ideas. You need to keep your emotions in check."

She meant it when she said she was sorry and thanked him for his candor and advice. "But—" she said.

"But nothing, Ally," he interrupted. "Don't do it again."

"Doesn't it bother you a little bit?"

"I'm not sure I follow."

"That the bill was designed to serve his donors, not the public."

He softened a bit and regarded her with a cross between amusement and pity. "Oh, Ally. That's the way these things work."

"Every time?"

Mark shrugged. "Not every time. Just most of the time."

"But why?"

"Because as of now, it's totally legal. Wyncott's not doing anything wrong by endorsing this. And it *will* help the public. Costs get driven up by high insurance premiums meant to protect businesses from overly litigious claimants. Once this passes, those costs will come down. Everyone will win. It won't happen overnight, but eventually it'll make a difference."

"That's not what I'm talking about, Mark. It's the intention behind it. The intention of the bill is to reward his donors, not to lower prices for consumers. It's the intention that matters, not the outcome."

Mark chuckled. "Oh no," he said. "Sounds like we're veering dangerously close to a theological discussion. Save your intentions for church. This is politics."

Ally smiled in spite of her misgivings. Mark had a gift for explaining things she didn't like in a way that made it easier to swallow. Though they'd gotten off to a rocky start, with Mark feeling understandably put out by having to take her on, he was probably the closest thing she had to a friend in the office. He made an effort to get to know her and occasionally stopped by to joke about how orderly her desk was or how it was decorated. With Mark she felt free to talk about herself, about her traditional upbringing and faith, without feeling judged and to share parts of Catholic history that fascinated her. One of her personal favorites was anti-Catholicism in the United States. Pinned to the back wall of her cubicle was a series of antique anti-Catholic and anti-Irish political cartoons that had come with her from her dorm room in Milwaukee. The only one she framed, a stunning illustration by Thomas Nast, had run in *Harper's Weekly* in the late nineteenth century. It depicted crocodiles rising from the river to gobble up a group of children huddled on its shores, their lanky snouts jutting out of the water and lined top and bottom with jagged teeth. Upon closer inspection, the crocodiles were not, in fact, man-eating reptiles, but Roman Catholic clergymen. Bishops with miters atop their heads and vestments on their backs slinking to shore, closer to their prey. Rising like a specter from the river behind them was Saint Peter's Basilica, labeled "Roman Catholic Political Church." Mark, who had never seen it before, had been at once shocked and amused. Knowing that Catholics had been discriminated against for their beliefs in the past made her feel more connected to and protective of her faith. It also made her understand why religion played such an important role for many of Wyncott's voters. Mark respected that about her.

So when he occasionally chided her about her moral and religious sensibilities, she knew it was good-natured.

"You're right," she told him. "I'd just like it better if helping corporations was the by-product. Not the other way around."

He rolled his eyes in mock protest. "Catholics," he muttered with a smile. "Just cancel your plans and be prepared to be on call."

"I never have any plans."

"You're pathetic, Ally."

"I know."

It was good advice. She wasn't senior enough to participate in any of the political maneuvering going on below the surface to guarantee the bill's passage. But in the weeks that followed, she spent plenty of time researching where to run ads for it in the home states of Congress members who were holding out. News coverage of the bill and the ensuing debates were a welcome distraction from the controversy that swirled around the Communion memo. An archbishop in Colorado became the first person to deny Communion to an attendee at church services.

He targeted Kathleen Bauer, the state's governor and an advocate for making RU-486 available over the counter. No one in the office said it, but the move garnered far less attention than it should have only because it was Colorado. Such a move in Boston or Philadelphia would have created a frenzy. And maybe that's why, thus far, bishops in those cities had refused to engage with the memo. Even though it had been perceived as a direct attack on Archer, he had yet to suffer being denied Communion. Still, news coverage had focused on the memo to the point that it eclipsed his press conferences on foreign policy and green-energy initiatives. Pro-life groups had taken to following him to Mass at his preferred church in Alexandria, Virginia, and peering through the windows, crying foul when his priest personally delivered him Communion. Not long after, the Church served them with a legal notice to cease trespassing.

Milton Casey wouldn't have admitted it to his staff, but he was irritated to learn Archer continued to receive Communion, despite his otherwise general disinterest in the inner workings of Catholicism. He was similarly disappointed that Colorado was the only place the memo had been followed since it was issued. He was beginning to think Feeney wasn't holding up his end of the bargain, and he told him so when they next met. "It's been close to a month," Casey barked. "I thought you said your people do what they're told. Why aren't they blocking Archer?"

Owen, who was carving the filet mignon on his plate, didn't bother to raise his head when he responded. "I never said they do exactly what they're told," he said, chewing loudly. "I said they take instruction well and their reactions are easy to predict. You don't want them to actually deny Communion to parishioners at large. Not even to Archer. That's going to land them in hot water with the IRS and anger voters in the pews. And the clergy don't want to be dictated to like four-year-olds. Compromise is the goal here." He paused to wash down his mouthful of beef with a sip of eighty-dollar wine. "You want them to meet the edict halfway. To reiterate *why* Archer's the wrong candidate every Sunday, in lieu of punishing the people who show up. They'll feel like they've met the spirit of the memo, and every week an authority figure will tell a closed audience of twenty thousand parishes, indirectly, to vote for your candidate. For the next six months." A petite blond waitress nearby rushed to replenish the supply in his glass. Feeney dismissed her with a wave of his hand. "Not even a Super Bowl ad could get Wyncott that kind of targeted exposure."

Casey left the meal feeling better. Feeney was right. Mulcahy hadn't been far off when he described him as having a sharp business mind. Casey assigned a few staff members to help gauge the impact. The important thing, he stressed to them, wasn't to get a sense of how many people—political candidates or John Q. Public—were being denied Communion. It was more important to find out if any parish priests were stressing Archer's inherent incompatibility with their faith from the pulpit every Sunday. Pulling this information together was going to cost the campaign even more money. He would have to go back to their corporate donors. Wyncott's allies in Congress were making progress on the bill, which would help. But Milton was starting to get an ulcer from robbing Peter to pay Paul. If the next six months of counting down to election night didn't kill him, he told his wife on one of the rare nights he got home before she was already asleep, it might certainly leave him maimed.

Milton Casey wasn't the only one worried about money on top of everything else. Peter Merrick's last paid gig, with the *Economist*, had ended several months ago. He'd gotten distracted with his research on Ingram's letters. Emma was patient about it, but her small therapy practice combined with consultation cases for the local family courts was only bringing in so much income. Peter watched the controversy over the Communion memo play out in the news, but his focus was elsewhere. All the same, when his phone rang with offers to write a few pieces on the controversy for some very well-respected publications, he put the mystery of James Ingram's letters aside long enough to pay the bills.

✴

Several days after the archbishop in Colorado had enjoyed his fifteen minutes of fame, Milton Casey received a call from Peter Merrick, a freelance journalist whose name he vaguely recognized from a series of articles in the *National Catholic Reporter*. Casey immediately disliked Peter. He was one of those journalists who pretended to be shocked and flattered when you said you'd read something by them. As if they didn't all *live* for that kind of acknowledgment from total strangers, let alone someone in Casey's position. They stumbled awkwardly through introductions and mutual praise for a bit before Peter revealed that he was interested in doing an article on the Vatican's unprecedented entrance into American politics.

"Thank you for calling, Mr. Merrick," he said by rote. "But Arthur Wyncott would prefer not to make a public statement about this. I can refer you to our communications office if you'd like a quote from them."

"Actually, I'm not interested in Wyncott's take on it. I understand he's not in a position to comment publicly about this. And the piece isn't specifically about the memo. I was hoping to speak with you."

Casey wasn't expecting that. "Me?"

Peter seized on his surprise to sell his pitch. "Everyone's saying this is an unacceptable manipulation by the Vatican, but I'm writing an article on how this isn't the first time it's happened and it won't be the last. People vote according to what their ministers say all the time. Evangelicals vote on abortion and gay marriage, issues their pastors frequently discuss as a moral imperative during services. But I don't see that attracting the same attention. So why is this particular memo muddying the waters so much?"

While he spoke, Casey had begun nodding in agreement. Only when Merrick paused to get his response did he notice he'd been doing it.

Peter went on. "Anyway, you've been in the campaign business for nearly thirty years. I'm sure you've seen your share of these scenarios, so I wanted to pick your brain about the role of religious leaders in previous elections. We're going to have to cover the memo to the US bishops, but it won't be the main subject. And the focal point isn't going to be Wyncott. More so religion and campaigns in general. Can I convince you to give me twenty minutes?"

A couple of days later, Peter arrived at Casey's office for a brief interview. True to his word, the interview lasted just about twenty minutes and involved Casey offering his analysis of campaigns he'd had no part of. It was a perfect opportunity for him to point out that the candidates in those cases were clearly not as strong or viable as Arthur Wyncott, who had already spent nearly four years leading our nation to greatness. Further, he argued, Wyncott had a strong moral compass, and if religious leaders and their church members agreed with his positions, well, then it was a sign Wyncott belonged in office for a second term. In truth, he was somewhat disappointed when the interview wrapped up. He could have talked about campaign strategy for hours.

As Casey walked Merrick to the door, they passed Ally Larkin's desk. She was hard at work on changes to her proposed religious-entity tax structure. Wyncott's legislative assistants had sent it back to Casey with a string of edits designed to shore it up in time for Wyncott to present at an upcoming town-hall meeting in New Orleans. As Peter passed, he spotted the Thomas Nast print out of the corner of his eye and couldn't resist stopping. The first time he'd ever seen it was in a class with James Ingram his last semester at Ignatius.

"Sorry to interrupt you," he said. Ally jumped at the sound of his voice. "Your print—" He regarded the tasteful frame. "Is it an original?"

Ally laughed. "I wish. I really wish—but no."

Milton stepped in. "That print gets more attention than if a goddamned unicorn were standing right here," he said good-naturedly. He turned to Ally, then back to Peter. "Mr. Merrick, allow me to introduce you to Ally Larkin, one of our dedicated staff." Turning to Ally, he continued. "Mr. Merrick is a journalist writing an article on campaign tactics."

Peter reached out to shake her hand and noticed the class ring on her finger. In the center rose the letters *IHS* from the seal of the Jesuit Order.

"Where did you go to school?" He blurted out the question before he could stop himself.

Ally blushed a little. "Marquette. You probably haven't heard of it. It's in Wisconsin."

"I know it. Of course, I know it. I went to Ignatius."

She relaxed immediately, he could tell. "So you're a member of the Jesuit Fan Club, too," he continued.

She laughed. "I guess so."

"Where did you find the print?"

"Oh." Ally looked disappointed. "I didn't, actually. Find it by myself, that is. It was a gift from the college newspaper staff when I graduated."

"The newspaper, eh?" Peter nodded his head approvingly.

Ally beamed. "I was the editor."

Casey cleared his throat. He wasn't interested in a prolonged discussion about either Peter's or Ally's college experiences.

Peter took the hint. "Hey—look. I've got to go, but here." He reached into his wallet and withdrew a business card like the one he'd left on Milton Casey's desk.

"Here's my card. If you ever want to talk about journalism or freelancing." He cast a deferential look Casey's way. "Once the campaign is over, that is. Give me a call. I'd be happy to help."

He shook Casey's hand once more, and with a quick nod to Ally darted out the door and down the hall to the elevator. He had just exited to the street when his phone rang. Mike Trencher, an old buddy from his days writing for the *Wall Street Journal*, had managed to track down the contact information for Kevin Garrity in Olmsted, Wisconsin.

CHAPTER 12

The rickety porch at 217 Anselm Street seemed to be a micro-cosm of Olmsted itself. What had once been a wholesome structure, perhaps part of a home to a middle-class family with children playing in the yard, was now depleted of color, strength, and form. Peter took large unwieldy steps to avoid breaking through the rotting floorboards, soft with pungent decay and streaked with paint that had long since chipped off or faded from its original hue. The house looked like most of the others in Olmsted, a small postindustrial town on the banks of a murky river that used to power its now-deserted textile mills. On his drive through the ten blocks that composed downtown, Peter noticed four churches, none of them Catholic, and a lot of shuttered shops. The houses on either side of this section looked to be the oldest in the area, large brick structures with covered driveways, and some with grandiose colonnades or side gardens. He spotted the sole Catholic church as he turned up into the hills, where the homes ceased to be standalones and merged into endless stretches of row houses with shared lawns and stairways. A set of battered wind chimes hung from the porch eaves of 217. Its decorative glass disks had broken into jagged shards, but most of the chimes remained, emitting tinkling notes despite their haggard appearance.

His phone calls to the house had gone unanswered. If Kevin Garrity was still living there, he didn't have an answering machine, and not once in two weeks of calling several times a day had Peter caught a live person. The idea of living in this modern world with no answering machine, no cell phone, and no e-mail address, as far as Peter was able to find, baffled him. Peter himself was defined by technology and the many gadgets that kept him tethered to the outside world, intruding on him and Emma at all times. It was a deliberate choice, he concluded, for Kevin Garrity to remain disconnected from the world around him.

Peter pulled back the screen door that hung unevenly on rusty hinges and knocked lightly. If this door was anything like the porch flooring, he couldn't be too careful. After waiting for over a minute, he raised his arm and knocked again, this time with a bit more force.

He heard a muffled grunt of recognition from inside the house but couldn't make out the words. The peephole flicked open long enough for him to see movement on the other side, followed by the sound of multiple locks turning. A disheveled, overweight man opened the door. His threadbare T-shirt (Bon Jovi's Slippery When Wet tour) couldn't contain a gelatinous midsection that spilled out from under its edge.

"Yeah?" he said.

"I'm looking for Kevin Garrity," he said.

"Don't know why that would be," the man responded.

Peter tried again. "I'm sorry," he said, smiling and extending his hand. "I should have introduced myself. My name's Peter Merrick, and I'm hoping to speak with Mr. Garrity."

The man sized him up through pupils that were a little too large to belong to sobriety. "Depends on why you wanna talk to him," he said. "You ain't a cop so you're either trying to sell me some shit or you want me to tell you my sad story." He blinked, letting his eyes linger closed for a moment like he was tired or bored. "So which is it?"

Peter took a deep breath. He knew this was going to be a hard sell. "Actually, neither. Honestly. I'm . . . well . . ." He dug into his pocket and withdrew the letter from Ingram with "Return to Sender" on it. "See, Father Ingram—he died recently and I found this letter among his belongings and I—" A loud bang interrupted him. He looked up to see Kevin Garrity holding the fist he'd just slammed into the wall. "Are you okay?" he asked with genuine concern.

Garrity shook his head and clutched his fist. "You fucking guys," he said quietly. "You always wanna know if we're okay. But me saying I am or I'm not"—he leaned against the lintel and rubbed the back of his hand—"that doesn't make it so. And you asking all the time doesn't either."

Peter nodded. He didn't know why, and he suspected doing so was another example of the empathy Garrity had to come to despise. But like Ingram before him, he felt the need to do or say something. "Let's get some ice on that and talk," he pleaded. "I promise you—I'm not here to make anyone feel better or worse about what happened to you. But Ingram was important to me. I looked up to him. And these letters—you're not the only person Ingram reached out to. He wrote letters to a number of people, and I guess I'm trying to figure out why. I *need* to know why. You can understand that, can't you?"

Garrity winced, and his lip trembled as though he were going to cry, but the tears wouldn't come. Peter knew they had probably stopped coming a long time ago. "Okay," he finally said. "Come on in."

The couch was as threadbare and worn as Garrity's clothing. Even though it was mid-May, the nights could still be cold. There didn't seem to be any heat in the house; it was freezing. Garrity's hand was swelling up fast. When Peter offered

to make coffee for them, he turned on the oven burner to find
it gasping and sputtering. No gas came out to ignite. Garrity
pointed to an electric teakettle in the corner. "Worth its weight
in gold, that thing," he said. He smiled for the first time, and
Peter saw the gaps—teeth missing from both the upper and
lower rows in a mouth that, like Garrity himself, would never
again be whole. A few minutes later, he set a steaming mug
down in front of Garrity along with an old bread bag full of
ice. ("Brownberry Whole Wheat," Garrity said. "My grandma
always said it was the best store-bought around and she was
right.") It was wrapped in a filthy towel, the only kind he could
find.

"I'm here," Peter said, "because I came across these." He
pulled the letters out and caught Garrity's stricken look when
he spotted the opened flaps. "I read them. I know I shouldn't
have and I'm sorry. I found them at his office after his death.
I thought it might make me feel better or something." Garrity
didn't look as upset now. "If you don't mind my asking about
it," Peter said gently, "I'm not trying to exploit this, I promise
you. I believe he contacted a number of people like you and
I—"

"People like me?" Garrity snapped. "What the fuck's that
supposed to mean? Broken? Damaged?"

Peter backpedaled. He hadn't meant for it to sound that
way. "Survivors," he said finally. "People who were broken, were
damaged by someone else. And who survived it."

Garrity calmed down a bit. He shifted on the couch and
stared out the window.

"Look, I knew Father Ingram for a long time," Peter tried
again. "A very long time. I thought I knew everything about him
that mattered. His values. What made him tick. But I found
a bunch of these letters." He pulled out the rest and showed
them to Garrity.

"The only thing I know about all the people who received them is that you've, every last one of you, been involved with suits and settlements filed to hold the Church responsible for what happened."

"Yeah, so what?" Garrity said. "I knew I wasn't special—these guys've been doing this stuff to kids forever. It's not like there was something in the water in Wisconsin."

"That's not what I'm talking about." Peter was struggling to make his point. "What I mean is, I can't figure out why Ingram was reaching out to you. Or to this person"—he tossed another envelope on the coffee table—"or this one. He never mentioned any of these parishes or towns in all the years I knew him. Was never even sent here—formally or informally—according to archdiocese records."

"I wouldn't believe a goddamned thing they tell you." Garrity almost spat the words as he stood up and walked to the kitchen. "They'll tell you they didn't know anything about any of this, but they knew. Hell, some of them were even here when it happened."

Peter took a breath. He was afraid to ask the question, afraid that the answer would destroy his memory of Ingram. "Was Ingram here? When it happened?" He closed his eyes and said the words. "Was he the man who did this to you?"

Laughter was not what he was expecting to hear. He opened his eyes and saw Garrity doubled over in the doorway to the kitchen.

"What are you talking about?" Garrity said between chuckles. Somewhere along the way, his laughter turned into hiccups and hyperventilating breaths he couldn't control. "Did you read any of those letters?"

"Only the few I found. I didn't know what to make of them. He kept apologizing in all of them. Saying he took responsibility for what happened and wanted to make things right."

Garrity grew serious. "Yeah, he did."

"How do you mean?"

"Do you know how many of them knew this was going on? How many times I told them? How many times my mom told them? She went to the other priest. I said something to a nun at my school. When I still had to see him every day, my mom went to see the monsignor. 'Don't worry about it,' he told her. 'We're taking care of it.' Taking care of it. Yeah, they took care of it—just enough so I didn't have to see him in school anymore. So he stopped talking to me. But I still had to see him around town. You've seen this place. It's not big or nothing. He was with a different kid every time, a little blond boy or occasionally one with brown hair. Like you could just swap us out for each other." The description made Peter sick to his stomach.

"He was gone, my dad. Took off when I was ten and it started not long after that." Garrity said the words like they were any other, a comment on the weather, a matter-of-fact observation about holiday shopping crowds. He pulled a cigarette out of a box on the table and lit it. "My mom was all over the place after he left. Couldn't keep a job, couldn't fucking think straight. My baby sister's sitting in her high chair for hours, with *shit* spilling out of her diaper she ain't been changed for so long, and my mom would just sit there with this dead look on her face. Like she didn't care, like she didn't see us there. I couldn't understand it then—how she could be so dead inside and still be walking around."

His hands were shaking as he lifted the cigarette to his lips. "I didn't like being around that. I hated having to come home after school. There was never any food. My kid brother always whining that he was hungry, or someone on the phone hassling us about money we owed them. I'd hang out at school for as long as I could. I wasn't supposed to be there late, so I'd follow the janitor around and get him new water, hold the door open, anything to keep him from yelling at me to go home. God, it was great. I'd get home and my mom would be mad, but it didn't matter 'cause by then it was only an hour or two before I could go to bed and forget all about it and wake up and get out of there again before she was up.

"My teacher, Sister Lucius, pulled me aside one day. Asked me the last time I'd taken a bath. Some of the kids were complaining I smelled. I just started crying. Like a fucking baby. She took me over to the rectory and made me a sandwich. While I was eating, she went into the office to talk to—" He tried to say the name but couldn't. "To the Father," he finally said.

"When she was done, they came out with big grins on their faces. He asked me how I'd like to come work at the office after school on Tuesdays and Thursdays. Said he could pay me a couple of dollars every week, and he'd drive me home after dinner. It was such a relief, you know? Like I didn't have to sneak around anymore. I had an excuse to be there all the time, and my mom wouldn't yell at me when I got home. She was proud of me for it. Didn't care what time I got home because every Tuesday when he dropped me off late, so much later than the other days, he'd bring bags of groceries. Cans of soup and stuff. 'You're too kind, Father,' she'd say. She acted like a complete flake when he was around. 'I don't know how we can repay you. It's too much.'"

Garrity leaned back on the couch with his hands behind his head.

"Well, I was already paying for the groceries. The first time he bought them, nothing happened. He smiled at her and smiled at me and said I was a good boy and it was no bother and he'd see her next week. My sister stopped screaming all the time and started sleeping better. My mom would clean up the house a bit on Monday nights so he didn't see how messy it was the rest of the time. It was kinda like before my dad left. That first Tuesday it happened, we went to the store. He always let me pick out something just for me. Froot Loops or Lucky Charms—the expensive cereal we could never afford. I helped

him load the bags into the back of his car. It was dark already
'cause it was winter and the day was over before you knew
it. We were about halfway home when he pulled over on the
side of the road. Asked me if I liked spending time with him.
I said it was great. He smiled and said he was glad. Because
he liked spending time with me. He put his hand on my thigh
and started rubbing it. Then he unbuttoned his pants with his
other hand. He took one of my hands—they were frozen at my
side, like—and stuck it down there. He made my fingers close
around it, around him, and starting moving my hand up and
down. I just stopped feeling, you know? I was staring out the
window but I couldn't see nothing, it was so dark out. So I just
stared at the dark, waiting for it to be over. He kept thanking
me afterward. Told me I was so good. After that, every Tuesday
he'd take me home a little late. My mom never asked why. She
was just happy with the food and the money I got."

He took a long drag on his cigarette, the ember burning
right down to the filter, flush with his fingertip. If he felt any
pain, it didn't register on his face. The smoke plumed from his
mouth in a heavy exhale.

"And then I knew how she'd done it. Be a zombie for so
long, get out of bed and do stuff without even thinking about it
because you can't. If you stop to think about it, to think about
anything, you can't pretend anymore this life isn't the piece of
shit it is, you know? That this is all there is for you. Thing is"—
his voice started to crack—"I know it's kinda my fault that it
happened."

Peter stood up in a flash. "You're wrong, Kevin." He didn't
mean to shout, but it came out that way. "This is absolutely not
your fault. In any way." He enunciated the words as clearly as
he could. "And the fact that you think it is—you just—Jesus,
you just need to know that it isn't. Okay? It isn't."

But Garrity wasn't listening. The tears were rolling down his face now, even without blinking. They just pooled in the corners of his eyes and streamed down his face.

"Oh, I knew that's what you'd say. What else can you say? I mean, all the therapy books, every counselor I've had—they all say the same thing. It wasn't my fault. But you only think that because you weren't there, okay? You weren't there!"

He began crying openly. "You see, all I wanted was a normal place to be. A place where the dishes were put away and the bills were all paid and there was food in the house and my clothes were clean."

"Of course you did," Peter tried. "What kid doesn't want that?"

"But that's just it," Garrity wailed. "When you're a kid, that's *all* you want. It's enough. You don't need anything more than that. You don't see how big this world is or what comes after right now. So when someone comes along and gives you that— makes everything around you feel normal—you don't fight the way you should've maybe. Or you don't say no soon enough. Because you don't want to lose that life. The one with the clean dishes and the movies on Sunday and a mom who gets dressed and changes the baby's diaper. You don't want that to go away, so you don't say anything. And see, once that happens, it *is* your fault."

"You have to know you're wrong about that. Somewhere in the back of your mind." Peter tried to get Garrity to look at him, but he stared into the distance. "Look at me. You wanting a normal life doesn't make this, any of it, your fault."

But Garrity wasn't listening. His vacant gaze indicated his thoughts were far away. He didn't stare at the wall so much as through it.

"You know the worst part of it all? Is that after it was over— after I finally said something to my mom and she went to the monsignor to complain about it and he stopped touching me—I didn't know what to do. At first, he still tried to see me. Tried to explain that I was confused and that he did what he did because he loved me and he wanted to make me happy. Then my neighbor saw him talking to me one afternoon and told my mom, and she went back to the monsignor to complain, and he never talked to me again. Just moved on. I saw him with other kids. Boys who were younger than me, cleaner maybe, and the worst part about it all is that I was sad. I missed him. I missed that he spent time with me and took me to the movies. I mean, how fucked up is that? Because once he was gone, I was stuck back at home with my mom and the messy house and the empty shelves. And I thought, you know, maybe he was right. Maybe he did love me. Maybe he was the *only* person who ever loved me because that's all the love I deserved. That kind of dirty love that you're not supposed to have. But sure, look at me." He gestured around the living room at the wallpaper peeling just below mold stains on the ceiling, and the pile of dishes in the sink that emitted the stench of sitting dishwater and rotting food. "Maybe he knew all along that I'm one of those people who don't deserve what everyone else has." He sank back into the couch. "Hell, I know it."

The two men sat quietly. Outside, a strong breeze whistled through the window frames. What remained of the wind chimes clanged against the porch posts, a discordant clatter that matched the air in the room.

After a while Peter spoke again. "Do you want to tell me what that was about?" He nodded at Garrity's injured hand. "When was the last time you saw Ingram?"

"Never met him," Garrity said. "He offered to come talk to me. Said so in every other letter."

"There are more letters?" Peter was surprised. "Letters that you read?"

"Hell, sure I read 'em," Garrity said. "Eventually. Just not at first. I couldn't. The minute I saw those initials after his name, saw the return address for Ignatius. It just turned my stomach, you know? But I finally opened one of them. Took me two days to get through the whole thing it hurt so bad, but I did it." He shrugged.

"What did you say when he offered to come visit?"

"Told him I couldn't take it. Not right now. Don't know if I ever coulda, to be honest." He rubbed his fist. "But, I don't know. It's kinda like even though I knew I wasn't ever gonna meet the guy, I liked the idea of it happening, you know? I liked thinking about how maybe someday we'd meet for coffee or something. I'd have a reason to get up that morning. Have a reason to shower and shave." He stood up, walked into the next room, and opened a closet door.

"I even, you know, knew what I'd wear." His muffled voice came from inside the closet. He pulled out a dress shirt still folded in its package—pale blue with thin red stripes. Garrity walked back in and set the shirt on the table next to the coffee. It was so new and fresh next to the grungy table with its water-mottled newspapers and empty beer cans. "I thought I'd take him to Saint Francis of Assisi church there in Belleville. Father Ingram sent me a letter once with a quote from him, and it stuck with me." He turned and faced Peter as though he were delivering an address to the Supreme Court. "'All the darkness in the world cannot extinguish the light of a single candle.'" He bobbed his head on the last word, his tone solemn and profound. His eyes closed for a moment, an added gesture of piety. Then they flickered open and a smile broke out on his face, a broad, enthusiastic grin that hit Peter square in the chest. Kevin came back around and sat on the couch, the pristine shirt in its package clutched in his hand.

"I thought maybe, as dumb as it sounds, we'd get together and I'd feel normal, you know?" The smile struggled to stay on his face. The lines of his mouth were still curved upward, but his eyes were going dim with disappointment.

"Like he'd be able to tell me why this happened and then it really would be okay. 'Cause I'd know—I'd get why everyone else got off scot-free. Why you never had nothing like this happen to you." His smile died, face frozen as he stared blankly at the floor.

"I thought he could tell me maybe I was special. Like God picked me because he knew I could take it." His voice trembled. "A couple of years ago when this all blew up? I was approached by the lawyer representing the other kids. See, my mom had copies of letters she'd sent, logs she kept of what days she visited who and what they talked about. This guy asked me if I'd sign on, turn over that information when I did. There'd be a payout at the end of it, he said. I got forty thousand dollars when my mom complained. They made her sign something saying we wouldn't talk about it. The money's long gone, but I told the lawyer I didn't want their money anyhow. I didn't want to have nothing to do with them ever again. All I wanted, I told him, was an apology. For letting him do that to me and the others for so long. For ignoring us."

He shook his head angrily. "It's been four years of going back and forth with that lawyer and twenty-five years since it happened, and I'm still waiting for an apology. I know what the lawyer says. That they can't because it'll be seen as an admission of guilt, and now that there's a civil suit they legally can't have contact with me. But it's tough to swallow. Ingram's the only one yet who's ever said shit to me about it being wrong. That's why I started reading his letters. I had sent the others back, and one day I was sitting here feeling sorry for myself and I thought, fuck it, just read what he has to say. It can't make you feel any worse."

Peter smiled. "Ingram was a master at saying the right thing."

Garrity nodded. "You're right about that. I finally opened one of them, and he started by saying that he knew nothing could fix it, that he wasn't writing to me to say it would be okay or that it would ever be anything other than what it is. But he wanted me to know he was sorry, as someone who gave his life to Christ and the Catholic faith, and that they had failed me. He said what drew him to God was His infinite capacity to forgive. That we could make mistakes or we could choose to do the wrong thing, the worst possible thing sometimes, but if we could find the strength to admit it and ask for forgiveness, it would be granted. His greatest disappointment in life, he said, was that the very men who sold that line for a living didn't really believe it themselves. But he believed it, he said. And he hoped I did, too. Because if one of them failed me, then they all failed me, and he hoped I could forgive him."

Peter folded into himself, the weight of relief and agony pinning him to the couch. Guilt, profound and powerful, washed over him as he imagined James Ingram sitting by himself in an office writing letter after letter, holding steadfastly to the belief that the right words uttered by the right man could heal the damage. That anything could. Snippets of their conversations through the years and the many hours spent philosophizing about sin and forgiveness converged with this newfound knowledge of the purpose behind the letters. Of acts that proved James Ingram didn't just *think* about these ideas, these definitions of sin and redemption. He lived them every day, until his very last breath. The tears came so quickly, so suddenly that they pinched the corners of Peter's eyes. He looked around the room in an effort to keep from blinking. When at last he did, tears splashed onto his shirt and arms.

"How did he die?" Kevin Garrity asked quietly.

"Alone." Peter grimaced as though he'd eaten something bitter. "He died alone."

Garrity inhaled sharply and dropped his head into his hands. "I hope that's not true. I have to believe that something—I don't know, a spirit maybe—was there with him, telling him it was going to be okay."

The scornful chuckle pushed its way out of Peter's chest before he had a chance to stop it. "Really? That's what you believe?"

Garrity smiled his broken smile again, one side of his mouth curling up faster than the other. "Every minute of every day? Nah." He nodded his head around the room. "But right now—what else do I got? What do any of us got?"

In that moment Peter felt like the fraud he'd always known he was becoming. He could write eloquent articles on the role of religion in society, participate in panels alongside esteemed theologians and professors. But for quite some time, long before Sheeraza Akhtar's arm landed on his terrace, he'd been a man of hollow faith. He knew the right things to say and how to put religion on a pedestal where he could tear it down just as quickly, but didn't know how to feel it. Over the years, his letters from Ingram had brought a momentary burst of renewed spirituality, a pride in feeling close to God and the way growing up Catholic had shaped that relationship. But Ingram was gone. And with him, Peter feared, went the last pieces of him that could believe. He wanted to think there were more Ingrams in the church than there were predators. Sitting across from Kevin Garrity, however, he found it difficult. He thought back to when Ingram had stopped wearing his Roman collar and the way so many servants of the church would forever be tainted by the shame, secrecy, and role of unknowing accomplice foisted on them by the others.

"Who did this to you?" he asked Garrity when at last he could speak again. "What was his name?"

Garrity shrugged. "Does it really matter? I'm not going get an apology or anything else that really matters. Not until it's too late anyway."

"I can't promise you money or an apology even," Peter said. "But I do know he didn't get away with this for years on his own. Someone else knew. And someone above that person knew. Think back to when you were a kid, Kevin. What was the one thing you learned more than anything about being Catholic? I don't mean about God. I mean about being Catholic."

Garrity scoffed. "You do what you're told."

"By whom?"

"Whoever's more important than you."

Peter nodded. "Give me his name, Kevin. Give me his name and I'll find out who let him get away with it."

Garrity's eyes clouded. He dropped his head, and his voice fell to a whisper.

"Hartnett," he said with note of fear. "Father William Hartnett."

CHAPTER 13

On Saturday mornings, Ally Larkin would rise early to go to
the farmers' market in Takoma Park before heading to the
office for a few hours. On the walk back to her apartment,
she usually stopped at a small Catholic church tucked away
near Sligo Creek Trail to light a candle for her grandfather, who
had died her senior year of college. It wasn't just the attractive façade of the church with its gabled rooftop that drew her
there. It was a deep and gradual connection to the space. To
the right of the entrance was a carving of the crossed keys of
Saint Peter, the gatekeeper of Heaven, while two saints flanked
the gothic arched entrance. The church of Saint Bonaventure,
Ally's local parish back in Piedmont, bore none of the overt
Catholicism of this structure. Sprawling and cavernous with
the indistinct modernism of many post–Vatican II churches,
Saint Bonaventure barely stood apart from the cinder-block
buildings of the local technical college. ("Gaston County
Tech! Where You Can Find Your Future!" the advertisements
squawked with undue optimism.)

Inside, this church was simply, tastefully decorated in
contrast to that one. Stark white stretches of vaulted ceilings

arched between sturdy dark-brown wooden beams. The cru-
cifix above the altar did not feature the sort of Soap Opera
Jesus that frequented the churches of Piedmont. Gone were
His sweaty curled locks, pink lips, and pale blue eyes. This
Christ, expertly carved from one piece of dark wood, twisted
and writhed with almost palpable suffering, the polished hol-
lows and contours of the wood casting shadows across a body
that seemed to sag with the weight of unbearable pain. Seeing
this carving was the first time Ally really considered the relationship between suffering and forgiveness in a more than
perfunctory way. Gazing at the body, she wondered if inflict-
ing such torture could really be forgiven. This was a question
she would revisit for the rest of her life. The line between her
Saturday visits to the church and her struggle to find a sense
of belonging in Washington was intimately drawn. The reliable
presence of Father Gutierrez, a middle-aged priest originally
from Baltimore, who greeted her with a smile and revived her
optimism, was an added benefit.

Her path to Washington, DC, had come with a host of
questions and doubts. In her last semester at Marquette, where
she double-majored in philosophy and economics, she began
the arduous process of looking for a job, along with all of her
classmates. The practical application of politics had never
actively attracted her. Growing up in Piedmont, she'd never
quite mastered it on a high school level. The notion of doing
so as a career was even more foreign. Her default mode was
to move quietly below the radar and hope she wouldn't attract
attention.

At Piedmont High School she'd gotten along fine with
the various social strata, but never truly connected with one
over another. As an academic high performer, she heard snide
comments from various factions and cliques counterbalanced
by unsightly exuberance from her teachers. Her Friday nights
did not include parties held by The Desirables, who usually

extended the kindness of ignoring her unless the need to pass calculus forced an uncomfortable tutoring alliance.

But nor did she belong to the less respectable class of students, boys with wads of chewing tobacco in their lower lips and girls who could most kindly be referred to as "rough-hewn," sporting different-colored hair every other day from the cosmetology courses they took in the vocational program. One of The Undesirables, Jackie Thomas, a rotund girl with red cheeks and a gap in her teeth ("You should see the fucker who did it," she said of the gap's source, a confrontation with her stepfather), was more often than not seated outside Principal Wharton's office when Ally arrived each morning to read the daily announcements over the PA system. Such students were usually lined up outside the door to pay for transgressions from the previous afternoon. Smoking under the bleachers. Beaning a fellow student with a roll of paper towels during Home Economics.

On the morning Jackie's dental gap made its appearance, she sat slumped and unblinking in the chair, an ugly purple bruise covering much of the left side of her face. She stared blankly at the gray institutional carpet, the red rims of her eyes swelled with moisture that threatened to spill if the lids dared close. Gone was the surly girl who routinely shouted profanities at Principal Wharton. Before Ally sat a broken being, the slouch of her shoulders exuding defeat.

A disheveled boy, maybe fifteen, exited Wharton's office, his face burning with shame, but Jackie didn't even look up. Wharton's stern voice summoned the office secretary, leaving Ally and Jackie alone in what promised to be an awkward silence. Ally reached into her backpack and withdrew a packet of the Twizzlers she was selling for the drama club's annual trip to Chicago. She placed it on Jackie's lap, where her fists sat tightly clenched. "Fuck Wharton," Ally said softly to the crumpled figure. "He's full of shit." The words stunned her, but she continued speaking, almost without control. "Besides . . . this"—she gestured around the room at the bilious butter- cream paint and disintegrating corkboards—"all this is just a blip. A short blip in your life; it doesn't really matter."

Even as her lips curled around the words, she was aware of how contrary they were to everything she'd ever done in her life. Her orderly goals, her nights spent studying or perus- ing college catalogs, her volunteer work during her spare time. But in that moment, looking at Jackie, whose eyes were wide with a mixture of shock and gratitude, Ally Larkin believed every word. "Doesn't feel that way now," Jackie muttered. The rest of her face turned as red as her swollen lip, and her voice strained with controlled emotion. Ally placed a nervous hand on Jackie's shoulder. "I know. But this won't last." She looked Jackie in the eye. "I promise you. It won't always be like this."

Jackie blinked at last, the pools of collected tears exiting in one silent splash. She clutched the Twizzlers and stuffed them into the pocket of jeans that were at least a size too small, pressing snugly against her hips so the excess tissue pushed up beyond the top button in a misshapen lump. "A blip," she said, looking at Ally one last time as the secretary called her name. Ally nodded. "That's some fucking vocabulary, Larkin." Jackie smiled, the jagged flesh around her broken tooth so apparent that Ally felt a shot of phantom pain. Shortly after the door closed, the string of profanities Ally knew almost by heart began seeping out in muffled tones from the space between the carpet and the door. On Jackie's departure, Principal Wharton shook his head. "Such a shame," he said to anything and anyone in the vicinity. "That one's probably going to end up pregnant by junior year, and she has such a head for math." Ally was too polite (and too Catholic) to say anything, but part of her wondered: If pregnancy really did signal the end of your life as you knew it, might that not mean something different for Jackie, maybe a path to leave behind her unexplained bruises and start anew?

A couple of weeks later, Ally stood dazed on the basketball court in gym class. Piedmont High was small enough that any attempt to split one class into two teams would necessitate a half-court game, so the third- and fourth-period classes overlapped. Ally spotted Jackie as her class entered and noted her subtle nod of acknowledgment. Ally Larkin, for all her intellectual prowess, was not an athlete, and her complete disinterest in winning a gym-class basketball game would not have surprised anyone who came to know her in her adult years. But by missing three plays in a row, she had raised the ire of a senior on the girls' soccer team. A preppy named Jami ("With one *i*," she would chirp between exclamations of "I mean, right? Right?") angrily shoved the ball at Ally's face. "If you can't catch the ball, get out of the goddamned way." Ally was contemplating the ugliness of Jami's sneer surrounding the perfection of her teeth when Jami's head snapped to the right. It was the result of the basketball bouncing harshly off her cranium. Both girls looked to the source—Jackie Thomas. "If you can't *avoid* the ball," she said matter-of-factly, "get off the goddamned court." Though never stated, it was clear Ally was unlikely to encounter trouble from The Desirables or The Undesirables ever again. She appreciated this unspoken protection, but never called upon Jackie to provide it. Knowing it existed was enough for them both.

Life at Marquette was immediately different. As a presidential scholar, she was lumped into a group of students just like her, but Ally still carried that social trepidation from high school. When she secured a summer internship with the Archdiocese of Boston based on a personal recommendation from the university president, she found herself in an even stranger social environment. Thrust into a world of cocktail parties and political functions, she struggled to fit in.

Catholicism in Piedmont, like everything else about the town, was largely a middle-class designation. In Boston, that seemed to be the complete opposite.

By day she worked with outreach coordinators in dingy sections of the city marred by graffiti and abandoned houses that reeked of decay. By night she mingled with businessmen and attorneys who spoke nonchalantly of homes on Nantucket and boats with more square footage than her parents' house. It was the first time she detected the palpable difference between Catholicism in America's cities and in the rest of the nation. If she stood by herself at a function, she might go unnoticed for an hour. But when Cardinal Mulcahy introduced her, guests seemed to glom on to her, hanging on her every word. When he inevitably spotted someone else, another admirer or an important connection, he would move on, and she was left to face an excruciating span of several seconds when her conversation partners would either politely stay or abandon her immediately.

The experience was like the anxiety she felt watching water skeeters swarm the Piedmont River every summer—their limbs stretched precariously on the surface, forced into an almost constant state of motion that seemed to save them from sinking. She stared at them, waiting with anticipatory horror for the moment when the spindly legs would tire and give out, leaving the water to swallow them whole. It never came. By science or will or other forces she couldn't comprehend, their ability to skirt the surface was more definite and reliable than the inevitable calamity she imagined, but it still did not and could not relieve the sense of imminent doom that filled her. However strong and steady something might seem, she worried it could crumble.

She returned to her studies at Marquette forever changed. If she'd been asked what she learned, she would have struggled to answer. She was now more aware of the challenges faced by a diocese of Boston's size and historical significance. But she had also seen the Church operate as a business and formidable political entity in ways her Jesuit professors at Marquette never had.

Not that she was ungrateful. She wasn't. She knew she'd gotten her job with Casey in DC because of that summer in Mulcahy's office, but the Church she saw in those months was at times vapid and vain, drenched in wine and artisanal cheeses. She was still trying to reconcile that version of it when she learned the job was waiting for her in DC if she wanted it. Her hectic senior year had deprived her of the chance to process everything—Boston, graduation, and the strange social strata of young, idealistic Washington—and she moved through her new life in somewhat of a fog.

When she first settled in Takoma Park, before she knew anyone or had established a sense of herself at the office, she visited the church near the Sligo Creek Trail every night. There was something comforting about knowing that, as a Catholic, wherever you were, you could always find a familiar place. It was on one of these contemplative evenings that she met Father Gutierrez. She had managed to get out of work at a reasonable hour that night and had an invitation from Mark to join him and some of his friends from college for a drink in Dupont Circle. Though she would never have said it to him, she was fairly certain he invited her only because he had a vision of her returning to a dark, lonely apartment plagued by the stench of fake floral air freshener and kitty litter. She didn't have a cat, but her apartment was usually dark. And she was occasionally lonely, but she did not view spending time alone as the same thing.

Her reticence toward DC was bound to dissipate. She would grow roots there, or she wouldn't. Then she could try life in a different city. Just as she had known that morning in the office with Jackie Thomas that high school was but one of many parts that make a life whole, she knew also the first city she landed in after graduation need not be her last. That those fearsome first years out of college, with their many bumps and bruises, would feel like high school gym class in another few.

Mark was correct that she craved company. He just didn't realize that she wanted the right kind of company, not simply warm bodies with vocal cords.

She declined his offer and boarded the Metro to return home, settling comfortably into a corner seat with her magazine. Looking up to spot the station stop, she caught her reflection in the window. In the sickly lighting of the train car, she looked small, slightly yellow, and utterly alone.

From the Takoma Park station she took a different route home specifically to walk by the church. To her immense relief, it was still open. At the candle station, she discovered she didn't have any single dollar bills to stuff in the donation box. She scrounged together enough pennies and other change to meet the suggested payment, suffering a momentary pang of guilt after the coins hit the bottom of the collection box. Normally she would have been lighting the candle in honor of her grandfather's memory. But this time, she lit the candle for herself. To ask for help in figuring out what she was doing with her life. She hadn't chosen the job with Milton Casey so much as followed along with Cardinal Mulcahy's suggestion because she deferred to his knowledge and authority. It did not occur to her that of the many subjects a career clergyman might be an expert in, the life desires of a young woman from Michigan was likely to rank quite low on the list. But with the exception of her strange alliance with Jackie Thomas and her future rejection of Steve Tilden, Ally had almost always done what was expected of her.

After a few false starts, she finally found the candle she was meant to light. Her sister had always chided her for being so fussy about the candles, but Ally believed from her earliest days that there was a moment when you spotted the candle and knew it was the right one to carry your prayer. This one, squat, crusty, and contained by the only dark red glass, was clearly The One. The wick took some patience, and she had just blown out the flame on the lighting stick when she heard a noise behind her.

Father Gutierrez introduced himself, welcomed her to the neighborhood, and invited her to the rectory for a cup of tea. Three hours later, she bid him good night, the Mass schedule tucked under her arm, and wandered home to the apartment. For the first time since her parents hugged her good-bye and began the long drive back to Michigan after helping her move into her apartment on Maple Avenue, she felt genuinely at ease.

The day Steve stole her idea, she came immediately to the church after escaping the office. She kneeled at the back pew and slumped her head into her hands. It wasn't the end of the world. She knew that. Casey had already acknowledged he was aware the idea sprang from her cleverness. That wasn't what exhausted and drained her so about the incident. It was the weight of the disappointment she felt in discovering that not only did people choose to behave this way, but it was accepted that the person in charge wouldn't feel the need to correct it.

When she explained this to Father Gutierrez, he nodded sympathetically.

"Well, Ally," he said, his eyes pinched, "I wish I could tell you you'll never encounter this again. But you will. You've learned a valuable, if painful, lesson."

It was no different from what her parents had told her about it, but it felt better coming from him. In her earliest memories, hearing news good or bad from a priest possessed an extra layer of importance and sincerity.

She had discovered this at age eight, when she was leaving Mass one Sunday morning with her family. Her father, his jocular laugh and eager handshake in full effect, walked beside her as they filed past Father Healy and onto the noisy street. The loud flower prints on the dresses of middle-aged women nearby made her want to look anywhere but up, so she fixed her gaze on the shoelaces of her father's wing tips, following him confidently and securely out of the church.

But at age eight, away from the nave of Saint Bonaventure's and the familiar scent of incense mixed with summer sweat, she felt small for her age and far from anything she knew but her father's wing tips. Exiting parishioners chattered around her. She heard "sodality meeting" and "bric-a-brac sale" and other phrases that held no meaning for her. All the while she watched his shoes intently, reluctant to let them out of her sight.

She reached up for her father, seeking out his warm hand with its wrinkles of experience and the knobby scars that told brave tales of camping or breaking up dogfights. Strong but gentle at once, he would squeeze her hand reassuringly and all would be better.

She knew immediately it wasn't him. This hand was frail, its skin like the leaves that fell from trees in autumn, its hair wiry and stiff, the ends of its fingers cold—almost dead. Ally released the hand, jumping back with a strangled cry. Looking up she saw an elderly priest she didn't recognize smiling down at her with curiously delighted eyes. She burst into tears at the shock.

"Now, now," he said. "There's no need for all that." She wailed even harder at the criticism.

"That's quite enough." The words were commanding, but not angry. "You've just wandered off course a bit and gotten away from your parents. Were you at Mass just now?"

She nodded, her lips frozen.

"And you were listening?"

Again she nodded.

"Good. Then you know it's possible to get lost and still find your way back. Right?"

Her panicked breaths became less shallow, growing into deeper inhales until at last she could speak. "You're not my dad," she'd said petulantly.

He broke out laughing. "Indeed, child, I'm not. If I were, it would require a good deal of explanation!" She didn't know what it meant at the time, but relaying the comment to her parents that night at dinner, she noted the way they, too, laughed. Thinking back on the moment now, she flushed with embarrassment at how little she had known. He extended his hand, but she had no desire to touch it again, to feel the papery wisp of it and the way the skin bunched and crinkled so easily in her grasp.

"Fine then," he said. "You don't have to hold my hand, but you do have to come with me." She did. And he returned her, as promised, to her parents.

Of course, with the recent developments in the Church, she couldn't help but wonder if she would have felt safe going with him now. If he would have returned her like he was supposed to. Over the past few years, she'd become aware how thoroughly corrupted this trust and bond had become. But never once in all her years alone with a priest had she encountered questionable conduct, and she knew that while not all clergy were to be trusted, nor should they be painted with the same brush. In her short time in DC, Father Gutierrez had proven himself a source of genuine support and comfort.

He blushed when she told him as much. Or when she said the bad apples were getting all the press now, but there were so many good ones out there like him. No matter how many new allegations popped up, which happened pretty often these days.

Father Gutierrez smiled and put his head down, hiding his face until the color had returned to normal.

"I appreciate the compliment, Ally. Really, I do. You have to know that. But I only wish it were that simple," he said. "Every one of these guys? Someone in their parish—most of them in fact—saw them the way you see me. That's the thing. They don't wear signs around their neck. If they did—if *all* things dangerous did—this world would be very different."

Ally knew that from a rational place in her mind, but she felt robbed of her ability to believe good things about all the priests she'd known in her life. From the earliest days of the scandal's eruption, back when she was still in high school, she hadn't been angry necessarily. She hadn't been offended like most of the people she knew, as they talked about it in the parking lot of Saint Bonaventure's or in the supermarket checkout line. It was naturally disturbing to her the way it was anytime a pedophile was identified, whether he was a random drifter or a respected baseball coach. But as the scandal moved on, growing larger and wider, she'd felt cheated the way she did when she was eight and Santa brought her a generic-brand Barbie doll instead of the real thing. Her parents tried to chase away her disappointment, explaining that it was just as good, but Christmas was never quite as special to her afterward. It so changed the way she looked at Santa, it was almost a relief to learn the truth of his identity a few years later. She no longer had to pretend she wasn't a doubter. And while she never personally experienced impropriety with a priest, she looked at the growing list of the guilty—from the men who committed the crimes, to the superiors who allowed it to continue—and felt the indelible impact of it on her sense of faith.

"Have you read the articles, Father?" she asked Gutierrez. "The statistics say it's possible one out of six do this. That can't be right, can it? Because if it is, that means I've probably met at least one. Eaten dinner with him, or sat in his class, volunteered with him. And the whole time, I was part of it. Helping him put on that face to the world while he did these things."

Their crimes didn't just physically and mentally damage their immediate victims. They stole the comfort of belief from every follower. Maybe her own belief was an optimistic version of what she *wanted* to think happened in Jerusalem two thousand years ago but was just as misinformed as her perception of priests and the Church in general.

"I want to remain faithful," she told Gutierrez. "About people in general. But it's not easy."

Gutierrez patted her hand. "You're allowed to have doubts, Ally. I'd be lying if I said I never had them. Realize it comes with the territory, not just of being a Christian, but of being part of humanity. You can't know everything with absolute certainty. It wouldn't be faith if you could."

"But what if I helped them? What if the signs were there and I didn't see them because I didn't want to?"

She expected Gutierrez to give her a standard line that would, if only in grammatical structure, absolve her of the inadvertent role she feared she might have played. But he didn't. Instead, he bluntly told her about being in high school back in Baltimore and about a charismatic young priest who did things differently. They didn't spend all their time at retreats talking about what it meant to be religious. This priest got them out working every weekend—repainting a building off the Belair Road corridor, tutoring kids, and teaching ESL classes. It was refreshing.

"My parents were traditional. Back in Cuba, you were supposed to spend more time in Mass than on these kinds of projects. But I thought it was great. I was devastated when he left. We all were. A number of years later, I learned he'd been transferred to Peru, and an accusation from one of my classmates was the cause. It didn't lessen the impact of what I learned from him. But it removed the wool from my eyes, there's no doubt about that. You can't know everything about a person, Ally. The best you can do is keep your eyes open."

She had spent a lot of time asking him for advice while she tried to settle into her new life in DC. If he tired of babysitting her, he never said so. It hadn't occurred to her that someone like Father Gutierrez could be dragged into a situation not of his own making, the way she felt dragged into the sexual-abuse scandal by nature of being Catholic. But that's exactly what ended up happening.

On the day the memo on withholding Communion was issued, Milton Casey gave the staff strict instructions not to discuss it outside of the office or a structured press conference. "Look, I'm not going to lie. Is this a good thing for Wyncott? Sure. But it's got nothing to do with him and, as you can see, it's stirring up a lot of controversy. So the best thing we can say about it is nothing. Or reiterate that Wyncott respects the rights of churches and how they care for parishioners."

So Ally hadn't discussed it with Father Gutierrez, even though she was deeply curious about his thoughts on the command. She didn't even ask what he thought of the archbishop in Colorado, when she could probably have gotten away with it and was sure he'd have had something interesting to say. Some months after he gave her the pep talk about priests, the memo controversy flared up again. This time it was over the archbishop of Saint Louis, Cardinal Keane. He'd publicly stated that he would not deny Communion to anyone in his archdiocese, pro-choice or not, unless they had been formally excommunicated. "While I defer to the knowledge of the Holy See and its commitment to protecting the faithful, I cannot, as a servant of God first and foremost, politicize a ritual as sacred as the Eucharist. If we are to promote the tenets of confession, we must trust that those who have sinned will seek their penance to preserve that relationship, not to avoid public humiliation."

That he spoke out about it was a shock. Nearly two months had passed since the memo's release, and according to the research firm Casey had hired, during a sampling of services, eight out of ten priests had reiterated at least once that Catholics were obligated to vote for a pro-life candidate. It was just assumed that everyone else in the American Church was doing the same or, if they weren't, their silence was tacit support. Keane's public challenge of the memo was definitely unexpected.

Shortly after Keane's announcement, a writer for the *St. Louis Post-Dispatch* penned an article announcing that the archbishop had received notification that he was concluding his appointment in Saint Louis and moving to the South Pacific to assume a role within the Archdiocese of Agana. The following day, a columnist questioned the connection between Keane's removal and his outspoken refusal to "play politics with people's faith," as he had been quoted describing the memo. "Does the Vatican Want to Control the American Election?" screamed the headline.

It was a ridiculous suggestion, Ally told Mark when he put a copy of the article on her desk. She spotted where he was going with it and decided she'd had enough. "I get it, Mark. You read *The Da Vinci Code* and you think the halls of the Vatican are teeming with sinister puppet masters. But it's not. Maybe your life is a little more interesting when you can cling to the idea that it is, but the Church has entirely too much on its plate to worry this much about an American election. What would they get out of it? Nothing. So what's the point?"

Mark clapped his hands. "Finally! After two years you're finally thinking like a true politician. This is a proud moment, Ally."

Ally grinned back at him. "Or a sign I need to get out of here."

"Not until after November, you don't."

Hours later, she was still thinking about their conversation and the article. Mark was right. Maybe it was a weirdly

Catholic tic, but intention and motive were cornerstones of her judgment.

But she would have to wait for another day to continue the debate with Mark. Casey had announced he was redirecting even more staffing resources to get Wyncott's bill on tort reform the support it needed. And that included Ally. She'd have to get up to speed with the team, which she did by staying at the office all night.

It was close to six o'clock in the morning when she finally got home. Only three of them, Mark, Ally, and Steve, had been left by five thirty. Even though he had (wisely) been avoiding any direct contact with her for nearly two months, Steve finally turned to her and said it was time for them all to go home.

From the Metro escalator, she started in the direction of home. Her body ached with fatigue. Pulling all-nighters in college had been stressful, but nothing compared to the aura of panicked preparation the office had been in since Casey announced the last push for the bill. She'd been walking for more than ten minutes before she noticed she was going the wrong way. Her dazed wandering had brought her to Father Gutierrez's rectory.

She stumbled back from the garden pathway in the front and had already turned to go back to her apartment when the door opened behind her.

"Ally? Is everything okay?"

She was embarrassed. "I'm so sorry. I got off the train and wasn't paying attention to where I was going. I'm fine. Just exhausted."

"Let me give you a ride home."

She nodded gratefully. "I hope I didn't wake you," she said through a yawn as she crawled into his modest hatchback.

"No, no. I'm up this time every morning. I saw a shadow move through the window and thought you were an enormous bird."

"I guess it's a sign I spend too much time here, huh?"

He laughed. "Not at all. And I hope you'll continue to come even after I'm gone."

The words startled her awake.

"Gone? What do you mean?"

He took a deep breath and turned to focus on the streets ahead of him. They were the only car around.

"I'll be leaving. In the next month or so."

"Leaving? To go where?"

"Alaska," he said slowly.

She blinked at him. "Alaska?" she said, incredulous. "There are Catholics in Alaska?"

He smiled patiently. "Evidently. I've heard it's beautiful there."

"It's a meat locker covered in darkness for most of the year."

He cracked a smile. "Thanks for the encouragement. Where's that optimist I know and love?"

"That optimist disappeared around four a.m., Father. But seriously," she said, "who did you upset to get shipped off there?"

She knew as soon she said the words that she'd hit a nerve. His smile dropped and he turned back to the steering wheel.

"Wait. That's not what really happened, is it?"

"It's not appropriate for me to discuss such matters with you."

"I don't care," she protested. "Tell me what's going on."

He turned the car down Maple Avenue and pulled up to the curb across from her building.

"It's complicated, Ally. I don't think there's any way I could explain it and do it justice."

"Try me."

He wasn't, he explained, the right match for this parish, and it was perhaps for the best that he was going to be moving on. His ideas didn't match the expectations here.

"What are you talking about? Everyone here loves you. Takoma Park is about the crunchiest place on earth, and you're the crunchiest priest I've ever known."

He laughed. "I'm not supposed to be crunchy, Ally. And I'm not supposed to win a popularity contest among my parishioners. I'm supposed to serve my church and, through it, God."

She understood immediately. "Your homilies are too liberal, huh?"

"You could say that," he said.

"So tell them how conservative I am and that I never miss your services."

"It's not so much what I say that's the problem. It's what I don't say."

She unbuckled her seat belt and turned to face him. "What does that mean?" she asked. He didn't respond. "Just tell me," she ordered. Reluctantly, he gave in.

After the memo on the worthiness to receive Communion was issued, his monsignor met with him and others about following its order. "I had reservations about it," Father Gutierrez said. "And I told him that. I wasn't the only one. A lot of us were uncomfortable with it. I mean, look around you, Ally. Look at the signs on the front lawns here. It's obvious where people stand politically. If I had to deny Communion to the ones who are pro-choice or the ones who think Jack Kevorkian's a hero . . . Well, I don't know who would be left." He cast her a sideways glance. "Other than you."

The monsignor told them they didn't have to single people out. He suggested they compromise. Insert a well-timed and well-placed reminder into the sermon that a vote for Thomas Archer was a vote for sin.

Ally cocked her head. "But I don't remember you ever saying anything," she said.

"That's because I didn't. I chose not to address it at all."

A few weeks after that meeting with his monsignor, he was writing notes for his next sermon when he received an unexpected visit from the archbishop of Washington, DC, Cardinal Curran. "He was polite," Gutierrez told Ally. "But there was no doubt about it. I was being ordered to campaign from the pulpit."

Ally felt that same tug of discomfort she'd felt that morning at Casey's office when Mark turned on the TV for coverage of the memo's release.

The meeting with his archbishop had ended with mutual dissatisfaction. Gutierrez refused to agree to endorse Wyncott over Archer.

"I've given you an order and I expect you to obey it," Curran told him. He didn't. The notice of his transfer arrived at the rectory several weeks later. He took in the look of shock on Ally's face.

"Don't be sad. I knew what I was doing. And I'd do it again."

It didn't matter. She hunched over and covered her face with her hands, muttering a string of profanities that continued for several seconds before she stopped and looked up at him.

"I'm not sad," she said between fast breaths. "I'm angry, Father. I'm so mad I can't think straight. I can't—I can't even talk."

He got out of the car and came over to her side. "Come on," he said, pulling her out and walking her up to the apartment door. "You're exhausted. Get in and get some sleep. All this—work, life, the world even, will look different when you wake up."

He was right. A few hours later when she pushed back the blankets and looked out the window, the world *did* look different. But for Ally, it held more questions than ever before.

CHAPTER 14

On the drive back to Mitchell International Airport from Olmsted, Peter kept swerving onto the soft shoulder. His behavior fit every bad driver tactic in the book. He thumbed words into the search engine of his iPhone, his eyes darting from the keyboard to the road to the screen to his rearview mirror. He scrawled in a notebook resting on the beverage tray while steering with one hand. He chatted on his phone without the headset, which he'd left on his desk, forgotten in the aftermath of an argument with Emma that started in the bathroom the morning he left.

"You're going where?" Emma had asked.

"Wiff-kahnshun," Peter shouted past the whirring of the electric toothbrush she'd gotten him for Christmas, the one that seemed to attack his mouth every time he used it, battering his teeth if he didn't hold it firmly the entire time. Given the war raging in his mouth, he thought he'd managed to pronounce it pretty clearly. Demosthenes he wasn't, but nor was he Elmer Fudd.

Emma popped her head back into the bathroom.

"Where?"

He removed the toothbrush long enough to say the word again. "Wisconsin."

The brush's head had continued to spin, spraying everything in front of him with a smattering of white film, and Emma tried to duck the splash. She was wearing his favorite bra. The pale blue one with maroon flowers embroidered on the trim. Her arms were in the sleeves of a shirt and she paused to give him A Look before cramming her head into the neck hole and letting the fabric shimmy down her torso.

"What article is this for?"

Peter should have answered immediately, said the first thing that came to mind. But he waited too long and she pounced.

"This isn't for an article, is it?" she said.

He switched off the toothbrush. That was enough carnage for one morning. He spat into the sink, wiping his mouth with his arm. Emma looked vaguely disgusted.

"It could be. I don't know yet. I have to get more information."

She didn't look irritated anymore, but she didn't look absolutely happy, either. "And this information requires you to fly to Milwaukee at the last minute, when we're supposed to spend the weekend with my parents?"

It certainly wasn't going to look good. He knew Emma's sister thought he'd lost his mind since returning from Kashmir. She'd told him as much, and he imagined that a similar lecture from his father-in-law couldn't be far behind. Especially if he skipped out on visiting them to chase what might turn out to be nothing.

"I'm really sorry," he said. And he was, in a manner of speaking. "It's taken me a while to track down this contact, and I can't get an answer when I call."

It was the wrong detail to share. She erupted. "Let me get this straight. You're blowing us off to show up at someone's house because they won't answer the phone? How do you know anyone's even there?"

"He paid his taxes on time last year according to the city records."

Emma flipped the toilet cover down and sat. "Peter, what is this? What's going on?"

"It's nothing. I just need to get some information."

"Why won't you talk to me?"

"Emma, honey. It's not a big deal. I'll be gone two days, max."

"I'm trying, Peter. I am. I know you need to work through this stuff on your own time and in your own way, but you have to help me out here."

He hated that. He hated the way she assumed every single thing he did or said was motivated by the explosion in Jammu. When he stayed up all night working on his article about Ingram for the *Hartford Courant*, Emma told him not sleeping wasn't going to make the nightmares go away. When he made small talk with the Yemeni shop girl at the local supermarket, she asked if she reminded him of Sheeraza Akhtar.

"Not everything in this world is about tragedy, Emma," he snapped. "I'm not some wounded bird you need to fix with a self-help book. I'm doing fine."

"What you're doing is shutting me out."

The back-and-forth was all so frustrating. "You're blowing this out of proportion. Seriously, hon. I just need to get some work done."

She didn't budge. "Why won't you tell me what this is about?"

"Because." He adopted a belligerent pose.

"Because why?"

"What, are we six? Because I don't want to right now."

Emma wasn't going to let him get away with that. She stood up and walked closer to him.

"Not good enough. Try again."

"Not now. Let me see what I can find out."

"Tell me," she pleaded again.

"Let it go, Emma."

"I won't!" The shout took him by surprise. He couldn't remember the last time he'd seen her so angry. She stepped right up to him, yelling the words in his face. "I won't let it go, Peter. What the hell is going on that you keep hiding everything from me? Why won't you tell me?"

Peter lost it. "Because he was a pedophile!" he screamed. The roar came out of nowhere, and he felt disembodied as he shouted the words.

"He sent letters to his victims, Emma. Ingram did. Apologizing for what he did to them. Okay? And maybe I'm not *hiding* everything from you. Maybe I'm trying to figure out what to do about learning the man I respected most in this world was a child molester the entire time I knew him. I'm *very* sorry that my schedule for mourning the desecration of his memory has been so incredibly difficult for you to deal with."

She shrank from him as if he'd hit her.

"I'm tired of holding your hand, Emma. Leave me alone to do what I need to do. Can't you do that? Just leave me alone until I figure it out!"

Emma crumpled onto the edge of the tub. Peter stormed out and slammed the door, bounding down the stairs and out the door to his car.

He drove around for an hour to clear his head. Turning down the street to his house, he paused a few doors away and left the car idling while he got out and peeked at the house to see if her car was still there. It wasn't.

He parked in the driveway and walked in the front door. The first thing he noticed was that Grady wasn't there.

"Grady?" he called out. "Gradeser?"

In the kitchen he picked up a box of dog treats and shook it. "Come on, G-Man! Come get a snack!" He paused to listen for the jangle of dog tags but heard only silence.

He climbed the stairs and turned down the hallway to the bedroom. A suitcase was on the bed. The sight of it stopped him cold, as though a force field had popped up to block him. He knew something like this would happen. Ever since that night drinking hot chocolate with Emma's father, he had suspected this moment would come. The suitcase was small, compact, and just the way he always imagined Emma would leave him—with nothing more or less than she'd had when they married.

Resigned, he took a deep breath and walked in. The duffel bag he used to go to the gym sat empty near his nightstand. He tossed it on the bed and started taking socks and underwear out of his drawer. As he stuffed the clothes into the bag, his eyes kept straying to the suitcase.

When he couldn't help himself any longer, he reached over and flipped it open. A few of his shirts and pants lay folded within. Three pairs of socks bulged from the mesh pocket lining the top of the case. And in the center of the case, on top of the clothes and next to a travel-size umbrella, was a folded piece of paper. He opened it. The message was short and to the point.

I'm sorry. I get it now. I love you, Peter Merrick. Come home soon.
E

He realized he'd been holding his breath when it came out in one solid burst. Back downstairs, he stopped in the kitchen to grab his cell-phone headset but got distracted when he knocked the wall calendar to the floor with his shoulder. He flipped it open to the right month and tacked it onto the corkboard. That very day was circled in red: *Grady Vet: 11:30.* He rushed out the door with his suitcase, completely forgetting the headset and feeling better than he had in a while.

The trip to Wisconsin had been a successful one. With so much to do in a limited time, he hadn't called her once. About fifteen miles from the airport he dialed her phone number. She picked up, the lightness in her greeting perking him up immediately. "Hi!" she chirped.

"It was a mistake, Ems. The whole thing. It's not what I thought it was."

He heard her sigh. "Oh, Peter. I'm so relieved."

"Me, too. I'm on my way to the airport now. I'll see you in a few hours."

"Okay. Talk to you soon."

"Emma?" He caught her just before he hung up.

"Yeah, babe?"

"Thanks."

A couple of hours turned into half a day, thanks to a tornado in southern Illinois that affected air traffic and connections all the way up to Milwaukee. By the time he got home, Emma had long since gone to bed. Packaged leftovers sat on the top shelf of the refrigerator. He grabbed the container and wandered down the hallway to his office. As he was waiting for the computer to start up, Grady shuffled into the room and plopped down right on top of Peter's feet. Soft fur tickled his ankles and Grady's warm belly acted as the perfect slippers, chasing off a chill that had settled on Peter. He was too focused on finding out what he could about Father William Hartnett to notice it until the warmth rushed up his leg.

So far, he'd managed to track down at least six civil suits filed against Hartnett, by three different attorneys representing more than fifteen clients across several states. Less satisfying, however, was his attempt to identify a clear trend or connection among the other cases and James Ingram. Why had Ingram reached out specifically to Kevin Garrity, and what connection did William Hartnett have to him? His calls to the parishes he had numbers for didn't yield results. When he identified himself and described what he was looking for, he was informed that they could not comment on pending litigation and referred him to Ted Mercier, an attorney in Philadelphia representing some of the claimants. The next day, Peter dialed his office. Mercier was delighted to get his call.

"You going to write an article about this dirtbag?" he asked, after Peter explained who he was. "'Cause if you are, you need to include all the dirtbags who kept fobbing him off on everyone else."

This was a man after Peter's own heart. "Believe me, I have no problem doing that if I find the information," he said.

He was trying to find out more about Hartnett's movements. Mercier was the right place to start. "Eighteen parishes in less than twenty-five years," Mercier told him. "And that's just the ones I've been able to track down so far. Every time I turn around, the church lawyers are filing another injunction to prevent me from getting access to their records." In the background, Peter could hear the clatter of a filing cabinet drawer sliding open.

"At the start, he was able to stay there for two years or more before rumors started. That was back in the late seventies. I mean, I look at it now and the evidence was all there. But I'm looking at it today, you know, with modern eyes that know how widespread this shit is, right? Guess they didn't really pay attention to kids accusing priests back then."

He was right. Peter was about the same age as some of Hartnett's victims. He could recall very clearly when public-service messages about sexual molestation started appearing, and schools started teaching kids about what to do if someone touched their private parts ("The parts covered by a bathing suit," his sixth-grade teacher had said) and to tell someone

("An adult, a teacher, or someone else you trust") immediately. He thought about the emphasis they placed on abusers being strangers and the idea that teachers, priests, and coaches were the kind of adult you should tell. It was an irony of epic proportions. By the mid-1980s, sexual-abuse information campaigns had reached the mainstream, but were still focused on stranger danger. Given that it had practically taken the start of a new millennium for people to speak out about priests committing abuse, he had no trouble believing, as Mercier did, that the uncensored annals of the American Church probably had thousands of cases never reported by Catholics too pious to conceive of priests being culpable.

"Toward the end, though, he got sloppy. Or maybe the kids just got a little braver. Whatever it was, he was transferred more quickly in those last couple of years. He'd get busted in under a year. In some case, just a matter of months."

Mercier agreed to fax a list of the eighteen known parishes as soon as he got off the phone. Peter found what he was looking for the minute he received it. At the bottom of the page, just a few rows up from the end of the list, was the answer: *Retreat Coordinator, Good Shepherd Church, Claremont, Pennsylvania.*

Hartnett had been there for just under two years. Peter took out the research he'd done on Erik Bader months before. Bader had settled out of court and, as part of the settlement, signed a nondisclosure agreement that prevented him from publicly naming his abuser. The court records were sealed, but based on the age he admitted he was when the abuse had taken place, Peter determined that it fell within the period William Hartnett was there.

He flipped through his notes for the *Hartford Courant* article and found the list of Ingram's clerical career locations given to him by Jane Kemp. A cross-check of the dates revealed that Hartnett arrived at Claremont to act as a full-time retreat coordinator around the time James Ingram gave up his part-time work there upon completion of his PhD at the University of Pennsylvania.

Ingram's letters suddenly made so much more sense. He had to have known about Hartnett, but maybe he didn't find out until long after he'd left Claremont. The letters to Bader, Terzulli, and Garrity all started less than two years before his death, many years after those particular victims had been abused. But once he found out, the guilt—the agony—of having created the opening filled by a predator would have crushed him. According to Mercier's records, Hartnett arrived at Claremont from a stint in Illinois. His time in Claremont ended sooner than expected, and he moved on to a small parish in upstate New York, where he was caught behaving inappropriately in under a year. From there he was reassigned to the Archdiocese of Milwaukee, which placed him at Our Lady of Sorrows church in Olmsted. He arrived there just a few months before Kevin Garrity's father walked out on his family.

A phone call to Claremont informed him that the current monsignor had only been there for eight years. The office secretary, a brash woman named Dorothy, gave him information with little prodding. Not only did she offer the names of all the monsignors dating back to the Battle of Brandywine practically, she gave him the dates of their tenures.

Monsignor Tom Sexton had left parish administration in the late 1990s to finish his PhD in theology and was now on staff at the University of Scranton. Peter decided an in-person interview might yield better results. He played the Jesuit college grad card when he called to arrange a meeting. Friendly Monsignor Sexton was eager to help a graduate of Ignatius who had written articles for the *National Catholic Reporter* and *America* magazine. So happy, in fact, that he didn't really press Peter for details on the scope of the article he claimed to be writing.

Sexton's office at Scranton was typically academic. Bland with limited character beyond that which Sexton gave it by hanging framed copies of illuminated manuscripts on the walls. The conversation was easygoing at first. An explanation of when and how Sexton decided he wanted to become a priest, where he studied. Peter used this to deftly turn the subject to a listing of where Sexton had worked and a summary of his work as a minister at each location.

When he began outlining his time at Claremont, Peter seized the opportunity. Sexton was completely unprepared, that much was clear. "And what about the presence of William Hartnett at Claremont during your time there?" The old man's face fell, a look of anguish more than shock crossing his face.

"I'm—well—" he sputtered. "William Hartnett was a—" He tried to offer an explanation, but the words weren't coming.

Peter softened the interrogation a little, allowing the man to catch his breath before he pressed on. "How did he end up in your parish?"

Sexton recovered suddenly, finding his voice and standing. "Mr. Merrick," he said curtly. "I think this conversation should end before it even starts. I can tell you I took care of the Hartnett situation as soon as it came to my attention."

Peter smiled, tried to calm him down. "I know you did. Look, Monsignor, I'm not here to pick a fight with you about this or blame you for what happened. I'm trying to figure out what happened. How William Hartnett ended up in Claremont."

Sexton sat back down, his body sagging in the chair. When he looked up, his face burned bright red and he blinked repeatedly. "I ask myself how I could have let that happen every day. Whether I shouldn't have looked more closely at his background before agreeing to assign him to Claremont."

He reached into the lower right-hand drawer of his desk and pulled out a bottle of scotch and two glasses. He set a glass down in front of Peter and poured a healthy amount of the amber liquid for them both.

"I should have. I know that now. I know that if I'd called around to a few of his other parishes, I probably would have found someone willing to tell me what happened there. Why he left. But he came with such impeccable references from people with impeccable reputations. There didn't seem to be a need to do more digging. I'm not sure that I could have asked any questions without causing an uproar and offending everyone involved."

"Wait. Let's start with the references. How did you hear about William Hartnett?"

Sexton had only recently been promoted to monsignor when he was assigned to the diocese governing Claremont. He was sorry to see James Ingram go, of course. He was certain that Peter, as a graduate of Ignatius, must understand why. Ingram assured him he would request permission to stay on until his replacement was identified and help with the transition any way he could. It was typical Ingram.

Hartnett, he explained, was assigned to Claremont by the archbishop of Philadelphia on the recommendation of Owen Feeney. Sexton remembered Feeney from his days at Villanova and knew that he had just returned to America after spending two years in Rome at the office of the prefect for the Congregation for the Doctrine of the Faith. At the mention of Feeney's name, Peter sat up straight, locked on every word. Hartnett was being transferred from the Chicago archdiocese, which also governed Parkchester, Illinois, by Cardinal Mulcahy. "Like I said," Sexton said with a shrug, "the man had impeccable references. Feeney sent a letter of personal introduction on Hartnett's behalf. Father Ingram liked Hartnett just fine and recommended him as well. It seemed like a perfect fit."

Peter nodded. It was completely understandable. "So what did you do when you found out what he was doing?"

Managing his removal had been slightly more complicated for the young monsignor. "I was shocked. When the first report trickled in, I did some investigating. I couldn't be sure what had happened. The boy who complained had a history of problematic behavior that predated Hartnett. Still, I thought it was better to play it safe. I contacted Feeney and asked him for advice on how best to proceed. I didn't want to ignore the child's complaint, but I didn't want to cause a problem for Hartnett on flimsy evidence. Feeney said I'd done the right thing by handling it discreetly, and he would look into it."

"Out of curiosity," Peter said, "what do you consider flimsy evidence?"

"In the first case, the child said Hartnett had made him uncomfortable by asking questions about how many girls he'd kissed. Did he like girls. That sort of thing."

"Any physical interaction?"

"No sexual contact. The boy said Hartnett put his arm around him."

"And that didn't seem unusual?"

"Not that unusual. Which made it difficult to determine how true it was. Part of it was that the boy had been caught masturbating in the back of the school bus. He was disciplined for that, and a few months later disciplined again for standing under the bleachers and staring up girls' skirts. The simple fact is that he had already displayed hypersexualized tendencies. And each time we disciplined him, he expressed confusion as to why. Hartnett denied it and with no one to corroborate the boy's story, I couldn't tell how much of it was truth and how much was fantasy."

The explanation didn't make Peter feel any better, but he had to admit it made a certain amount of sense. He told himself that if he'd been in the same position, he would have acted immediately. But the truth was he couldn't know that. He wasn't in that situation, and the calculation each person made in each situation was just that: a decision made based on a set of factors unique to the circumstances.

"What about the second incident?"

Sexton nodded. "That was a lot more clear-cut. A clerk working the drive-through window at the local Dairy Queen spotted Hartnett with his hand in a boy's lap when she leaned out farther than usual to hand them a milkshake. She saw enough to mention it to her mom. When I was notified, I called Hartnett in to ask about it. He didn't deny it, but wouldn't admit it either. This time, Feeney didn't even need to hear the whole story. He told me to file the formal transfer request with my archbishop and that I could rest assured it would be handled."

"So who had him moved? Feeney or the archbishop?"

Sexton leaned forward. "That's the thing. Feeney handled so many things for the archbishop, it was hard to tell."

Peter didn't tell him as much, but in his experience, that had always been the case with Owen Feeney.

"Do you know where he was transferred?"

Sexton nodded. "A small town outside Rochester."

Peter wrote some notes. When he finished, he rose, held his hand out to Sexton, and thanked him for his time.

He was almost to the door when he turned once more to the priest.

"One last question—did you inform the monsignor at his new parish about his behavior?"

"No," he said humbly. "Feeney said he would take care of notifying them on behalf of the archdiocese." The monsignor dropped his head in shame. "But I should have followed up myself. Just to make sure."

Peter didn't respond. There was no use telling someone something he already knew. He slipped quietly out of the office and headed back to his car.

By the time he got to the New York State Thruway, he'd already contacted the parish near Rochester where Hartnett was transferred after Claremont and spoken with a Monsignor Behrend, who was assigned to the diocese at the time. The story was remarkably similar. Hartnett came with personal letters of introduction and impressive credentials. He became a staple of the community, helping to build a shelter for battered women, and helping an out-of-work father whose car had broken down. Only this time, the first child to come forward wasn't a behavioral problem. He was the son of a member of the city council, who immediately involved the police. Hartnett's transfer was arranged immediately, and in exchange, the father agreed not to press charges. Hartnett had been placed with a parish somewhere in Wisconsin. As he listened to Behrend, Peter realized why the story sounded so familiar. He'd read parts of an article about it out loud to Ingram that day a few years ago when they'd had their most frank discussion about the scandal.

"So, no one from the Philadelphia archdiocese informed you that Hartnett had been removed for inappropriate conduct?"

The monsignor scoffed on the other end of the phone. "Not a peep. If they had, I damn well would have refused to accept him."

But the biggest similarity of all was the one Peter already saw coming. "Who wrote the letter of introduction?"

"Big player in the church now," the monsignor said, not without a trace of jealousy. "Bishop Owen Feeney."

CHAPTER 15

Peter stared at the phone for several minutes before he picked it up to dial. He had to admit that a small part of him was going to enjoy grilling Feeney. But that didn't mean he wasn't intimidated by the prospect of confronting the good bishop via telephone. In person would have been preferable, but Peter knew how much Feeney cherished his status and that he probably had a gatekeeper to protect him from the riffraff. Without Ingram around to arrange it, an in-person meeting, was next to impossible. In fact, without Ingram so many things now felt impossible. Trying to catch Feeney for a meeting seemed like a waste of time. He settled instead for the telephone.

The minute he'd gotten off the phone with Monsignor Behrend from Rochester, his instinct was to call Feeney up and taunt him. But he wanted to do more research first. By piecing together publicly available biographies from Feeney's many media appearances, he was able to create a poor-man's timeline of the events surrounding Hartnett's arrival in and departure from southeastern Pennsylvania. When Hartnett arrived in Claremont, Feeney had been a monsignor for a couple of years. He was appointed to the title just prior to serving at the Vatican. That he had become very well connected during his time in Rome was clear. By all accounts, he may have returned to the American Church with the same title he had when he left, but he wielded significantly more power and influence than before. News articles featuring information on the Philadelphia archdiocese almost always quoted Feeney more often than they did the archbishop himself.

The Cardinal Mulcahy connection from Feeney's time in Chicago also spoke volumes. Peter called around to journalists from Mulcahy's previous parishes. They were happy to share truth, rumor, and everything in between about Mulcahy and his considerable influence. Since his early days in Baltimore, Mulcahy had developed a reputation as a "cleaner": someone who fixes problems in a parish, whatever those might be. When the Baltimore archdiocese was teetering on the edge of bankruptcy (moral and financial), Mulcahy was handpicked to replace the current leadership. He moved quickly, closing struggling schools and reducing operating expenses by consolidating parishes and auctioning off property to the highest bidder, which in this case happened to be McIntyre Industries, a defense contractor. It was generally accepted, but never explicitly stated, that Mulcahy's personal connections to the McIntyre CEO, a bullish man who grew up in Mulcahy's South Boston neighborhood, had come in handy.

At his next stop, Chicago, Mulcahy trained his sights on restoring the reputation of a parish on the North Side, where a monsignor had been charged with accepting monetary kickbacks in exchange for recommending that the church purchase property that directly benefited the man who paid him off. "They were gifts," the monsignor had maintained. "Perfectly legal under IRS law."

"But not under mine," Mulcahy had supposedly told him. "You're going to donate every penny of it to a charity, and I'm going to make sure you don't go to prison." And he did. At least, according to people Peter spoke with who'd worked in the office at the time. He was aware that if he'd tried this even two years ago, parishioners, employees, and believers wouldn't have talked to him. But by now, everyone but the church leadership was talking.

Like a good little foot soldier, Mulcahy had moved to Boston just after his predecessor was whisked away to Rome to avoid further investigation into what he knew about the amount of sexual abuse in his archdiocese or, more importantly, whether he had contributed directly to covering it up. In exchange for taking on the least desirable jobs, Mulcahy banked IOUs with anyone he spared from embarrassment and aggravation.

William Hartnett was transferred to Claremont from Parkchester when Mulcahy was with the Chicago archdiocese. Then he was transferred to Rochester just weeks before Mulcahy arrived in Philadelphia to be keynote speaker at the annual United States Conference of Catholic Bishops symposium.

Six months to the day after the archbishop of Philadelphia approved Hartnett's transfer, Feeney was promoted to bishop. Peter knew he was drawing specious conclusions that probably couldn't be substantiated. Not at this stage. But there were just too many coincidences, and deep down, he knew someone had struck a deal along the way. He just didn't know which one of them initiated it or why.

The rudimentary flowchart he made following all these connections sat in front of him as he stared at the phone, preparing to dial Feeney. On paper, it made him look like a crackpot conspiracy theorist. He was beginning to feel like one, too. Even if he was, he felt no doubt that Feeney played a role in Hartnett's overlap with Ingram. And that whatever had transpired before and after, it prompted Ingram to spend the rest of his life reaching out to people who never understood why he felt responsible and for whom his apologies may have come too late. Taking up that mantle, continuing with Ingram's mission—that alone was worth a phone call to the Bishops Conference.

Feeney's assistant, an unpleasant woman named Sister Anne Marie, didn't so much speak as she did cackle. The sound was so harsh that at first he thought it was a digital recording gone awry. He couldn't quite place her accent. It was somewhere between Brooklyn and the Furies. After two minutes of limited success with her, he concluded it was probably the latter. She didn't budge until Peter mentioned that he was hoping to speak with Feeney for a magazine piece he was writing about the late James Ingram, SJ.

While her voice remained the hard, shrill nightmare it had been from the moment she answered the phone, her demeanor did soften. She expressed her sympathies and agreed to transfer the call. When Feeney picked up, it was obvious he had been prepped for the conversation. "Mr. Merrick, lovely to hear from you. I'm sorry it's not under better circumstances." They exchanged a few pleasantries, Feeney complimented him on the *Economist* series, and then Peter shared a few memories of Ingram to break the ice.

"I want to thank you for taking the time to speak with me."

"Of course, of course. Anything I can do to pay tribute to James."

"I was hoping you could help me flesh out something I'm looking at for the article."

"I'll certainly try."

"James, you recall, was an avid letter writer."

"Yes. He was." From the way Feeney said the words it was obvious he was looking at or reading something else. Peter could probably have said Jesus was a Muslim and gotten the same response.

"Well, he sent a series of letters to people in different states. Pennsylvania, Illinois, Wisconsin."

"Mmm-hmm," Feeney said dismissively.

"And I've been trying to figure out the connection between them. But the only thing I can find is someone named William Hartnett."

That got Feeney's attention.

"I'm sorry, who?"

"A Father William Hartnett. Actually, you might know him." Peter was kind of enjoying playing dumb. "He spent some time outside of Philadelphia when you were with the archdiocese there."

There was silence on the other end.

"Your Excellency?"

"The name does ring a bell, but as I'm sure you know, Mr. Merrick, the business of an archdiocese involves a lot of faces and names in a short amount of time."

"The business." Peter repeated the words, thinking about how much the Church in America had begun to resemble a corporation with the way it downsized, sold off pieces of itself for profit, and covered up mistakes. "Yes, I understand. This one might perhaps have stood out more than the others."

"Why is that?" Feeney asked coolly.

"Well, he arrived to replace James when he finished at the University of Pennsylvania."

Feeney's voice picked up immediately. "Yes, of course! Father Hartnett." He lowered his voice to a conspiratorial whisper. "He wasn't with us for long, Mr. Merrick. I'm not at liberty to discuss the specifics, but he wasn't an appropriate fit for our parishioners. He was removed as quickly as the archbishop could effect a transfer."

Peter decided to take his lead. "That's a shame, really. He wasn't an appropriate fit, you say?"

"Unfortunately," Feeney said breezily. "No. He wasn't."

"Very helpful, Your Excellency. That helps clear up a lot. If I can trouble you for one more clarification?"

"Certainly."

"If Hartnett wasn't an appropriate fit, then why did you recommend him to the monsignor in Claremont in the first place?"

"I beg your pardon?"

"And why did you recommend him to the archbishop in Rochester after?"

Silence again greeted him.

"What do you want, Mr. Merrick?" Feeney said after some time. He was all business now.

"The same thing we all want, Your Excellency."

"Money, I suppose," Feeney said wearily.

"Answers," Peter corrected. "About why you let this happen."

Feeney spoke after a pause. "Ah, Mr. Merrick," he started, his baritone voice oozing condescension. "That's the source of the confusion, I'm afraid. You see, I don't answer to you. Not now. And not ever."

Peter was dumbstruck. He opened his mouth to respond but couldn't.

"That's all for today, Mr. Merrick. And for the foreseeable future. But thank you so much for calling, and may God's peace be with you."

Peter was still holding the phone to his ear long after Feeney had hung up.

The next day he called back. The secretary would not be moved this time. Or the next day. Or the day after that.

He didn't really know why he kept calling. Maybe it was to get under Feeney's skin a little bit. Or maybe he wanted to tell him what a failure he was next to James Ingram and always had been. He threw some clothes in a backpack and headed for his car. He was going to have to go back to DC. If Emma disapproved, this time she didn't say anything. Since the blowup before Milwaukee, he'd been making an effort to clue her in, and she'd been making an effort to keep some distance.

"I know what I'm doing," he assured her.

"I'm not sure you do," she said, not unkindly.

"There's more to the backstory with Hartnett and Ingram. I need to find it."

She stood up on her toes to kiss him. Her hair smelled like lemons. "Just manage your expectations," she said, giving him an extra squeeze. "And try not to get arrested."

She stood in the driveway waving to him until she'd dwindled into a speck in his rearview mirror.

His first two days following Feeney around didn't yield much useful information. Feeney liked to swim in the morning, although Peter didn't want to think about what style of swimwear he wore. He used his chauffeur service to travel four blocks to a CVS. And in a turn that seemed contrary to everything else about him, he was a resolute Dunkin' Donuts man and could not be tempted by Starbucks despite its closer proximity to his office.

On day three, Feeney exited his office building in the middle of the afternoon. It was the first time he wasn't flanked by at least two assistants. Peter decided this might be his only chance to catch him one-on-one. Feeney's sedan traveled down Rhode Island Avenue, cutting down R Street and onto Sixteenth until, eventually, it came to a stop by the Pembroke Hotel on P Street. There, Feeney exited the car, pausing to smooth the folds of his simar, and headed for the entrance. Peter had been hanging back a bit and didn't want to approach the hotel until the sedan pulled far enough away. His only hope was that in jeans and sneakers he moved slightly faster than a sixty-five-year-old in a dress.

He slipped past the reception desk and rounded the corner to the elevators in time to see the doors closing on the carriage with Feeney in it. He stood for a moment watching the floor marker tick up. It stopped on the fourth floor. Peter sprinted up the fire stairs and slowly opened the door on four. The elevator had already closed, but Peter could hear the rustle of clothing as someone, Feeney he assumed, moved down the hall. He waited a few seconds to establish a safe distance before stepping into the hallway and looking around the corner.

There was no sign of Feeney. Just a series of conference rooms with pompous naval names like "The Admiral" and "The Waterloo." He had no idea how he was going to figure out which room Feeney was in short of interrupting the meeting and causing a scene. He paused outside the first room, pushing his ear up to the door in an effort to detect Feeney's absurd speech pattern within. He couldn't discern the voices. After a few minutes he resigned himself to the failed effort and headed for the elevator bank. A loud chime announced the arrival of the elevator. The person exiting bumped into Peter, and when the man spun to apologize, Peter saw it was Milton Casey. For a moment he panicked, unsure what he should say or if Casey even remembered him. Casey answered the question for him.

"Mr. Merritt, is it?"

Peter's heart jumped into his throat.

"Uh, it's Merrick, actually. Peter Merrick," he managed.

Casey shrugged apologetically. "Merrick, of course. I read your article after we talked. Excellent work. What brings you to Washington, DC?"

"Nothing much." He scanned his memory for any plausible explanation. One finally presented itself. "I'm on the selection panel for a journalism scholarship."

"That's great," Casey said with a broad smile. "It's important to mentor young people at the start of their careers. A word of advice, though." He leaned in. "Don't try to steal our Ms. Larkin away. Not until after the election."

The laughter that spilled out of Peter's mouth was 80 percent relief and 20 percent amusement. "Oh no, Mr. Casey. I won't. She's all yours."

Casey patted him on the back. "Good man. Now, do you know which one of these is four thirteen?"

"Third one on the right."

Casey gave him a nod and turned down the hallway. Peter was about to press the elevator button again, but gut instinct told him to hold off. He heard Casey's muffled steps slow, followed by the click of a door handle. He peered around the bend, careful to keep out of sight. Casey slipped into the conference room. As the door swung shut, Peter saw it: the floor-length black fabric of Owen Feeney's simar.

He got back to his car mere moments before a traffic cop would have caught him with a long-expired meter. When he was safely away from being ticketed, he turned down a side street in Dupont Circle and pulled up to the curb at the end of the block. He searched through his phone and dialed the number he had called to arrange the meeting with Milton Casey. He asked to speak with Ally Larkin and was redirected. Ally's line rang three times before she picked up.

"Ms. Larkin?"

"Yes," she said with a trace of suspicion.

"This is Peter Merrick. We met a few weeks ago at your office. The reporter and Ignatius University grad."

Her voice popped up an octave with recognition. "Yes! Hello! What can I do for you?"

"I'm in town for a day and wanted to take you to lunch. Maybe talk about your interest in journalism."

"Right now?" She sounded confused.

"If it's possible."

"Let me see what I can do."

The phone clacked a bit as she moved it away from her mouth. Her voice murmured through whatever she covered the speaker with, but he couldn't make out what she was saying.

"Okay—that'll work," she said when she returned.

"I'll be at your office in a few minutes. Meet me out front."

Soon they were seated at a casual café a few blocks from her office. Peter put in the requisite fifteen minutes of small talk before bringing up what he really wanted to discuss. He'd asked her to lunch, he explained, because he had an awkward question to ask her. She frowned and leaned back into her seat, looking at him as though she were scared he was going to hit on her. It would have been entertaining if she hadn't seemed quite so terrified. He corrected her misconception, explaining that he was trying to find out about the connection between Milton Casey and Owen Feeney. She frowned again. She didn't know what he meant.

"I really don't, Mr. Merrick. I mean, they've met at social functions, of course, but I don't know what kind of connection you're asking about. And even if I did, I'm not sure I could tell you. I'd lose my job."

Peter tried again. He didn't need her to reveal any sensitive information necessarily. He just wanted her to think back and see if she remembered Feeney in the office. She didn't. Did she have any recollection of Casey meeting with Owen around the same time as significant developments in the campaign?

"No," she said. "But again, Mr. Merrick, if I did, I couldn't tell you. It's not just that I'd probably lose my job. I wouldn't want to do that to Mr. Casey. He took a chance on me and offered me work when I couldn't get anyone else in this city to hire me. And he did it entirely because Owen Feeney and my old mentor from Boston asked him to."

"Who was your mentor?"

"Cardinal Mulcahy," she said, unaware the name would make Peter sit up and listen.

"You worked with John Mulcahy?"

She nodded. "The summer before my senior year I worked with his outreach office. So you see, I'd love to help you. But I can't betray the trust these men put in me."

Peter reclined slowly into the plush bench of the restaurant booth. "I can understand that, Ms. Larkin. Believe me, I wish I didn't have to ask you these questions. I stumbled on it entirely by accident."

That seemed to pique her curiosity. She wanted to know what this was all about—he could tell. She leaned forward with an expectant pose.

"I can't tell you anything about Milton Casey," Peter started. "I've only met him in passing, and he seems like a nice enough guy. And I've never met John Mulcahy. But Owen Feeney is someone I do know a lot about. And I think you deserve to know what kind of man you're dealing with." She didn't reply, but she also didn't try to leave. He took it as encouragement to continue.

"Feeney's been around the block, and he's been a leader in the Church for a long time now. He's also a man who deliberately covered up the sexual transgressions of a priest who served under him in Philadelphia and then recommended that same priest to parishes in other cities without uttering a single word about why he was being removed. Quite the opposite, in fact. He wrote glowing letters of introduction about what an asset this priest would be to his new parish."

Ally sat in silence, her mouth slightly open in shock.

"Oh, and he did it, most likely, in exchange for a promotion to archbishop. Now, I don't want to tell you what to think or what to do. As it happens, I know that your boss and Feeney are meeting this very moment at the Pembroke Hotel. But this is who these men are, Ally. I just thought you should have the full picture before you decide whether you have anything you want to share with me." He pulled some money out of his wallet and put it on the table, enough to cover lunch for both of them. "Think it over. I'm going to be in town for another few days. If you remember anything, you have my card."

She was still sitting in the café, eyes wide from the implication of what he'd told her, when he turned the key in the ignition and pulled his car away from the curb.

CHAPTER 16

Three days later, her conversation with Peter was still playing off and on in the back of Ally's mind. It was at its most distracting when she was at the office. She looked at Milton Casey differently now. It was hard not to wonder if what Peter said was correct. That there was some sort of strange connection between Feeney and Casey. She thought back to when Casey made them all watch the news segments about the Vatican memo on suitability for taking Communion. She thought about how the whole office stopped what they were doing to watch Owen Feeney address the cameras and explain why he was endorsing Arthur Wyncott for president. Nothing overtly unusual sprang to mind about the sequence of events, and even at the cocktail party where she last saw Feeney, Casey hadn't spoken to him longer than to say hello. Still, Peter's story had shaken her. If it had been about anything else it wouldn't have packed the same punch. But for some time now, doubt had begun to seep into her about her church. After several years of one incident after another coming to light, she had begun to believe nothing was impossible no matter how far-fetched it might seem.

She struggled to readjust her focus to the tasks at hand. The major push to gather final support for Wyncott's tort-reform bill had succeeded. Their efforts had targeted two senators for support: Walter Bingham, a Republican from California, and Mary Ryan, a Democrat from Pennsylvania. Both were respected across party lines and carried significant influence. Bingham's son was planning a run for governor of West Virginia and needed assurances for the mining companies backing his campaign. An affiliation with Wyncott could help with that. Ryan was rumored to be sniffing around for a presidential run in 2020. With the endorsement of Ryan and Bingham, Wyncott had secured the necessary number of promised votes to ensure the bill's passage. It was now on its way to the congressional hopper, where the physical bill would be retrieved, debated, and eventually voted on possibly as early as Friday morning.

Casey had directed her to resume work on her proposal to create economic development corporations to regulate funds earned by churches engaged in for-profit activities. Wyncott would be making campaign stops in Michigan and Indiana in the upcoming weeks, and Casey wanted to know how the proposal was likely to go over with audiences there. Ally wasn't thrilled by the idea of having to work alongside Steve again. Once or twice he'd tried to make amends, as much as someone like Steve could. It started with a few fumbling invitations to join him and his friends for drinks at exclusive restaurants. "There will be a lot of good people there for you to meet." Each time she declined. Father Gutierrez would probably have told her she was cutting off her nose to spite her face. But she'd already had more than enough of Steve Tilden, and if he thought they were "good people," she was fairly certain she wouldn't. More recently, he'd attempted to curry favor by bringing her a frothy coffee beverage. "I only drink tea," she told him. This morning, he'd told her not to make any plans for Fourth of July.

His parents had rented him a boat for the summer. Everyone in the office was going to come to a party he was throwing on it. They'd get a great spot out on the water and watch the fireworks from there. It was going to be, he concluded with a phrase that didn't make sense to Ally no matter how many times she heard it, "just sick."

"Bring your swimsuit and a toothbrush. We'll head downriver after."

"*We* won't be heading anywhere," she said without looking up from her work. "I've already got plans."

"No, you don't. I don't believe that for one minute."

When she made eye contact she was shocked to see him smiling. Not smirking. Not mocking. But smiling.

"Okay then, Steve. I don't have plans. I just don't want to go."

"Come on, Ally. Don't you think it's time to end the deep freeze? I mean, we're adults and we're colleagues."

"Yes, we're colleagues. Not friends. I have work to do."

He lingered at her desk as if waiting for her to change her mind or speak to him again. She didn't. After several minutes of dedicated ignoring on her part, he shuffled away. She overheard him talking to another colleague later when she walked past the break room. "I wish she'd just yell at me already and get over it," he whined.

That was where Steve Tilden was wrong. Ally had stopped imagining what she would do to him with a branding iron. Now she was just waiting for the right moment to reveal him as the incompetent buffoon he was. For the preparation on Michigan and Indiana, Casey had mercifully divided the contacts list between them. Once they'd gotten a chance to speak with community organizers in each state and hear their takes on the Church tax restructuring, they'd have a chance to present their ideas on framing the discussion to best appeal to voters in those states.

She spent most of the day on the phone with a range of organizations. Even the ones who said they planned to vote for Archer, and thought most of their members would as well, were polite and took the time to listen to her proposal. In general, the various groups said they liked the idea. But Archer's camp had been selling the idea of transparency more effectively than she anticipated. "When he said it," an executive director named Sam told her, "it's like a lightbulb went off. I thought, well, what *are* they doing with the money? I mean, half my time here is spent begging people for money or trying to convince them why we're a good cause for them to support. Then I read about these megachurches where the pastors make six figures. Or a real estate developer buying an old school for millions."

Sam wasn't the only one she heard saying that. A number of her conversations came back to the metaphor Archer had used about how it was time for churches to stop behaving like corporate profiteers. The organizers Ally spoke with liked his idea, they liked what he had to say, but most of all they liked the idea that the money trail would be easier to follow. After rereading her notes from all the conversations, it became clear that presenting her original proposal was going to be a tougher sell for Wyncott than they thought. A few times she looked toward Tilden to get a read on what kind of response he was getting. Nothing in his body language indicated positive or negative feedback. She still had some time before Casey expected her finished analysis, and she knew she'd have to get to work. Based on the timeline they were looking at, Wyncott didn't have to sell a completely new idea. He just needed to offer his variation on Archer's. She called around to the team handling tax issues and got the exactly the answers she wanted. Under her modified proposal, Wyncott would be able to address concerns about churches abusing tax breaks and the question of transparency all at once.

Her fingers flew over the keyboard. Churches and other religious organizations would be required to convert the tax savings resulting from their special status to a set-aside fund. Use of these funds would have to be reported quarterly, including a breakdown of transactions, which would provide greater transparency. The privacy of other funds would be respected, but the amount saved each year through special status would be made public via IRS filings, along with how it was spent. A group could still pay for its leaders to travel to a conference, for example, but if they paid with money from a tax break, they'd face public opinion.

She wasn't sure if Casey was going to go for it, but she was confident that Wyncott could make a stronger impression walking in with this idea than with a proposal that voters in Michigan and Indiana were already saying didn't do enough. It would give Wyncott the opportunity to say he was prepared to challenge churches running themselves like corporations while reaping the benefits of nonprofit status. Casey had been clear from day one that the chances her idea would ever be more than a sound bite were slim to none. "But dress it up with some nice words," he told her. "Make it look pretty." So she did.

She didn't know how long she'd been typing at her desk, but when she finally looked up, most people in the office had left. It was late. This time she didn't feel the same sense of accomplishment she had in the past when she managed to throw something together ahead of schedule. The conversation with Peter Merrick still lingered in her mind and made it difficult for her to look at what she'd written without the nagging feeling she was becoming a little too much like Casey. That by deliberately crafting something meant to pay lip service long enough to secure votes, she was officially a cheat.

The printer's fan whirred and blew hot air in her face as she waited for it to spit out her document. The few people who remained in the office appeared to be winding down. She hadn't seen Casey in over an hour. It wasn't clear whether he intended to return. His door was still slightly ajar, and a small desk lamp burned brightly, splashing fingers of light onto the unremarkable wall-to-wall carpeting. Ally wanted to hand him the summary personally. At only 10:00 p.m. he might still show up. She slumped in her chair, lolling her head back to stare at the ceiling. It was throbbing from too many hours spent staring at the computer screen, and her stomach rumbled in a reminder she hadn't eaten since lunchtime. DC was the kind of place where delis didn't seem to stay open past 6:00 p.m., and tumbleweeds wouldn't have seemed out of place in the neighborhoods dominated by offices and bland federal buildings at this hour. She needed a break from the office—someplace she could keep an eye out for Casey and inhale a tasteless (but caloric) sandwich as quickly as possible. When she got outside, she took off toward E Street, hoping she could find something cheap, fast, and not completely revolting.

Success eluded her. A bookstore café was still open, with a bleak selection of pastries and sandwiches that sat in the case like the last children picked for the kickball team. Even that was too good to be true. She took a seat but never had a chance to order. Although the shop listed its hours as 8:00 a.m.–11:00 p.m., by 10:20 the passive-aggressive barista had begun hovering around her seat, sweeping the floor and shouting more loudly than necessary to her colleague in the book section, "Hey, Danny? Grab that TRASH BAG there would'ja? I'm stuck CLOSING alone again!"

Dejected, she gave up and decided to head back to the office. One of her coworkers, a staffer on the international relations team, was exiting as she came around the bend. She caught the door before it clattered closed and slipped into the room silently. Twenty feet ahead of her, with his back turned, Steve Tilden stood at her desk flipping through what she could only assume was her church tax proposal. Everything in her wanted

to tackle him and pummel him. He was absolutely unbeliev-
able. A shameless, spineless reptile. But she knew better this
time. She knew that the best way to take care of someone like
Steve Tilden was to wait, figure out what he was planning, and
then cut his legs out from under him, just like he'd done to her
in that meeting.

She darted down the hallway to the break room and hung
out there until a few minutes had passed. She opened and
closed the microwave. She pressed the buttons loudly and
often. She ran the water and clanged the coffee mugs around.
And when she walked back to the bullpen afterward, Tilden
was back at his desk looking like the cat that ate the canary.
They were the only two people left in the office. She gave him
a begrudging nod.

"I thought you left for the night," he said.

"Nah—grabbed a sandwich and hung out watching TV
with the donor relations team. Have you *seen* their media
lounge?"

Steve was clearly relieved. "Oh yeah," he said. "That thing
is *sick*!"

She nodded at his notepad. "How'd it go with your calls
today?"

"Fine. Not much to report."

"Really? Nothing?"

"Nope. Just more of the same."

"Yeah," she looked him straight in the eye. "Mine, too. The
same as the others. Guess we can keep to the original plan." For
an instant, Steve's brows pinched together in confusion. Ally
saw it—saw that he wanted to ask her about it, ask her why
she'd changed her proposal. But he couldn't.

She shrugged and sat back down in her chair. The set-aside
summary was still on her desk, exactly where she'd left it. But
the sheaves of paper were uneven and misaligned. She nonchalantly straightened the pile and went back to typing. From

time to time, she felt Steve watching her, trying to read her reaction perhaps. She didn't give him one, just focused on her computer screen, typing randomly on the keyboard between reading recaps of shows she missed by not having a TV.

Tilden was typing furiously, and Ally had a pretty strong notion that whatever he was working on was going to closely resemble what sat on her desk. After a while, he stood up and retrieved something from the printer. Out of the corner of her eye she watched him read over it. He was a mouth reader and a loud one at that. She couldn't make out any of the words, but the ghostly whispering was as annoying as Tilden himself. After a few more rounds of printing and mouth-reading, he stuck the document in a blue folder. With a measured glance her way, he slipped into Casey's office. She couldn't turn to watch him without making it obvious what she was doing. But when at last he exited the office, the folder was no longer in his hands. He lingered around his desk after, watching her intermittently. She could feel it. Midnight came and went with no sign of Casey. Then one o'clock. She desperately wanted to go home and get some sleep, but she had to wait out Tilden. Why hadn't he gone home? As far as she could tell, he wasn't typing anymore. Finally, at one thirty, she heard him sigh and the creak of his chair as he pushed back from his desk.

"That's it," he said. "I can't take it anymore. I've got to get out of this place. You want to share a cab home?"

She blinked at him. "I don't think we live near each other."

His face flushed. "Oh, yeah. You're way out in Takoma."

"Yes, way out," she said drolly. "Thanks, though, for the offer."

It was the first genuine thing she'd said to him in weeks. He smiled. "Don't stay too late."

He grabbed his bag and headed out the door. She remained at her desk for a full twenty minutes after he left, even though the curiosity was killing her, just to make sure he wasn't coming back. There was no way he was going to get away with taking her ideas and passing them off as his own this time.

Bleary-eyed and exhausted, she finally pushed open the door to Casey's office. It was a disaster area. His moratorium on e-mail had left documents, binder-clipped, spiral-bound and loose-leafed, piled up like Jenga towers waiting to tumble over. In the desk-lamp light, she could make out the colored folders but the blue and purple ones were indistinguishable. She picked up the first one. Plans for Wyncott's roundtable with a green-energy coalition. The language had too much scientific content to have been written by Tilden. The next one was on a comprehensive campaign to address the crystal-meth pandemic. Definitely not Tilden. She spotted the corner of a dark folder sticking out from a pile on the far side of the desk. With its awkward angle against the rest of the more orderly pile, it looked like it had been put there in haste. Pulling it from the pile, she noticed it felt somewhat heavy and bulky. Initially, it looked to be related to the tort-reform bill. The first few lines talked about excessive expenses incurred by large awards from civil litigation and the need to cap payouts. She glanced at the second page and was about to put it back in the pile when a word caught her eye: *churches.* For a moment she contemplated the idea that Tilden was smarter than she'd given him credit for.

Peeking her head out of the office, she confirmed she was still alone and took the folder to her desk. The summary laid it all out: Churches and religious entities had fallen victim to the litigious nature of American society. Despite special status, they were being targeted by lawsuits for damages that far exceeded their capacity to pay. In its conclusion, the paragraph made reference to an addendum to Wyncott's tort-reform bill that would limit the amount churches or other religious organizations would be required to pay in the event a court found in favor of the plaintiff in civil litigation against

them. To minimize the negative impact on citizens as a result
of litigation—school or community center closures, for example—this amount, the summary stated, should not exceed
$200,000 per claimant. If the case had been brought on behalf
of a collective of parties, similar to those brought against Big
Tobacco, the award couldn't exceed $200,000 per party, or $50
million, whichever was less. The addendum would be inserted
under Division C, Title II, Section 101, a.6. Ally returned to
Casey's office and dug around on his desk until she found
a copy of the bill. It wasn't difficult to spot. At nearly eight
hundred pages single-spaced, it was competing with a nine-
teenth-century English novel for detail. She flipped through
the pages, stopping on 657, Division C, Title II, Section 101,
a.6. She scanned it and, sure enough, there was a line offering
protection to churches.

She wrote the page number on a Post-it and returned to
the materials in the blue folder. The rest of the first document
outlined the estimated impact of the tort-reform bill. A table
provided sample savings based on projected models for exist-
ing companies. Defense contractor McIntyre Industries would
save an estimated $380 million in damages and legal fees. Fall
River Energy Corporation stood to hold onto $520 million it
would otherwise have paid out. And at the bottom of the table,
the recently added clause projected to save the Catholic Church
nearly $700 million. She unclipped the rest of the materials.
The second document didn't have a title, but a date/time stamp
in the footer indicated it had been printed in February. It was a
timeline. Important polling days and town-hall meetings were
in bold. The due date for Wyncott's tort-reform bill submis-
sion was highlighted in red. So also was a possible date range
for the vote on it. *Election Day* appeared in purple. And there,
between Wyncott's bill and election day was a three-word line:
Vatican Memo Released.

Ally looked at the date stamp. It definitely said February 22nd. But the memo had been released in April. On the page behind the timeline, a strange footer darkened the margin. She flipped to it and recognized Bishops Conference stationery. The page was stamped "DRAFT" and predated the formal Vatican memo. It was addressed to bishops and monsignors. Referring to the Vatican memo, the letter reminded them of the Church's teachings and directed them to take every possible opportunity to advocate voting for the presidential candidate whose position on abortion was in line with the Church's:

Before us we have two candidates vying for President of the United States. One stands with us in preventing sin. The other, despite his claims of devotion to our Faith, supports that which goes against our central tenet of respect for life. Voting for a candidate who endorses rights in opposition to our teachings is a sin. As Shepherds to your Flock, you must protect them from committing the sin of formal cooperation in evil. It is your duty and obligation to encourage them to vote their conscience on Election Day.

Part of her knew what she would see next even before she looked. Scrawled across the bottom right of the page was the signature of His Excellency Bishop Owen Feeney.

Reading the letter seemed to suck all the air out of the room. Ally leaned against the door of Casey's office to collect herself. She moved hazily toward the copier, the packet of papers still in her hand. The clickety-clack of the machine made her eyelids heavy. Finding what Steve Tilden left on Casey's desk was now the furthest thing from her mind. While she was unsure what her next move should be, she was certain she needed to get a second opinion. She tucked her copy of the documents into her backpack and dashed out of the office.

Before the elevator had reached the ground floor, she was on the phone with Peter Merrick.

Per his recommendation, she walked a couple of blocks away from the office to meet him. He pulled up to the curb. They drove back to Takoma Park and settled down in her apartment. She made tea while he sat at the table, reading the documents in silence. When he was done, he put the packet down.

"Crazy, right?" she said after he sat there for several beats without saying a word.

"I'm still trying to process it."

She sat down opposite him and scooted up to the table. "Did you read it the way I did?"

Peter sighed. "You mean, do I think Casey struck a deal with Feeney to campaign for Wyncott in exchange for getting out of paying civil damages? Then yeah, I did."

"Or maybe Feeney struck a deal with Casey."

Peter nodded. She was right. It could've come from either side.

"What I don't get," he said, "is why this is the first I'm hearing about this clause in Wyncott's bill."

She shrugged. "It's almost eight hundred pages long. People are busy focusing on whether it lets large companies and corporations off the hook or not."

"With net assets of close to five hundred billion dollars, hundreds of hospitals, and investment portfolios with the biggest Wall Street banks, I'd say the Catholic Church has *got* to qualify as one of the largest corporations in the world," Peter countered.

"Yeah," she said, "but everyone's talking about the bill in relation to Big Tobacco or companies responsible for pollution and oil spills."

"Maybe," he agreed. "But it still seems strange given all the coverage about abuse cases out there and the way Archer has been scrutinizing nonprofit statutes. This would definitely have gotten negative attention. Unless . . ." He tipped his chair and balanced on its back two legs. His eyes were closed, but Ally could see his eyeballs moving back and forth behind the lids. Suddenly, they popped open and he flopped the chair back down. "Unless it wasn't there before," he finished.

"I'm sorry?"

"When did they send the bill to the hopper?"

"The final version? This morning."

"And you got notice you'd secured enough votes to pass it when?"

"Two days ago. On Monday. They tweaked it one last time to incorporate changes the holdouts wanted before they'd come on board. Then they sent it out again. They all agreed to support it and Wyncott's legislative team put it in."

Peter stood up and began pacing. Daylight streamed into the apartment. Birds chirped loudly outside the windows. He scrolled through the contacts on his phone. At five in the morning it was a stretch, but he was going to try. He dialed his friend Mike Trencher, who had helped him track down Kevin Garrity's information. He was with the *Washington Post* now, covering politics. The phone rang a few times before Mike picked up, clearly a little annoyed.

"What the fuck are you doing, Merrick?" Trencher griped.

"Amateur," he replied. "What are you doing asleep?"

Mike wasn't amused. "I'm serious, Pete. Why'd you wake me up?"

"Who's covering Wyncott's tort-reform bill?"

"Not me. Now let me go back to bed."

"I know it's not you. I need to see a copy of what's been preapproved by the majority. What went out to congressional aides to drum up votes. You guys got a copy of the final version, right?"

"You can wait 'til the vote like everyone else, Pete."

"I don't like waiting. Just do me a favor—I promise you'll thank me for it later."

He heard the creak of the bedsprings as Mike sat up. "Okay. Shoot."

"Take a look at Title II, Section 101, a.6. It's on page 657."

"Why?"

"It gives churches an out for paying high damages to victims of sexual abuse."

"It *says* that?"

"Of course it doesn't say that. It caps the amount that can be awarded in civil litigation. But you and I both know what that means—with statutes of limitation on criminal charges, the only recourse victims of sexual abuse have just got slashed in half. Take a look at it and tell me when you've seen it."

He hung up and turned to find Ally staring at him.

"What's wrong?"

"That's the first time I've heard the words out loud. I mean, I knew that's what this was about, but hearing it . . ." She looked wounded, so surprised.

"Well, look." He tried to soften the blow. "I don't know. Maybe we're wrong. I can't say that for a fact. Not yet. I *do* know that the Catholic Church has spent the better part of the past fifty years covering for criminals and the last ten refusing to take responsibility for it."

"But it just seems so far-fetched, doesn't it?" she said. He thought back to when he was her age and wondered if he'd ever possessed her brand of naïve optimism. He didn't honestly know. "Like I'm turning into a conspiracy theorist with all this stuff. Would they really do this? It's just money, right?" she asked.

He stopped pacing and turned to her. "You know priests used to marry all the time, right?" She nodded.

"I mean, celibacy was always preferred, but they never really blocked priests from marrying before. Do you know when that changed?"

"Not really," she said. "The Middle Ages sometime, maybe?"

He nodded. "That's right. Gregory VII issued an encyclical on it in 1074. Then the Second Lateran Council reinforced it years later. And do you know why?"

"To strengthen the bond between Christ and the priest as a mediator," she said, reciting almost verbatim from her Sundays studying catechism.

"Not the ideological argument, Ally. Not the party line. The *practical* reason."

She shook her head.

"Because," Peter explained, "when married priests died, everything they owned—property, riches—went to their firstborn."

She blinked at him.

"And know what happened when they stopped letting them marry? It went to the Church. All of it—money, jewels, property. Everything left behind when they died. It went to the Church."

He sat down across from her. "They changed the terms of committing your life to God to make money, Ally. Not because Christ ever said to. Not because the apostles did it. But for money. What makes you think they wouldn't do this?"

She couldn't give him an answer. His cell phone rang, a welcome interruption. He picked up.

"What's the word, Mike?" he asked. There was a pause. "Is that so?" Then another.

"Then I guess I gave you one hell of a story. Get someone over there today to see which version got put in the hopper."

He hung up and turned to Ally. "He checked the copy of the bill Senators Bingham and Ryan agreed to sign off on. And guess what? It doesn't have a Section 101, a.6. No mention of churches at all, in fact."

He carried his mug over to her sink to wash it. When he finished, he picked up his car keys. He needed to get over to the *Post* and help Mike. "Don't worry," he said, gesturing to the materials she'd copied and shown him. "I'll do what I can to keep this part quiet." He was almost to the door when she called after him to stop. In her hands was her copy of the timeline and letter from Casey's office. "Here. For your friend at the *Post*."

He looked at her. "You know Casey's going to fire you, right?"

She nodded. "Yeah," she said. "Take it."

After he left she climbed into bed and stared at the ceiling. There was no way she was going to fall asleep. After a few hours, she got up, took a shower, dressed, and set out on her walk to the Metro for what would likely be her last employed day for a long time.

When she got to the office, the phones were already ringing off the hook with members of Congress calling to rescind support. Casey was ricocheting around the room, shouting orders and generally panicking.

"Well, fucking try him again!" he screamed at a staffer who told him Senator Bingham was unavailable for his call.

Finally another staffer got someone on the line. Ally could hear whoever it was screaming from two feet away. "It's a misunderstanding, sir," Casey tried, suddenly submissive and deferential. "We got the versions mixed up and sent the wrong one."

He repeated that phrase to anyone he could get on the phone. Someone called from across the room, "Vice President Eldridge on the phone." Casey didn't say a word. He stalked into his office, picked up the phone, and kicked the door shut.

Mark changed the channel in time to see NBC showing two copies of page 657. Title II, Section 101, a.6 was circled in red in the copy on the right.

"Again," the reporter was saying into the camera, "the source of the discrepancy hasn't yet been identified. Senators Bingham and Ryan maintain that they were told their copies were the final version before they agreed to vote for it and that this clause was *not* in the version they agreed to. At this point, all we know is that the version placed in the hopper for today's vote contained a surprise line no one recognized or, according to Arthur Wyncott's camp, authorized. White House spokesperson Walter Gillen maintains that is the first time Wyncott has seen the clause."

Mark changed the channel to CNN, where Jack Caffrey, the head of an abuse survivors' advocacy group called Justice Now, was speaking with the anchor. Caffrey, a lanky man in his early forties, was red with rage. Article 6, he said, was clearly an attempt by the Wyncott administration to protect churches from taking responsibility for years of criminal neglect. The anchor interrupted him to quote Walter Gillen's "no prior knowledge" statement. "Not good enough," Caffrey barked. "Why didn't he know? Isn't it his job to know what he's legislating? It's one of two things here. He knew and was fine with it, or he didn't and he's asleep at the wheel. Either way, why would I want this guy in office for another four years?" A public opinion poll graphic popped up on the screen with a live-feed arrow charting Wyncott's near-hourly descent in popularity.

"TURN IT OFF!" Casey roared from the door to his office. Everyone stopped and turned toward him in shocked silence. He was holding a list. He called out the first name. A young staffer who worked on health care stood up. Casey called him into the office and closed the door. Ally turned to Mark in confusion. "He's going to find the leak," Mark explained. "He'll bring everyone in one by one. I've been through it a few times now. It's downright terrifying." In between phone calls, Casey continued to call them in.

By lunchtime, Casey was on the letter H. Every time the door opened, Ally watched shell-shocked staffers stagger out, some of them in tears. Casey called in the next person and closed the door. Mark turned only one of the TVs back on, and everyone huddled around it. Wyncott was giving a press conference. Standing there poised and looking into the camera, Wyncott disavowed any knowledge that the clause had been included in the bill or that it could be manipulated in the way victims' advocates claimed. An enormous number of people worked to craft these bills, and numerous versions were always floating around, he explained. He couldn't be expected to be responsible for every word in it, but was grateful that this error had been caught in time to prevent further problems.

He called on a reporter in the third row. "But you are responsible, sir," the reporter started out. "You're the president—responsibility rests with you, doesn't it?"

Staring confidently into the camera, Wyncott said his tort-reform bill was meant to protect American consumers from high prices passed down by companies forced to pay egregious amounts in civil damages. But, he conceded, it was obviously too loosely written, too open to potential abuse and would need to be clarified further before resubmitting it for passage. He thanked them for coming and stated he wouldn't be taking any more questions. The camera zoomed in on Walter Gillen for comment as Wyncott exited the podium.

Mark heard the turn of the door handle on Casey's office and snapped the TV off just in time. The staff scattered to their desks, but not quickly enough. Casey looked around the office. The angry man from a few hours before now stood hunched in defeat. He pushed his glasses up and rubbed his eyes before returning to the staff list. Ally took a deep breath and walked over to him. "Can I speak with you for a moment, sir?" She stepped into his office and closed the door.

She stumbled through her confession, tripping over words and stuttering. When she finally stopped talking, she saw how violently her hands were shaking. Casey just stared at her. She couldn't tell whether he was angry or murderously calm.

"Why?" he said after what felt like an hour of excruciating silence. "I just don't get it. You're smart, Ally. You have a strong instinct for this stuff. Why would you ruin everything?"

"Because," she started to explain, even though she knew it was something a man like Milton Casey would never understand. Tears of exhaustion bubbled to the surface. "I wanted my church back, sir. The way it was supposed to be. And I wanted to stop wondering if this"—she gestured at the campaign posters and framed copy of the preamble of the Constitution on the wall—"all of it, is a sham." If her words had any effect, Casey didn't share it.

She felt like her body was moving in slow motion as she walked back to her desk. Everyone was watching her, but no one would speak. She didn't touch anything in her cubicle. All of it, even the framed Thomas Nast illustration, stayed in place. She just grabbed her backpack and turned to leave. The elevator chimed when she was halfway down the hall. Arthur Wyncott rounded the corner flanked by a Secret Service detail and walked briskly past her, a grim expression on his face. She looked back just in time to see him enter the office. In nearly two years, this was the first time he'd visited their office. Even two weeks ago, this encounter would have thrilled her. Now, she felt nothing.

CHAPTER 17

Peter Merrick read the headlines about Wyncott pressuring his campaign manager to resign with mixed feelings.

In sound bites flooding cable news programs, the radio, and newspaper headlines, Milton Casey claimed sole responsibility for the line in the bill. Thus far, they had managed to spin the entire affair as a mix-up and the sort of thing that was apt to happen from time to time in the legislative process. "Still," Casey announced, "Arthur Wyncott trusted me to make important decisions on his behalf and to act responsibly and in accordance with his values. I failed to do that. And it is therefore that I resign my post." Within hours of Casey announcing his resignation, Wyncott's polling numbers began climbing again. With over two months to go, it was possible he might recover what he lost from the controversy, but most political analysts agreed that without Milton Casey driving things, it would be tough to pull off.

Much to Peter's dismay, coverage of the scandal didn't draw any connection to the United States Conference of Catholic Bishops or the Vatican, just the impact Title II, Section 101, a.6 would have had on the ability of sexual-abuse victims to get compensation for their suffering. "No direct evidence," Mike told him. "I think you're probably right about the quid pro quo, but what do we have? A timeline and a draft of a letter every bishop got. Big deal."

The surprise clause and Wyncott being out of touch was a more reliable story. And it was the one the press ran with. The journalist in Peter knew Mike was right, but it didn't help him feel any better about it. "Why so glum, Pete?" he asked. "We got the bad guy in the end." But they hadn't. He was certain Feeney was behind most of this and, just like he'd managed to get away with moving William Hartnett around like a chess piece, he'd come out unscathed. People like James Ingram would always be left to pick up the pieces. Meanwhile, Feeney would most likely be rewarded, possibly even made cardinal, for dodging yet another bullet.

Archer's campaign didn't miss an opportunity to take advantage of the situation. Peter had to give him credit for being more restrained than he himself would have been—Archer refused to suggest Wyncott had attempted to trick Americans or that he was a puppet president, incapable of thinking or acting for himself. Instead he said Title II, Section 101, a.6 was another sign that America had lost its way and become too corporate under the leadership of Arthur Wyncott and men like him. Under his proposals, America would retain the entrepreneurial spirit that built the nation and made it so great. "But we can no longer sacrifice the values that made us Americans in pursuit of wealth," he said. Part of Peter was relieved to see Archer capitalize on the scandal. Archer had seemed, for most of his campaign, to be a little too good to be true. It helped to see him use someone else's misfortune to promote himself. For better or worse, it made Peter respect him a little more.

Even though he knew Casey had obviously made a deal with someone to take a fall for Wyncott and Feeney, he couldn't help but think of the irony. An oily, amoral campaign manager showed more integrity by admitting his wrongdoing and suffering the consequences than Feeney or any of the other church leaders had since reports of the widespread sexual abuse first emerged. Following his resignation, Milton Casey was offered a lucrative deal with McIntyre Industries to be their chief lobbyist. It was hard to feel bad for him and his untimely exit from the world of presidential campaign strategy.

Some nights, Peter would pull out his copy of the smoking-gun file Ally had given him and read it over and over, searching for anything he could tie Feeney to. Nothing concrete enough ever materialized.

His continued pursuit of Owen Feeney would have to wait for another time. A few weeks after Milton Casey's resignation, Patricia Roedlin called to ask him to write a full-spread article on James Ingram for the university's biannual alumni magazine. Her deadline was surprisingly tight, she said, because the new university president was going to be announced soon, and they wanted to publish one last celebration of Ingram's life before moving someone else into his office.

So he shelved Feeney for the time being. He recognized that, like evil, Owen Feeney and men like him had existed since humanity's creation. And that sooner or later, they all slipped up. He would just have to keep an eye out for the opportunity.

Emma knocked on the door to his office and came in. She leaned against his desk, half sitting on the ledge, half standing.

"You're looking thoughtful," she said. "What about?"

Peter chuckled. "Take your pick."

Emma rolled her eyes good-naturedly. "Not Feeney again. Please, enough with him. Just for a little while."

Peter reached over and pulled her to him, sitting her on his lap so he could bury his face in her side. "No more. I promise."

"What do you think about Ireland?" she said.

"What for?"

"For vacation."

Peter felt himself tense up. He hadn't been on an international flight since his return from Jammu. It was completely
irrational and he knew it, but his physical response was what it
was. Emma noticed immediately.

"What's wrong?"

He thought about their last big fight, about how she told
him she could take almost anything that happened, but not the
way he shut her out. He took a deep breath and decided to
tell her about Jammu. He told her everything. About carrying
the arm through his apartment, dripping blood the whole way,
down the stairs and across the street to the school. People were
shouting all at once, and he couldn't understand more than
a few words, they were speaking so fast. The bodies far out-
numbered the stretchers, and two ambulances weren't nearly
enough. He didn't harbor any misconceptions that Sheeraza
Akhtar, whoever she was, might still be alive. That's not why
he was wandering around like a madman with a limb in his
hand. He wanted to make her whole, if he could. So that when
her family came to claim her, if in fact anyone could before the
searing heat baked the corpses beyond recognition, she'd be
there. All of her would be there. Soot and gore covered much
of the scene. Some bodies were charred and black while others
were nude, their clothing ripped off by the force of the blast.

More than twenty-five feet from the entrance of the
school, he found a torso missing its head, a right leg from the
knee down, and a right arm. The upper portion of the body was
covered in a pheran that matched the fabric remaining on the
arm. Pale blue with swirling designs in dark red. Her top was
tangled up under her arms, revealing her waist and stomach.
Men and women rushed past him to and from the explosion
site. Even as they helped carry the injured out of the school, the
Kashmiri women remained covered head to toe in accordance
with expectations of modesty. He crouched down by the body
before him and put the arm in its rightful place. Then he pulled

what remained of her pheran down, covering her exposed skin, and pushed the full leg together with the other one. When he walked back to the apartment complex, he passed the section where they'd corralled the family members looking for news. There were a disproportionate number of children in the line, crying and wailing. The full impact of the attack hadn't hit him before then. The NGO was working specifically to educate Kashmiri women of all ages. By his quick count, Peter estimated, the bombers had managed to leave twenty-five children motherless.

He went back upstairs to his apartment, sat down in front of his computer, and started typing. When he finally finished and filed his coverage of the explosion, he went to wash his face, looking in the mirror for the first time since that morning. Caked-on blood, vast quantities of it, was spattered across his forehead and shirt. That's when he started vomiting.

Finally, he told Emma about how he'd encouraged a teacher from the school, someone he chatted with every Wednesday at the market, to start the training program. How he'd given her the contact details for the NGO that came to help them set up the classes. And how the bodies all around him that morning, the wailing children and the carnage, were his fault.

It was the first time he'd spoken to anyone about the incident. It just felt disingenuous to need to "talk" about it when he'd watched the whole thing from a distance, never in harm's way, knowing that after he filed his story, he'd pack a suitcase and leave for America. The carcass of the school and the holes in entire families left behind would be there long after he was gone.

Emma was quiet when he was done.

"Thank you," she said after a while. She got up from his lap and leaned against the desk again. "I don't need to know what you're thinking or feeling at all times, Peter. Really, I don't. I just need to know you're still feeling."

He nodded. "I know. I want to try harder. I'm *going* to try harder."

They agreed to work on it. And to get away—go on a real vacation, together for the first time in a while. Emma had her heart set on Ireland, and he couldn't think of any good reason not to go there.

"Just as soon as I finish this article for Patricia."

She leaned over to kiss him. "Then you'd better get working on it."

He shut his laptop and reached over to unplug it. Stuffing it in his bag, he told her not to wait for him at dinner. He'd get something on his own.

"Where are you going?" she asked.

"Somewhere I can get the inspiration I need." He tossed the bag over his shoulder and headed down the hallway, patting Grady on the head as he passed by. He was at the front door when she called out to him. He turned around in time to catch the miniature soccer ball he kept on his desk as she threw it his way.

"For when you hit a block," she said with a grin.

"I love you. You know that, right?" he said.

She nodded and blew him a kiss.

When he reached Ignatius University, he bit the bullet and paid eight dollars to park closer to the theology department. Walking across the main quad, he remembered clearly the first time he'd come to Ingram at his office. The department secretary had sent him to the newer office, nestled in the corner with huge windows and a perfect view of the quad. The office was empty. He poked his head in to look around and noticed it was also immaculate, as though it hadn't ever been used. After waiting for twenty minutes, he had finally given up and left. On his way down the stairs, he ran into Ingram coming up.

"Mr. Merrick!" he boomed. The words echoed all the way up to the ceiling, where corpulent cherubs struck coquettish poses from the chandelier molding. "I wasn't sure you knew where the theology department was!"

Peter blushed. "Actually, I was just looking for you."

"Of *course* you were," Ingram ribbed.

"No, I was!" Peter protested. "I went to your office, but I didn't see you there."

"You wouldn't have," Ingram said, not bothering to offer further explanation. "But if you're not in a hurry, we can talk now." He gestured for Peter to follow him. They went down to the ground floor and then down one floor more to the basement. It smelled of mold and lemon Pledge. "Ahh, the site of God's work, Mr. Merrick," Ingram said. "And God's humility." He pointed to an orange-seeping moisture stain on the wall.

Peter wandered with him down a poorly lit hallway with a few scattered rooms. Inside one, what appeared to be large computer servers buzzed loudly. At the end of the corridor, Ingram keyed into the last office. The interior could not have been more different from the office his secretary had directed Peter to. There on the wall was the brass rubbing of the German knight. Books sat everywhere, on the floor, on the windowsill, and stacked in triplicate on the already overburdened bookshelves. In the corner sat a potpourri bowl from which the aroma of peaches rose. Ingram gestured for him to be seated.

"Now, then, what can I do for you?"

They started with Peter's questions about an assignment, but veered quickly off course to everything from immigration to *Beowulf*. When Peter finally managed to end the conversation, not because he wanted to but because he had his first meeting for the Ignatius University *Gazette*, Ingram had loaded him down with books. "You must read them. They're fantastic, each of them. No rush, but return them when you can."

Nearly fifteen years later, the stairwell to the basement of the theology department still possessed that musky scent of mold and decay. The computer servers had long since been moved and the offices converted to cubicles for graduate students. There was a good chance the basement hovel where Ingram used to sit had also been converted. But it was spring break, and with any luck, not many students would be around. Even if he couldn't get in, taking a stroll around the building for a minute before settling at the library might help increase his concentration.

Down the musty hallway behind the last door on the right sat Ingram's office, door closed. As it turned out, there were no graduate students in at all. At first he thought Ingram's door was locked, but it was just swollen with the basement damp, lodged hard against the frame but not closed all the way. After some impressive effort, Peter managed to move it.

Despite the months that had passed since Ingram's death, the smell in the office was just as Peter remembered it. It was the power of memory, he suspected, but it was a comfort all the same. He was surprised to find the office nearly untouched. He wondered if Patricia and Jane hadn't known Ingram had continued to use it, but didn't see how that was possible. They struck him as the kind of colleagues who relished knowing everything going on with everyone else at all times. Then again, James Ingram had been their complete opposite. He would have cultivated the ability to steal a certain amount of privacy for himself, despite the best efforts of those around him.

Books, though not as many as Peter remembered, filled the shelves, and an electric teakettle sat on a mini fridge, which hummed with unnecessary energy use. He examined the kettle with amusement. It spoke of affluence and sophistication with its stainless steel casing, digital temperature display, and preset brewing options like "Green Tea" and "Chai." It must have been a gift. He could only imagine what Ingram would have said if he'd seen it on the shelf of a store or how he would have struggled not to make a similar comment when it was presented to him. A coffee cup sat on his desk, glued to the surface by a dark ring of sugary liquid that had hardened practically to cement on the bottom. It was, perhaps, Ingram's last drink ever in the office. Peter touched the edge of the cup as if doing so could make him feel closer to his friend. As often as he thought of Ingram, he was already starting to slip away. The anecdotes, the conversations—those remained etched in Peter's memory with impressive clarity. It was the other details that were fading from prominence. The gentle earnestness with which he shook your hand when he hadn't seen you in a while. The gifts and other packages that would arrive at the most random times, because, he would write in the cards that accompanied them, he saw it and thought of you. But most of all, the sound of his voice, deep, rich, and comforting even when it was expressing disagreement or admonishment. It was a voice that conveyed in tone and quality everything about the power of forgiveness represented by the Church he'd devoted his life to.

When Peter arrived at Ignatius University as a freshman, he would have identified himself as Catholic if you asked him. But it wasn't part of him. It was more like a physical fact, like the color of the mailbox in front of his parents' house (red) or how many siblings he had (two). He knew Catholic rituals, history, and teachings, but hadn't personally connected to its beliefs. In truth, he'd gone to Ignatius not as an expression of his faith, but because it gave him the most money. He hadn't expected to leave any more religious than when he entered. While he wasn't a constant attendee to Mass, and even now his Lenten resolutions lasted as long as the ones he pledged for New Year's, he had left Ignatius University a more spiritual man. This transformation was perhaps what he was the most grateful to James Ingram for.

Not long ago, Emma had asked him just why he was so angry at Feeney and about what had happened to Kevin Garrity. "I mean, it's horrible. I get that. The man's life was ruined. But I see that more as sad and tragic than infuriating. I worry when I see you get this angry. What's the source of it, Peter? Did something happen to you?"

If Peter had been the victim of abuse, it would have made explaining his feelings instantly accessible and understandable. But he hadn't. His childhood memories of parish priests were unmarred, his time with Ingram in college among the brightest spots in his life, and in all his years of providing news coverage in some of the most unpleasant corners of the world, he had never ceased to be impressed by the dedication of nuns and priests working on the ground. Including in Jammu, in the aftermath of the bomb. His anger came from the way Feeney and others like him cheapened the work of James Ingram and maintained a sense of entitlement.

It came from the way their lies and prevarications turned everyone who still believed into accessories to the cover-up. Most of all, it came from the double standard held by Church leaders in their prescriptive dogma that applied to everyone but themselves. It offended Peter's core sensibilities as an American who valued equality. Maybe it was true the America characterized by opportunity and level playing fields had been gone since the 1980s. Maybe it had never fully existed in the first place, despite Thomas Jefferson's eloquent words claiming it could. If in recent years America had lost its way, falling prey to gluttony, abdicated responsibility, and special treatment at every turn, then it was precisely this kind of moment when religion could have helped. Instead, Peter realized, it was part of the problem. And maybe it always had been.

He lifted the chair out from behind Ingram's desk, sat down, and pulled out his laptop. In his eagerness to flip it open, he knocked something off the desk and winced when he heard breaking glass. Leaning over to pick it up, he felt a pang in his chest when he realized what it was: the framed photo of the hound urinating on the Anglican bishop.

Gently, he removed the broken glass, shaking the remaining shards into a nearby trash can. He placed the frame on top of his work bag. The bulk of James's personal papers and letters may have gone to Owen Feeney, but this was going home with him. Away from his home office, in a basement where his cell phone didn't get service, his writing got off to a strong start. It helped that from time to time he could look up at the bookshelves to make reference to the titles there and incorporate other characteristics represented by Ingram's tchotchkes. As the article wound down, he found himself struggling with how best to end it, just as he had when he was working on the *Courant* article. More than an hour passed and he hadn't gotten more than a few words out. The truth was that he didn't really want to finish the article. It felt as though by writing these last lines about James Ingram he would be closing the book on him forever. He reached into his bag and pulled out the miniature soccer ball, grateful that Emma knew him well enough to have foreseen this exact scenario looming long before he did. The office resembled a bomb shelter with its books and knickknacks piled high, but Ingram's desk chair was a thing of plush luxury. Peter entertained himself with it, rocking way back, nearly to the floor, and talking to himself while bouncing the miniature soccer ball against the wall.

He overestimated the flexibility of the chair (and his own body) when he tossed the ball too hard. It shot back down toward him at a sharp angle, causing him to duck to avoid its path. He heard it make contact with the concrete floor, but when he looked down, he couldn't see it. He bent down into the leg space of the desk. It wasn't there. He stood up and walked around to the other side of the desk—still no sign of it. Dropping to his knees, he peered under the desk and spotted it in the narrow space between the floor and the bottom drawers. He learned the hard way that his arm was long enough but not thin enough to reach it. After some difficultly dislodging his arm and losing a wrist button, he decided to try another approach. Attempting to shove the desk yielded little success and reminded Peter he was out of shape. Several times he heaved his body at the desk but it was too heavy. He'd barely moved it half an inch after ten minutes of trying. It was time to give it a shot on the other side of the desk.

The floor in the leg space was filthy. He could see clumps of dust spilling out from under the desk. On his knees, he reached under and grabbed blindly for the ball. No luck. He pulled back to see if he could spot it when the top of his head grazed something. It crinkled like paper. Running his hands along the underbelly of the desk, he found it and tugged hard. An envelope came off in his hand. Crawling out from under the desk would have been easier if he'd been a circus contortionist, but he managed to do it. The envelope had seen better days. Coffee rings dotted the exterior and the corners looked ready to give out at any moment. Inside was a packet of papers held together with a bright red binder clip that seemed totally out of character for Ingram.

The top layer was a series of letters, all signed by Owen Feeney. They were in chronological order spanning fifteen years, starting with Feeney's signature as a monsignor serving the archbishops of Chicago and Philadelphia and ending long after he had been made a bishop, just prior to his placement as head of the US Conference and talk of possibly being made a cardinal. In some of the letters, Feeney addressed his superiors. In others, he issued orders to those serving under his leadership. The subject matter of the letters, by this point, was unfortunately not unfamiliar to Peter.

They generally began with a description of the alleged incidents of abuse, a summary of any investigation and interviews conducted to corroborate the report, and concluded with a recommended course of action. Not surprisingly, with the exception of one letter recommending that the accused priest be entered into a residential treatment program, every other letter suggested immediate transfer to a new parish. "At this time," nearly all of them concluded, "we consider it to be in the best interests of our servant to protect his privacy in this matter and will be making transfer arrangements with this in mind." Far more surprising were the objects of the transfer. In a collection of twenty letters, only six referred directly to William Hartnett. The rest referred to different priests serving under Feeney at various points in his career. In total, four pedophiles caught a break with Feeney, who pledged to handle each situation with the utmost discretion and decorum. By comparison, copies of letters sent to the parents of children who made complaints were a fraction of the length and provided far less detail, although in each instance they did commend the parent for raising their children in the Catholic faith.

A second set of correspondence, between Monsignor Feeney and Cardinal Mulcahy, then still the archbishop of Chicago, outlined Feeney's belief that there were reasonable grounds to deny a subpoena requesting church records related to Father William Hartnett's time in Parkchester, Illinois. Feeney recommended a delayed response to the subpoena until other options could be considered.

The last set of documents, however, really packed that Owen Feeney magic. Peter could see his strategic planning all over it and it convinced him, more than ever, that Feeney was the architect of the deal with Milton Casey. The document was beautiful. Professionally bound, it looked like it could have been put together by a top consulting firm. McKinsey, BCG, or Bain. It was a business proposal offering guidance on financial transactions related to abuse victims. For victims who seemed inclined to settle for quick money without involving the authorities, the report recommended the Church should act quickly. It should offer them $40,000–$50,000 in exchange for a signed agreement not to file additional claims, either in criminal or civil court, and a completed nondisclosure agreement. Victims who pressed for more money or had settlements negotiated by attorneys who pressed for more should be compensated up to, but not exceeding, $100,000.

They, too, would sign both agreements about no future claims and nondisclosure. The funds would not be paid in one lump sum, but rather broken out over installments of $25,000 to avoid drawing unwanted attention. The Church should be prepared, he cautioned, for victims who would refuse either type of settlement and instead press for exorbitant amounts or their day in court. Every effort should be made to convince these claimants to settle out of court. In the event that this failed, he concluded, it would be appropriate for the Church to protect its financial interests by any tactic recommended by legal counsel, including the filing of multiple motions and nuisance appeals. Doing so, Feeney asserted, would stem the flow of other victims motivated to come forward by the allure of easy money and save the Church valuable funds.

The piece of paper attached to the back cover of the proposal was dated one month later. It commended Feeney for his service and informed him of his promotion to bishop. Clipped to the back was an old newspaper article. The same one Ingram had borrowed from Peter that day when they discussed the scandal a few years ago. The same incident he had discussed with Monsignor Sexton. Only now, when Peter looked at it, he recognized parts of it immediately. He recognized the town of Parkchester and the quote from the single father near Rochester who'd borrowed William Hartnett's car in his time of need. He recognized the description of Hartnett's crusade for a battered women's shelter. And finally, he understood how Ingram had pieced together what happened.

Peter stacked the papers back together and shoved them in the envelope. Halfway in, they encountered resistance. He pushed a little harder and felt the crunch of paper at the bottom of the envelope. He reached in and pulled it out, attempting to smooth the wrinkles and creases. It was a formal response to a subpoena filed by Ted Mercier demanding that Feeney turn over all e-mails related to sexual-abuse matters for a span of eight months in the previous year. It was printed on Conference stationery. Feeney explained that he was very sorry, but that Mercier was likely to be dissatisfied with the records. He was not a member of this so-called electronic generation, he explained congenially, and therefore used e-mail only sparingly. He reminded the attorney that he had already complied with a request for official hard-copy correspondence on this matter. Nonetheless, he assured him, he had the IT department retrieve all related e-mails from the office servers and they were attached. At the bottom of the page, three names appeared under the CC list.

Something about the letter didn't sound right to Peter, but he couldn't quite put his finger on what. The tone seemed unusually conciliatory, for one. Feeney struck Peter as someone who played hardball, particularly when he was challenged. He was surprised by how cooperative Feeney was being. But it was more than that. He tried to think back to the conversations he'd had with Feeney. There weren't many and they usually took place at cocktail parties where conversation was surface-level only. That's when it hit him—Feeney's comments about being a technophobe. The last face-to-face conversation Peter had with him was at a Saint Patrick's Day celebration hosted by the mayor of New York City in a hotel ballroom. The event was swamped, jam-packed with everyone from the Irish ambassador up from DC to the owner of an Irish bakery in Woodlawn. By the time the FDNY pipes and drums unit rolled in, Peter was on the verge of a claustrophobic breakdown. He darted away from the ballroom dance floor, seeking refuge in the wings. A few feet from him stood a man dressed officiously in a black robe with a velvet-rimmed shoulder cape and black skullcap. Peter couldn't see his face, but he could see the man was holding a BlackBerry. It reminded him of when Ingram finally broke down and got a cell phone. No one had been more surprised than Peter when Ingram called him from it. And no one had been more amused when he got his first text message from Ingram, in all caps and full of mistakes:

DEXTER THE TEXTER HERE!1

PROVING I'"M NOT A DINOSAUR

While he never quite got the hang of texting quickly, Ingram, ever the stickler for grammar, did eventually master the nuances of punctuation. He told Peter about the time he was showing a clip from a documentary on an excavation at Masada to his students. He noticed that one of them, a pleasant enough young woman named Kelly, had spent the better part of the class texting instead of watching the clip. He'd noticed because all but one light was out in the room, and her phone left a ghostly trail of illumination as she repeatedly pulled it out of her pocket. He quickly checked his attendance sheet and located her phone number. It took him a good few minutes to get it right, but he managed to send her a message that said:

KELLY. STOP TEXTING DURING CLASS.

NOW.

FATHER INGRAM.

He'd watched, Ingram told him, as she received the message. What must have been the initial buzz of the phone vibrating in her pocket. Her meager attempt to surreptitiously look around the room to see if anyone was watching. Best of all, the way her eyes popped wide open as she gaped at Ingram after reading the message.

Even now, Peter laughed at the memory of how Ingram told the story. He'd been equally amused when he'd encountered this man, clearly an elevated member of the Church, using his BlackBerry at the mayor's party. When the man turned in profile, Peter saw the mousy little mustache, the odd spectacles resting on his nose, and knew immediately it was Owen Feeney. To his surprise, Feeney also recognized him, even though it had been years since they'd seen each other. Peter suspected Feeney met more new people in one hour at a party than Peter met in a month. They even talked about the BlackBerry. Feeney complained that he'd only just gotten comfortable using the roller ball scroll and now they'd switched to something they called a "touch pad." That was under two years ago. Feeney's claim that he didn't really use e-mail when he'd been conscientious enough to check it at a public cocktail party was ridiculous. The thin pile of e-mails Feeney returned to Mercier couldn't be all there was.

It might turn out to be a wild goose chase, but he decided to try to track down information on the recipients at the bottom of the letter. He had no idea if he'd be able to get in touch with them or even how he'd explain his call. They certainly weren't going to answer polite questions about their boss's e-mail habits from a complete stranger who also happened to be a reporter. But it was possible he had a friend in common with them. DC was the biggest small town Peter had ever encountered, and if you know more than fifteen people who lived there, six degrees of separation could put you in touch with almost anyone.

He started the same way he had started with Kevin Garrity. He entered the first name into a search engine. The first one, Charles Miller, appeared to be an attorney in the Conference's Office of Legal Counsel. He dug around but didn't find anything outstanding about Miller. Next up was Sheila Kenner, communications director at the Conference. Last was Martin Austin. The first few hits that came up clearly identified him as an IT guru. He'd been quoted in a few articles about some software platform Peter knew nothing about. Peter scanned the first page of search results and was midway through the second when he saw Austin's name attached to a web page for someone named Luke Rutkowski. He clicked on the link and was brought to a PDF of Rutkowski's resume. From an IT perspective, Peter thought it was probably fairly impressive. His resume read a little bit like Martin Austin's comments— technically knowledgeable but eminently incomprehensible. His credentials talked a lot about implementing secure servers and designing systems to safeguard sensitive information for clients.

Martin was listed as his supervisor for an internship with the US Bishops Conference. Peter cross-checked the date of the letter with the dates listed on Luke's resume. They overlapped. Of course, that didn't necessarily help Peter. When he was in college, he'd been honored to be selected for a summer internship with *GQ*. He felt slightly less honored after a summer spent largely photocopying and watching other people do the kind of work he wanted to do. But when he got to the end of Luke's resume, he felt a tiny rush of adrenaline. Listed under his professional references was Bishop Owen Feeney. That changed everything. Peter was fairly certain the editor in chief of *GQ* wouldn't have known he spent three months roaming the halls of his building, let alone offered to act as a professional reference. And Feeney didn't offer to do anything unless there was something in it for him.

With a little digging, some articles from Luke's hometown paper, and the help of a few privacy-violating people-search services, Peter was able to determine that Luke Rutkowski was in his second year of an MBA program at the Mendoza College of Business, University of Notre Dame. He graduated from high school in Wooster, Ohio, where he grew up with his mother, who worked as a bank teller, and four siblings. His father, a factory foreman, appeared to live in Nescopeck, Pennsylvania. A credit check on Rutkowski showed no loans taken out currently or in the past. No Stafford or PLUS loans for his undergraduate education at Ohio Dominican University and, more tellingly, no such loans taken out for business school. According to the Mendoza website, the estimated cost of the program was over $50,000 per year, with scholarship aid that generally didn't cover these costs in their entirety. He didn't know what, if anything, Luke had to do with any of this. But if he'd been working in IT for Feeney when Mercier sent the subpoena, then Peter wanted to talk to him.

When he announced to Emma that he was going to South Bend for a few days, her response was not at all surprising. She thought he was insane, but if it was connected to Ingram and it would help him move past all this, then he should get going and she'd see him when he got back. Even as he tried to call it "research" in his mind, he knew that "stalking" was a more appropriate term. He hung around the halls of Mendoza trying to recognize Luke based on some fuzzy photos in a few online issues of the Dominican University newspaper. He gave false credentials as a business journalist when a secretary stopped him to ask what he was doing there. He finally spotted Luke leaving the graduate athletic center. He introduced himself as a reporter and said he was doing an article on how effective internships were. He was wondering if he could ask him a few questions over a cup of coffee. Luke eagerly agreed. At times Peter *did* actually feel bad about lying so readily and often to get people to talk. It was one of the things Ingram said he didn't like about the profession his protégé had chosen. "Ah, but I wouldn't have to lie if people didn't lie to me," Peter had retorted. Ingram had patted him on the shoulder with a smile. "You don't want to get into a debate on moral imperatives with a theology professor, Peter," he told him. And wisely, Peter hadn't.

They sat down and Peter asked a few introductory questions. Where Luke was from, where he'd done internships, how helpful they were. Then he just went for it.

"So—let's talk about Owen Feeney," he said.

Luke looked away. "Oh. I, uh, I didn't really work for him." He tried not to sound nervous, but it didn't work.

"Really? I must be mistaken," Peter said. "I saw him listed as a personal reference on your resume."

Luke tried to backpedal. Explained that he'd met Feeney but didn't really work with him a lot that summer. After watching him founder, Peter laid it out. He knew he worked in Feeney's office. He knew Luke was an accomplished computer programmer. He was also aware that Feeney had responded to a subpoena with a total of sixteen e-mails for an eight-month period. Why was that? Luke shrugged. Peter tried again. Didn't Luke think it was odd that Feeney never used e-mail? Luke didn't know what Peter was talking about. Peter stayed firm. "You don't know or you don't want to say?" he asked. Luke responded first with silence. Then he started to stand up. "I think I should probably go, Mr. Merrick." He turned and walked away.

"Okay," Peter called after him. "Then let's talk about paying for business school."

Luke stopped. When he turned, his eyes were wide again. He walked slowly back to Peter's table and stood there staring at him.

"Business school isn't cheap," Peter went on. "And from what I've seen, you're not taking out any loans." Luke sat back down.

"I can fill out a formal request to review your financial transactions at the school," Peter bluffed. "It's going to be messy. A real pain in the ass for everyone and I might get turned down in the end. But not before it turns you into damaged goods. Or you can tell me how you're paying for business school and why I think that trail is going to lead to your buddy the bishop."

Luke didn't last much longer after that. He told Peter all he knew was that he was an intern and Feeney was his boss and had instructed him to expunge information from the servers.

"Which servers?" Peter pressed.

"The e-mail exchange servers."

"Did he say why?"

Luke shook his head.

"And did you? Expunge the information?"

Yes, he admitted. He had. Most of the e-mails went, except for a few. "Feeney sat next to me and we went through them. He handpicked the ones not to erase."

Peter sat quietly, letting the boy talk. The more he talked, the more information Peter got. Luke couldn't remember what the e-mails were about, but Feeney seemed to know what he was looking for.

"And what did he offer you in return for helping out?" The question kicked Luke's nervousness into a full-blown panic.

"Nothing," he started. "It wasn't like that. I was just doing my job."

Peter repeated himself. "What did he offer you in return, Luke?"

Luke's cheeks flushed. He was tapping his foot now. "He said he'd write me a letter of recommendation for business school, and if I needed help paying for it, he didn't see why his office couldn't offer some assistance."

"Define 'some.'"

"So far?" the boy asked. Peter nodded. "Most of it," Luke finished.

"And you didn't think that was weird? That your boss asked you to delete a bunch of e-mails then offered to cover an enormous expense for you?"

Luke groaned. "I know, I know." He buried his face in his hands. "Am I in trouble?"

Peter ignored the question. He needed Luke to focus. "When did Feeney ask you to do this?"

"I don't know," he whined. "I don't remember. The end of the summer maybe."

"Luke." Peter said the name forcefully. "Think hard about this. I need you to give me a date."

"Mid-August. I always went to visit my dad then. For the Poconos Raceway."

Peter pulled out the papers he found at Ingram's desk. It looked like Feeney got the first letter from Ted Mercier at the beginning of August. Luke blanched when he saw the Conference letterhead.

"Calm down," Peter told him. "The subpoena didn't come in until August 29th, so you should be fine." Luke gasped. "*Will* be fine." Peter tried to clarify, but it was too late. Luke had begun breathing heavily and muttering "Oh God" over and over.

As much to make himself feel better as anything else, Peter walked Luke back to the graduate dorms. He couldn't really blame Luke. There was a time when Peter would have looked at a man like Feeney with awe, and some people, younger and less versed in the nature of human failing, still did.

When Peter got home from Indiana, he reviewed the materials again. It was circumstantial at best. Even if he were to successfully get records from the college showing Feeney paid for Luke's business school, it all looked unusual, certainly, but not criminal. That was, he realized, how Owen and people like him had managed to get away with it for so long. They operated in a land of shadowy in-betweens hovering right at the line every time, but only crossing it ever so gently and never long enough to get caught. He decided to call Ted Mercier anyway. Even if Peter couldn't prove it, maybe Mercier could. Mercier was happy to hear from Peter again and thanked him for passing along any information he thought might be helpful. The worst part about his job, he told Peter, wasn't what happened to the victims he represented. It was knowing that no matter how much money he might get them, or how many apologies, there would never be any way to get them true justice. Peter knew how he felt and, for the first time, understood what life was like for Ingram in those last few years of trying to right so many wrongs.

He typed up a summary of what he'd discovered, along with a timeline. He recommended that Mercier look into the tuition payments to Notre Dame as a means to get some leverage over Feeney. Maybe if he felt caught out, he'd offer up someone else. These guys always did. It was a twisted kind of code they seemed to follow, and when it worked, there was no way to beat it. But when it broke, it cracked completely, falling immediately into disrepair and taking anyone around down with it. He stuck the summary and copies of the letters in the mailbox at the post office in Tarrytown and walked back home. A card from Ally Larkin was waiting for him. She wanted to thank him for giving her a recommendation. She'd been offered a job with a community center in Waterbury, not far from where Peter grew up, and so far she loved it. "It's going to be okay, isn't it?" she asked at the end of her note. Peter hoped it would be. A few days later, he waited at the bottom of the stairs as Emma came down with her suitcase. The taxi would be there any minute. Halfway out the door, he reached into his pocket and took out his phone. He wasn't going to bring it with him. This time was for him and Emma.

CHAPTER 18

Ted Mercier was more than willing to continue the crusade in Peter's absence. He'd been instantly skeptical every time he received something he had requested from Owen Feeney's office. In fact, he felt that way about most paperwork furnished by Church representatives on the rare occasions he received them without an extended battle. The materials always seemed entirely too benign. It was impossible to believe that, with the voluminous number of cases reported and suits filed across the United States, not once had Feeney ever mentioned anything about these cases in correspondence, electronic or otherwise. But yet, like so many of the records he'd requested from the Church—at the local level and even as far as Rome—responses were excessively slow in coming, and when they finally did, the information provided was impossibly clean. He was willing to acknowledge that someone as clever as Feeney knew better than to discuss sensitive information via e-mail, but he also knew that others did not, and there was a good chance Owen had received e-mails referring to cases and correspondence that Mercier could use to establish prior knowledge of inappropriate conduct. And if he could establish that someone at Owen's level knew, he hoped to use it to follow the trail back to Rome. It wasn't enough to lay the blame at the American Church's door. He wanted someone at the Vatican to take responsibility. He hoped to set up a circle of complicity. Lean on the Vatican to give him Owen, then get Owen to retaliate by giving him someone higher up, maybe even at the Vatican.

Mercier did not possess the manpower of a top-shelf law firm, but his instincts about what to look for were good. In the case of Feeney's reply to the subpoena, he'd known what to keep an eye out for. Even the slightest mention of another case or a date could help. He just didn't know *where* to look in the absence of fuller access to the Church's personnel records. He had filed the request for Owen's e-mails with an eye to scanning them for mistakes made by others. It was a crapshoot, really, an effort to cast a wider net with the hopes it might catch something marginally helpful. But with Peter's new information, Mercier now felt confident that he would find something. There were limits to how he could use the letters Peter found at Ingram's office as direct evidence, but at least now he knew specifics to ask about. In his time working on the William Hartnett case, this much was clear: Owen Feeney was not a man who did anything by accident. If he'd taken the time to manipulate an intern into doing his bidding, it was because he knew there was damaging information out there, and he knew he could intimidate Luke.

Of course, Feeney wasn't concerned in the slightest when Mercier contacted him. And given how effective the Church had proved at stalling any number of his previous requests, Feeney had good reason not to be. At the mention of Peter Merrick's name, Feeney smoothly dropped his voice to hushed, concerned tones. James Ingram's death had been hard on everyone, he explained to Mercier. But it had seemed to hit Peter Merrick particularly hard. "He is, Mr. Mercier, very

THE SHEPHERD'S CALCULUS 237

clearly suffering from some sort of trauma from his time overseas. That much is clear, and while I wish to help him and be supportive in any way I can, I'm afraid I can't be held responsible for what his broken mind fabricates."

Mercier listened to the explanation patiently. He was aware of Peter's background and had even read a number of the articles he filed from abroad. But if Peter's enthusiasm for implicating Feeney went beyond what some would consider normal, it still seemed reasonably motivated by rage at the Church's obfuscation. And as far as Mercier could tell, any emotional problems Peter might be grappling with hadn't affected his investigative abilities.

"Be that as it may," he said, interrupting Feeney's character assassination, "I'm afraid my conversation with a Mr. Luke Rutkowski compels me to request access to your IT staff."

The name caught Feeney by surprise, but he recovered. "Mr. Mercier," he began, "I've tried to be as cooperative with you as possible, but I'm sure you understand that these requests are really wearing on the goodwill of this office and its staff."

"Look, Mr. Feeney—"

"That's *Bishop* Feeney, Mr. Mercier. Your Excellency, to be even more accurate. But definitely not Mister."

"Mister or not, I'm still going to file a motion to have independent experts examine your servers unless you're willing to give me permission."

"And why would I do that?" Feeney huffed.

"To spare yourself and your bosses more embarrassment when I have to drag them into this."

Mercier heard the squeak of a chair as Feeney shifted in his seat.

"You're not going to find them any more cooperative, Mr. Mercier. It'll be a waste of your time."

Mercier shrugged. "Maybe not, but I'm sure going to enjoy being the cause of their inconvenience." After he hung up the

phone, he looked at the rest of the materials Peter sent him—
including copies of the files Ally Larkin had given Peter the
morning before the Wyncott campaign scandal broke. Feeney
didn't know he had it, which meant there was a good chance his
bosses didn't know either. Mercier wasn't above leaking photocopies of the correspondence between Feeney and Milton
Casey. It wasn't a strong story, but it would still create more
negative publicity the Church didn't need. So far, the Church
had managed to stonewall him with a united front. It was time
to pit its leaders against one another and see whether preservation of the Church or preservation of self won out. He looked
at his watch and calculated the time difference in Rome. Then
he wandered down the hallway to make some coffee. It was
going to be a long night.

⁊⬲

Several days later Ted Mercier arrived at the offices of the
United States Conference of Catholic Bishops to arrange
deposing members of the IT department. Feeney strenuously
objected to traveling to a neutral site. He assembled his legal
team and a few external attorneys, who greeted Mercier like
soccer players during a penalty kick—a grim wall of antago-
nism and dislike. Feeney explained that he wouldn't be making
any of the IT staff available even for informational discussions
until both sides had met and laid some ground rules.

"Fine with me," Mercier agreed. He wasn't sure he was
going to need them anyway.

Feeney took control of the meeting, quieting the murmur
of conversation with a pious lowering of the hand. He was
accustomed to being obeyed.

"Now, then, Mr. Mercier, perhaps you could describe for us
the scope of what it is you wish to discuss with our staff today."

Ted pushed a piece of paper across the table. "It's all here in the initial request." He pushed a second piece across. "And it's reiterated here, in the second request."

He was flipping through his pile to pull out the third request when one of the attorneys spoke up. "We get the point, Mr. Mercier."

Ted nodded. "We're requesting all formal correspondence related to Owen Feeney's involvement with the clerical career of Father William Hartnett, particularly between the years of 1982 and 2002."

"Mr. Mercier, my assignment to the Conference doesn't cover that entire period."

"I understand that, sir, but your affiliation with William Hartnett, from what we can tell, does. To the extent that you have any documentation related to this that was created or sent during your time with the Conference, we're requesting access to review it. We'd also like to speak with your IT staff about the electronic files and your servers."

Feeney leaned back in his chair. "From what you can tell? And just what do you think you can tell, Mr. Mercier?"

Mercier glanced sideways to the Conference's general counsel, Charles Miller. "It's all in the materials we've submitted to Mr. Miller. According to interviews with staff at various of Hartnett's parishes, you recommended Hartnett and sent letters of introduction on his behalf on at least two occasions of his relocation."

Feeney smiled. "I don't recall seeing any of these letters in the materials you've provided us, Mr. Mercier." He leaned forward to look at the papers in front of Mercier. "Do you mind?"

Mercier pulled the papers out of Feeney's reach. "The letters were not included in those materials."

"I see. And why not?"

"Parish staff were unable to locate them."

Feeney smirked. "Unable to locate them," he repeated. "That's unfortunate, Mr. Mercier. But I'm afraid I don't understand what you hope to gain today. Clearly you have no evidence that these letters actually exist, and I've already provided you with all we have that complies with your request." He rose from the table and smoothed the folds of his simar. "I think we're just about done here." Around him, his Conference colleagues rose in unison as though attending Mass.

Mercier remained seated. Glaring up at Feeney, he nodded his head. "See, that's the funny thing. Documents have a way of disappearing anytime you're around, Mr. Feeney." He deliberately punctuated "Mister." "So the reason I'm here is to make sure that's just a coincidence. Because according to Luke Rutkowski, there used to be a lot more e-mails floating around about making problems—past and present—go away."

As before, Owen Feeney lost composure, if only momentarily, at the mention of Luke Rutkowski. "Mr. Rutkowski was an *intern* in this office, Mr. Mercier," he said with contempt. "I highly doubt he can have any authority on how an organization of this size and prominence runs itself. You can hardly expect his explanation to be thorough enough to pursue this."

"Then why did you pay for his education in exchange for his assistance scrubbing the e-mail servers?"

Feeney scowled. "I did not *pay* for his education in exchange for anything," he hissed. "I did my Christian duty to assist a worthy individual in need through perfectly reasonable means."

He sat back down in his chair, waiting for the moral superiority to silence Mercier.

Mercier turned to the Conference's lawyers. "And he's legally authorized to spend money that way here?"

"I don't *need* their permission." Feeney seethed, leaning across the table to shout in Mercier's face. "I'm the head of this organization. The only permission I need is from Rome, Mr.

Mercier, and I *get* it anytime I *need* it. Anytime I *want* it. And I certainly don't require approval from you or anyone else in this room. What I want and what the Church wants are one and the same. What I do and what the Church does are one and the same. Are we clear on this?"

"Then show me the records."

"I'll show you what I'm told to show you when I'm told to, not when you demand it."

"Then I'll just have to contact your superiors directly."

Feeney blinked at him. "Be my guest. You won't find them any more cooperative. When I speak, Mr. Mercier, it is on behalf of the Church."

Mercier silently shoved a piece of paper across the table to Feeney. His assistant simultaneously passed copies to the other people at the table. It was a copy of the proposal Owen had created for Milton Casey on Conference letterhead. Feeney's eyes flickered with recognition. Before he could speak, Mercier slid another set of papers across the table—copies of Feeney's letters about William Hartnett from Ingram's files. Owen hadn't yet grabbed it when Mercier aggressively shoved his last piece of paper across the table. It was a formal letter from the office of the prefect for the Congregation for the Doctrine of the Faith. It denied any knowledge of Feeney's proposal or involvement with Milton Casey and the Wyncott campaign. It repeated that Feeney had acted entirely on his own in this matter without permission from his superiors. As such, they likewise thanked him for bringing to their attention that Feeney may also have used Church funds for an unsanctioned purpose. The letter closed by approving his request for financial records related to Bishop Owen Feeney's management of the United States Conference of Catholic Bishops and granting him permission to review all requested materials.

"Apparently, not anymore," Mercier said quietly, but firmly.

Feeney looked suddenly pale. "There must be some sort of misunderstanding," he said. "They wouldn't grant permission. They wouldn't want this."

"What they wouldn't want," Mercier said, "is another scandal related to the election. I know. I spoke with them."

Feeney looked around the room at the attorneys. "Can you please excuse us for a moment?" he asked. His voice was calm. If he was nervous, he showed no sign. The others shuffled toward the exit. Feeney looked to Mercier's assistant. Mercier nodded for him to leave as well.

When the room was cleared, Feeney sat back down.

"What do you mean you spoke with them?"

Mercier pushed his chair back. "Come on, Owen," he said sharply. "These guys are selling you down the river. They're pinning the Wyncott mess on you and backing it up by making sure you go down for misuse of funds. They're painting you as the lone gunman. But it doesn't have to be this way. It doesn't have to be you who takes the fall."

Feeney shook his head. "No. You have it wrong."

Mercier pulled his chair closer to Feeney. "I don't. Give me the records. Give me the evidence I need to find them responsible. To nail who told you to sweep it under the rug and who authorized you to protect Hartnett by moving him around. I'll say you were following orders. But I need someone bigger than you, Owen. It has to be someone at the Vatican. Give me who ordered you to cover for Hartnett and any others. Let me help you."

But Feeney wasn't listening. He'd begun wringing his hands. "You're wrong. They wouldn't do this. Not to me."

Mercier reached over and tapped his finger on the prefect's letter.

"They already did, Owen."

He moved back to his papers and gathered them up. "Just think about it. I can help you."

Feeney stared with his mouth open, unable to speak. After a few moments of silence, Mercier walked out of the room. Feeney remained at the table, completely and utterly alone.

Thousands of miles away in his room at a cozy bed-and-breakfast in Kinsale, Ireland, Peter Merrick would see it on the news. He would hear about how the head of the United States Conference of Catholic Bishops, Owen Feeney, had been implicated in Wyncott's tort-reform scandal and was now being investigated by authorities for misuse of funds. In the papers he would read that according to investigators, records showed Feeney had made a number of personal transactions using Conference funds for a range of unauthorized activities, including payment for a former intern's education. A portion of these funds came from a federal grant from the Department of Agriculture, elevating the crime. The more salacious news outlets had hinted at an improper relationship between the bishop and the intern. Such irresponsible journalism disgusted Peter. Feeney had resigned immediately, and the Conference had issued a statement saying it would no longer tolerate abuse of Church authority and cover-ups of any kind.

It was, they said, a new dawn for Catholicism in America. Just a few weeks later, in November of that year, Thomas Archer echoed those same sentiments in a speech following his election as the next president of the United States—only the second Catholic president in its history.

CHAPTER 19

Weeks later, Owen Feeney stood before a judge, preparing to sign a waiver of indictment and plead guilty to misappropriating part of a $500,000 grant awarded to the Conference, in exchange for a reduced sentence: three years at a minimum-security prison with eligibility for parole after fourteen months. It was a small comfort to Kevin Garrity and others like him—so little to pay for his role in so much destruction. But for someone like Feeney, it wasn't bars or a cell that would break him. It would be the loss of control and the inability to command respect by the nature of his title, instead of what kind of man he was. Peter sat in the back of the courtroom on the prosecution's side, watching as Feeney croaked "Guilty" and nodded at the sentence pronounced by the judge. It was not lost on him that Owen's side of the courtroom was bare. No priests, no nuns, no devoted protégés sat hanging on his every word. The gravitas he had always projected was gone. So also was the stately purple-edged simar Peter associated with him. Without it, he seemed small and inconsequential. Not at all the criminal mastermind Peter had built him up in his mind to be, but a diminutive, frail, and achingly human figure. He shuffled out of the courtroom as he entered it—alone but for the court officers acting as his escorts. The church he had sacrificed so much for hadn't returned the favor when his time of need came.

There would be no return to exclusive parties and chauffeur service when he finished his time at Hattonvale Federal Correctional Institution in Pennsylvania. After agreeing to plead out, he was offered the choice of resigning his post or being removed. He chose to resign quietly and began serving his sentence the same way. The world that would greet him at the end of his sentence was bound to be harsh and unforgiving. The long stretches of silence between his job assignments in tutoring and landscaping would leave little to do but reflect on his choices and search for anything that might quiet the ugly truth buzzing in his head. That the only person who would have stood by him throughout this—in the back of the courtroom, during Hattonvale's visitor hours—was no longer there in part because of his failings.

Owen would ponder this irony every day in his cell, as he thought about James Ingram, a man he admired, loved even, but could never emulate. In the same way Jimmy had unwittingly tortured him by being born with an intellect that would always best him, Owen had come to accept that there were men in this world who were simply better. More true, more righteous, and just more *good* than everyone else. And that God had created them that way. He was less sure how it all would've turned out if he'd only faced Jimmy that last time, on the freezing cold night that he died. But of Jimmy's God-given superiority, at least, he was certain. Just as he knew Jimmy would still be alive if he'd had the courage to face him.

The many long hours in his office at the Conference had presented him with distractions from this truth following Jimmy's death. So also had the media appearances, the meetings, and the ever-present adrenaline that coursed through his body when faced with another challenge to the Church's authority. Now, from the confines of his squat habitat, where, two months on, the bland gray jumpsuit still chafed his delicate skin, he spent nearly every waking moment reliving those lost twenty-five minutes on the night of Jimmy's accident.

It seemed strange and anticlimactic that Jimmy had died, not surrounded by friends and loved ones as Feeney always imagined he would, but alone, in a random battle against chance and nature. Someone as "chosen" as he'd always viewed Jimmy to be should certainly have passed away in the middle of a papal audience or while addressing a crowd of admirers. But perhaps that was the purest expression of earthly relationship with God. That when our time came, we could only ever be what we made of ourselves here, not what the opinions and reverence of others created.

On the night he died, James Ingram brought a gust of wind into the diner on Kraft Avenue in Bronxville. He hadn't planned on going to a movie by himself. He had driven down earlier that afternoon from Connecticut to meet Owen for dinner, but got a call from Owen's overbearing assistant to say his meetings with the archbishop of New York were running late, and he would be unable to join him until closer to eight or nine. The local theater was showing the original *Sabrina* with Audrey Hepburn as part of its romantic lead-up to Valentine's Day. He'd always liked Audrey—in part for her smile and in part for her roles as a nun—and he also had a weakness for movie popcorn.

When the film let out, James looked at his cell phone. It had never failed to amuse the Ignatius students when they saw him wandering across campus chatting away. They were even more amused when they heard his ringtone—a movement from *Carmina Burana*—and the sense of impending doom it created. There was a missed call from Owen and a message. Owen, slightly out of breath, explaining that he wasn't blowing him off, that he'd thought about what he said and that they could discuss it tonight. He'd make it to Bronxville by about 9:00 p.m. at the latest.

So Ingram wandered from the movie theater, down the block, across the alley where he'd parked his car, and to the diner at the next corner. He'd asked the shop owner by the alley if he'd be towed. She promised him he wouldn't. He entered the diner and shut the door as soon as he could, noticing the thin fabric of the waitresses' uniforms and the way most of them wore sweaters to protect their exposed forearms.

Since waking that morning, he'd been battling a stomachache—a dull churning that had even managed to temper his enjoyment of popcorn. The delay in meeting Owen didn't help. He expected it would be a less than friendly encounter. In truth, the intensity of Owen's anger when they discussed it the week before had shocked him. He hadn't meant to issue that ultimatum. Even as he pushed the folder across the table ("Do the right thing, Owen. Do it or I will.") it felt so forced and unfamiliar to him. But he was unprepared for how blasé Owen was about it all. The way he shook his head and told him he simply didn't understand how these things worked because he'd spent too much time serving academia, not his church. That's when James realized he'd have to set a deadline.

He knew Owen had a temper—on more than one occasion he'd seen it when they were in high school, and he'd definitely recognized the rage simmering below the cool surface when Owen appeared on television shows and at press conferences to address anything from Roe v. Wade to the latest lawsuit filed against a diocese. But what surprised him about this recent flare-up was that it hadn't come in response to a headache caused by someone else. No, the rage had erupted as James matter-of-factly presented the information he'd assembled. Based on the evidence he'd managed to amass, not without some difficulty, the range of Owen's involvement in numerous cover-ups was clear. It was equally clear that Owen needed to formally turn it over to the attorneys representing the plaintiffs. Not just because he was legally obligated to do so according to the rules of exculpatory evidence. But because, as Ingram bluntly put it, after allowing the lives of so many to be irrevocably damaged by not putting a stop to it sooner, it was simply the right thing to do.

"The right thing to do, is it?" Owen had said, not even opening the brown envelope James gave him. "And what about the rights of all the people who will lose a place to worship when we have to close a parish to pay for this? What about the spiritual abandonment when we have to file for bankruptcy?"

Ingram smiled good-naturedly. "Practicing our faith began in clay chambers thirty feet below the ground, Owen. You must remember that feeling—the first time you went to the catacombs in Rome. It amazed you, didn't it? That what we've devoted our lives to began there by candlelight. And despite that, it didn't just take hold—it spread all over the world. People don't need a physical church to practice their faith—they need their belief in the convictions of that faith to be honored. To be upheld."

Owen shifted in his seat, rolled forward with his elbows on the table. "Come on, Jimmy. You know it's not that simple. It's never been that simple."

Ingram nodded. "It hasn't been in a long time. You're right. But to say it was *never* that simple is more than a lie, Owen. It's a denial of the very things that made our faith what it became." He looked at the envelope, at the way Owen had managed to avoid acknowledging it. "It's not going away just because you pretend it's not there. None of this is."

They were testing the limits of their friendship, he knew. And deep down, a part of him knew that Owen was unlikely to do the right thing on his own. But he hadn't wanted to just assume that. He had needed to give Owen a chance to prove otherwise.

That's why he'd come today. When they had parted that last time, after Owen calmed down and stopped shouting, James made him take the brown envelope containing evidence he had collected along his journey to right all those wrongs. Notes from conversations with parishioners where Hartnett and others like him had poisoned the community. Photocopies of letters secretaries and rectory matrons gave him despite explicit instructions not to share them.

"You're not just anyone, Father Ingram," one of them, Dorothy Bailey, had said when he visited Claremont looking for answers. He remembered Dorothy from his days as the retreat coordinator. She was older now, with the hunched posture of burgeoning osteoporosis, but that wasn't what struck him. It was her changed attitude. Years before, she moved through the parish offices with an expression of awe. Everything Ingram said was the most important thing she'd ever heard. She followed him around like a lost puppy dog, trying to anticipate his every need and mothering him in a way that made him at once grateful for the Church's restriction on marrying, but also deeply touched. In those days, Dorothy didn't speak unless spoken to, and whatever was requested of her was performed in the same fashion—with no questions and absolute supplication.

He prepared to give her his pitch. By the time he got to Claremont in his travels, he'd already met with resistance in other offices. Places where the secretaries were reluctant to help and always wanted to "check with the monsignor first." He'd had to learn how to read the situation very quickly and size up how sympathetic the women were to the object of his quest. With the older, more severe ones, manipulating their antiquated notions of male superiority in the Catholic tradition worked well. On being told no, Ingram gave a stern look and asked them to repeat what they had just said. Invariably, the second time around, the refusal was significantly less firm.

With others, he lied. It wasn't something he was proud of, but he sensed he would be forgiven for the transgression. He was just looking for sample response letters since they were dealing with a similar situation up at Ignatius, he told them, dropping his voice to a conspiratorial whisper to indicate just how special they were for being made privy to this information. He was driving back from a conference, you see, and thought he may as well stop by in person and pick their brains, since they were so clearly more advanced than his staff and worked in an office far better run than his own.

He began this way with Dorothy. A charming stammer, embarrassment at having to impose. She interrupted him halfway. "It's about damned time someone started looking at this stuff," she bellowed before clapping both hands over her mouth. "Pardon the language, Father." He barely contained a laugh.

"Can you believe this mess?" she went on. "I mean, growing up we always made jokes about it but now—I didn't think it was true, you know? I wouldn'ta joked about it so much if I thought it was. I promise you."

"It's okay, Dorothy," he said. "I don't imagine you would have." She led him down a musty hallway, far from the main rectory office, to a storage closet.

"But it's all over the place. Everywhere I turn," she called over her shoulder, the hallway too narrow to accommodate both her girth and his broad shoulders at the same time. "I think that's what makes me so mad about it. How they used me—used everyone in this office. It's like they were laughing at us. Here we were, showing up every day, doing what they told us to do. And they were laughing at us, Father."

She pulled open the drawer of a filing cabinet with some effort and blew off a layer of dust. "I don't mind telling you—five years ago? If you'd come here telling me you needed to look up these records, I wouldn'ta let you near them. I'd have been nice, of course. I always did like you, Father Ingram." Her fingers flipped through folder after folder with expert speed and ease. "But I wouldn'ta let you back here to see these letters. You couldn't've convinced me there was anything wrong with them letters. With doing a good turn for the new guy at his new job. Making him feel welcome, you know?" She pulled out one file and tucked it under her arm. The other folders sped by, her eyes darting at the first page of their contents before returning them or pulling them out. "But now? Just thinking about it makes me sick. Thinking about how many times he did that in how many other places, and we got such nice letters from the people who sent him here, even though they knew. They *knew*, Father. A*ha*!" she whooped. "Here we go!"

The exclamation surprised him. She half pulled a folder out of the cabinet and tilted her head sideways to look at the first page of the contents. Then the second page. Then she spot-checked a page in the back. "You're going to want to see pretty much everything in here." She took off down the hallway with all the folders and headed straight for the copier in the main office.

"Used to be I didn't believe a priest could do this. But I know better now, Father. And no offense to you or nothing, but these days you'd have a harder time convincing me a priest was innocent than you'd have telling me he was guilty."

It was a remarkable shift and one Ingram had felt stirring for quite some time, this loss of the immediate respect that was once as much part of the role as the Roman collar. His decision to enter the priesthood had never been connected to the automatic deference it earned from total strangers. In his youth he held the opinion, and still did, that respect was not something you acquired by wearing vestments. It was something you had to earn in order to be worthy of the clothing. In his days as an altar boy, it wasn't the grand ceremony of Mass that attracted him the way it had Owen. It was the confidence the priest at Saint John's exuded. The confidence in his belief and his role as a servant to his parishioners.

His personal connection to Claremont, the way he felt in many ways responsible for having inflicted this upon them, made Dorothy's comments that much more welcome. But they couldn't assuage his guilt. Not even forcing Owen to acknowledge his role in it could do that. Justice was a prismatic experience, unique to each person seeking it and only fully reached when they could forgive. He was prepared to spend the rest of his life finding justice for the Erik Baders, Kevin Garritys, and Anthony Terzullis of the world. But first, he had to forgive Owen.

To passersby at the restaurant where they quarreled the night he issued the ultimatum, it would have seemed like he and Owen were locked in a profound theological debate. Owen reiterated, with very little variation each time, the idea that one's vocation applied as much to answering his church's call as it did the grandiose notion of learning your place in this world directly from God Himself. With eyebrows peaked in incredulous arches, Owen leaned forward on the table so he was mere inches from James's face. "Of course I don't like it, Jimmy. I'm disgusted by the entire thing. But I'm not, in fact, the one who did this to these children, and I did what I had to do in order to remove them."

"What you *had to do*, under the laws governing the nation where you live, Owen, is report these men to the authorities. Make them face the same justice system that governs everyone. Barring that, you had an obligation to warn anyone who might come into contact with them."

"I did what was asked of me, and I did what was best for the Church. That's all anyone can demand, Jimmy. Even you.

You're losing sight of the true culprits in all of this. The sin rests squarely at their door."

"Am I?" Ingram replied. "And what of the sin of omission?"

Owen rolled his eyes. The exaggerated gesture hit its mark, landing like a kick in the gut to James. "For Chris'sakes, Jimmy. This isn't catechism. I'm not a twelve-year-old, and I don't need to be reminded of the Church's teaching. I live it, breathe it, and spout it every day."

"Tell me, Owen," Ingram said, standing up and digging in his pocket to throw money on the table. "Was it worth it?"

"Was what worth it?"

"Becoming a bishop? Was it worth all those kids? Those ruined lives?"

Feeney glared at him.

"But you're right," Ingram continued. "Maybe this isn't a sin of omission." He reached out and rubbed the edge of Owen's simar between his thumb and forefinger. "Maybe it's a sin of commission."

Feeney threw his hands up in mock defeat. "Fine, Jimmy. You found me out. I like being a bishop and would like, one day, to become a cardinal. I'm a fundamentally flawed person."

"Flawed is not what I would call it," he'd said at the time. "Flawed implies that some part of it is beyond your control, Owen. We're talking about negligence here—the willful and deliberate refusal to act even though you knew you should." He'd pushed a battered brown envelope across the table at Feeney. "You have a chance to do the right thing now," he said. "Don't make me wonder if you got lost in your zeal to become cardinal, or if you were this way from the start." He put on his jacket and looked at the date on his watch. "I'm giving you until next Friday to come clean. To make it right. And if you don't, I'm going to turn over the evidence myself."

So after all that, the many hours spent in a car traveling to the homes of victims, the afternoons holed up in dingy rectories in small towns from Connecticut to Wisconsin, James Ingram sat at a diner table in Bronxville on the coldest night of the year, waiting—hoping—that his friend would come. After ten minutes and the third inquiry from the waitress, Ingram ordered a cup of coffee. He nursed it for as long as he could, taking tiny sips until he grew close to letting it go cold altogether, morphing into a bitter, tepid soup. At every jounce of the sleigh bells still attached to the front door from Christmas beside a cardboard Jolly Saint Nick, Ingram looked to the entrance, filled with momentary hope. But Owen did not arrive. An hour passed. Then another forty minutes.

After nearly two hours in the mostly deserted diner, James swallowed the reality so prominently before him. Owen was never going to come. The friend he thought he knew—the one he had defended all these years—was no longer, if ever he was at all. He thought of all the times Owen had mocked him for being naïve. Having too much optimism to see the inherent selfishness of human nature. "It exists, Jimmy," he said. "In droves. Why do you think we're here? Everyone needs a moral structure, a pillar to lean on for support. Otherwise, we degenerate into animals." Maybe Owen was right. Maybe human beings were no better than wild beasts, as desperate, vicious, and self-serving as any animal backed into a corner. Or maybe James had made Owen what he wanted him to be in his mind, not what he actually was. But as long as such a thing as free will existed, he couldn't buy Owen's argument. He had to believe that no matter how far down a road you got, you retained the ability to choose to continue in that direction or turn around.

He stood up and lumbered to the door, the weight of disappointment visible in his shoulders. He paused once more to look around the diner and felt in his pockets for everything he

needed. The keys to his car in the alley. The keys to his apartment in the Jesuit residence hall at Ignatius. And the phone
where his last communication from Owen would live until
the university had his service formally discontinued. When
he finally finished with his fastidious checking, he peered out
the window once more, as though the additional two minutes
would provide the magic moment for Owen to show up at last.
But he did not appear.

Stuffing the ends of his scarf deep into his down-filled coat
and zipping it all the way to the top, he tucked his chin under
the flap and took a deep breath to prepare for the wintry blast.
His steps fell lightly, slowly as he walked down the stairs to the
street. His gait continued haltingly as he walked the length of
the sidewalk and turned down the alley to his car, hoping as
he dragged his feet that he'd run into Owen along the way. He
didn't. After one last glance around, squinting into the beam of
the alley's security spotlight, he turned and disappeared into
the desolation of the alley, the shadow cast by his body growing long and lanky until it seemed as large as the influence he'd
wielded over everyone who met him.

Owen noticed this about the shadow from where he was sitting
across the street from the diner in the warmth of his rental car
and the shadow of an office building. There was no chauffeur
this time, no taxicab from the Metro-North. This time he had
driven himself, feeling certain he would need the privacy before
the night was through. He'd been sitting in the car for the last
two hours, trying to will himself to go in. Beside him on the
passenger seat lay the envelope James had given him and told
him to provide to the victims' lawyers. He couldn't bring himself to do it, but he couldn't bring himself to face James either.
Despite the heat turned up high, the windows had fogged from
the cold. Wiping away the moisture, Owen had observed James

through the diner window. Witnessed the way he checked his watch multiple times, the jolt of his body every time someone entered the shop, and his concerned expression when he peered into the darkness from the warmth of his red vinyl seat. Owen kept telling himself to go in. To turn off the engine and just walk the easy twenty feet to the diner, where James would forgive him like he always did. Because he'd explain it and James would understand. Because he was Jimmy Ingram, who didn't have to agree with you to believe you were worthy of his friendship and devotion.

James's shadow stretched taller and thinner with every step until at last he disappeared from view and took his shaded twin with him. Owen's pulse quickened. He felt he was watching his window of opportunity close. That his assumption he could skip tonight's meeting and things would go back to the way they were was deeply miscalculated. Even if he couldn't tell James what he wanted to hear (*Yes, I turned the evidence over to the attorney*), he needed to go to him, if only to buy more time.

James continued to walk to his car, his mind cluttered with emotion. His thoughts swirled with a vision of him and Owen at age fifteen, wandering along the railroad tracks by the Harlem River at 225th Street. A memory of the two of them clambering to the top of a huge rock outcropping there, painted with a pale blue *C* by the Columbia University crew team, and jumping feetfirst into the rushing depths below. Of one afternoon when he felt himself get caught in a current, swimming as hard as he could against it, but not hard enough. The big blue *C* swiftly grew distant as the tide carried him toward the whirlpools by Spuyten Duyvil Bridge, until he felt Owen tug on his arm and yank him with surprising strength from the current's grip.

How, he wondered thinking back on that moment, had he been unable to fix all this despite his best efforts? He climbed into the driver's seat and reached for his seatbelt. His coat, always so bulky, would not be contained by it. He shifted one way then another but could not fasten the buckle and still reach the steering wheel. Popping the trunk, he stepped out of the car. With the trunk propped high, he stripped off his coat and tossed it in the trunk before turning to race back to the driver's side, to escape the biting cold that had seeped into his bones in mere seconds. The trunk hood didn't take. It bobbed up, cushioned by an errant sleeve of the coat. He lifted it fully open again, stuffed the sleeve in, and this time gave the hood a great heave as he slammed it down. The right heel of his shoe lost its grip on a patch of black ice with the effort, swinging up and wildly off-balance. His legs clattered against the bumper, and his body fell with a thud, the base of his skull battered by the impact with ice and macadam.

Across the street, Owen remained in his car, working up the nerve to follow James down the alley. To have it out right then and there, if that's what it was going to take. His right hand remained on the ignition. He told himself he wanted to turn it off, exit the car, and jog to James before he got too cold, but his hand wouldn't turn. Whatever Owen was telling himself or needed to believe, like in so many moments in his life, his thoughts and words failed to translate into action.

At last he landed on an answer. Maybe he wasn't meant to solve the world's problems with his old friend tonight, but there was always tomorrow and the day after that. There were two ways for James to exit the alley and begin the drive home. If he came out on Owen's side, he couldn't help but pass him. It would be a sign that the chance was not gone—that he could still flag James down and talk to him. That their reconciliation was meant to be. A minute passed. Then another. He craned his neck to see if he could make out headlights beaming from the alley, but the glow from street lamps and floodlights perched on the sides of buildings blended into one through the haloed sheen of his windshield. Another minute passed. He waited. Then waited some more. After close to ten minutes, there was still no sign of James.

In a crumpled heap not far from the back left tire of his car, James Ingram began to stir from his spot on the ground. He didn't know how much time had passed. He knew only that he was awakened by the pain in his head and the dull throbbing of limbs that were too cold. He tried to sit up, but his body wouldn't listen. The head wound was too great and his disorientation too severe. When he rolled over to his stomach and managed to get to his knees, he noticed the blotch of blood, spread wide in a haphazard stain across the snow and ice. The car was still there and he could see it—even reach out and touch it if his body had been willing to obey his commands—but it was no use. His synapses could not make the necessary connections. He saw the car, but did not perceive it to be a car. He heard the keys jangling in his pocket but did not identify them as such. With a deep breath that ignored the sharp pain in his head, he rocked himself back then pitched himself forward, struggling to stand. He got only one knee off the ground before he lost balance and came crashing down again.

Owen waited nearly twenty-five minutes. In roughly the same amount of time he could have been at James's apartment at Ignatius. He could have noticed that the car wasn't there and that James wasn't picking up his cell phone. But he neither called him nor went to his home. He sat in his car, not willing to face the rejection he felt certain awaited him. Finally, he concluded that James was in all likelihood long gone from the alley and had taken the other route home. That the moment of reconciliation he had built into a groundswell of renewed support and sealed fissures was never going to happen. And maybe, after all he and James had faced together, the vastly diverging paths of their careers—in which one expressed his love for God and other his love for the Church—it was better that way. The hand on the ignition had gone numb from its frozen position. He shook his arm, waiting to feel sensation, its return announced by the sharp pain of pins and needles. The knuckles wrapped awkwardly around the gearshift. He pushed it out of "Park," released the emergency brake, and drove slowly away.

At the far end of the alley, James Ingram lay on his back again, gazing at the sky. Everything was getting dark, but his arms and legs had finally stopped hurting. The bone-chilling cold, the ache that had seeped into his entire body, no longer plagued him. He didn't feel anything. Just the dizzying spin of fatigue and the weight of his lids opening and closing slowly over his eyes as though brass coins had been placed on them. He stared into the sparkling sky and thought about this world, what it was made of and what we in turn make of it. The life that awaited him—beyond the stars that were growing dim, darkness encroaching from the sides of his eyes and narrowing to a focal point—was one he had built his entire life around. One he used to comfort so many others for so long. But it occurred to him, as he lay there in the freezing night, that no matter what warmth, what bliss awaited him, he would end life as he began it. In a haze of confusion and the inability to know or understand what would happen next. The sky grew darker and darker. The world moving around him became muffled, like the stark quiet of being buried in snow. The last light of the stars disappeared. All became black. And all, including James, was now still.

ACKNOWLEDGMENTS

When I started this project, I thought finishing the manuscript would be the hardest part. It turns out that figuring out what, if anything, to do next was equally tough. I'm learning something new every day. I'm grateful to many people who have played important roles in making *The Shepherd's Calculus* a reality. To Trina Vargo for a life-changing year in Ireland that encouraged me to write. To Elisa Balestra for her friendship, integrity, and creative way of connecting dots. To Mary Lou Hartman and Cliff Sloan for their example of making a difference in the world and for their feedback and encouragement. To George Heslin and Origin Theatre Company for keeping me connected to creativity in critical ways. To Louise Runge, Heidi Sulzman, and Samantha Housman for reminding us all of the many complex and compelling stories out there to be told. To numerous friends and family who have read drafts and provided feedback: Ginny Buckingham, Malachy McCourt, Laura Gallo, Neil Grunberg, Patricia Hartwell, Kurt Gottfried, Jana Lang, Kathleen Romig Krepps, Greg Palmer, Tom Fox, and Charles Arrowsmith, to name a few. To Emilie Sandoz-Voyer, Laura Whittemore,

Meghan Harvey, and Girl Friday Productions for being everything I could have hoped for and more. To the staff at Fordham University's Edmund J. Walsh Library, where I spent many hours doing research. To Sara Shepard for making that long summer on Wall Street bearable, for making the world brighter with her novels, and for her moral support while I got this project off the ground: Pennsylvania and Penny Super Ponies Forever. To Mark Massa, S.J., Jim Fisher, and Jeanne Flavin for embodying the best of Jesuit education, shaping my worldview, and connecting me to my faith in critical ways. To my father, Gene, for his example of "doing right" instead of "being right," and to the Pearl River Farrellys for their humor, loyalty, and support. And finally, to my husband, Matthew, for the many cups of tea while I was writing, for reading every draft, for helping me with research, for wrangling Fintan, and for supporting me through setbacks with love and humor.

ABOUT THE AUTHOR

C. S. Farrelly is a writer whose career has spanned investment banking, government and international relations, and higher education. Her stage plays have been produced in New York City. *The Shepherd's Calculus* is her first novel. She lives in Pennsylvania with her family.

CPSIA information can be obtained
at www.ICGtesting.com
Printed in the USA
BVOW06s0816260118
506046BV00001B/13/P